INCANDESCENT

CHRISTINA LEE

Published by Christina Lee in the United States of America

Cover Design by Sleepy Fox Studio

Professional Beta Read by Karen Meeus Editing

Additional thanks to Erin for your beta read and Kelley for your sensitivity read

Edited by Keren Reed

Proofread by Abbie Nicole, Judy's Proofreading, and Lyrical Lines

1

DELANEY
SEPTEMBER

I PULLED INTO EDGEWATER PARK, glad the rain had held off. Planning an outdoor event in Cleveland was always tricky, even in the late summer months. A storm could blow over the lake at a moment's notice, but given the stifling humidity in the air, it might almost be a welcome change.

The upper pavilions were located near the auxiliary entrance, and the beach was down below, which was a sight all its own. Even if sunbathers weren't in view from this location, Lake Erie was a glorious, sprawling backdrop, the smooth surface glinting like diamonds in the sun.

My cell buzzed with a text from my friend, Marcus.

Good luck.

I breathed out and quickly fired back a thanks once I'd pulled into a space.

My sixteen-year-old son, Grant, was sitting stiffly in the passenger seat, holding a plate of brownies we'd made using his late mother's recipe. It'd been a tough twenty-two months since Rebecca passed due to long-term complications from a stroke she'd suffered after his birth. There had always been the risk of another occurrence, a topic we'd tiptoed around for

years, and in the end, it'd been a powerful enough one to take
her life.

I'd stepped in to fill her shoes as much as I could, but it definitely wasn't enough—it would never be enough—because
she'd been the rock of our little family and the love of both our
lives. She and Grant had connected on a level he and I never
would. He was quirky and brilliant, just like his mother.
Whereas she geeked out on science, he loved history, and when
their passions overlapped, they were a force to be reckoned
with. Grant went all in, collecting relics he'd found in various
locations, and she indulged his hobby more enthusiastically
than me. Not that I didn't make an effort, but he could tell I was
trying too hard—and failing miserably.

Grant adjusted his colonial-era tricorn hat, which was a bit
snug on his head. I could already see the sweat forming at his
temples, but I kept my lips in a neat, straight line, hoping to get
through the day without much fuss. Not that Rebecca's family
wasn't used to him wearing one period piece or another,
despite the temperature. Thankfully, he'd left his militia coat
with the hundred silver buttons in the back seat, possibly
deciding the humidity might do him in.

I glanced toward the pavilion, spotting her parents and
various aunts and cousins already gathered there. My father-in-
law, Howard, was in his wheelchair for this event, but around
the house, he normally used his walker. His health had deterio-
rated the past few years, and now that he needed dialysis, he
was mostly homebound.

My gut tightened. It was bittersweet coming to their annual
family reunion. We'd nearly passed on attending last year
because we just...weren't ready. We'd only stayed an hour,
Grant swiping at his eyes the whole way home. We were a
disaster, and it took time to process our sorrow.

I tried to stay strong for Grant, breaking down only after he
was in bed. But he'd called me on it more than once. *"Mom*

always said to get stuff out and not hold it in." So now, I tried to be more open when I was having a bad day. *Tried* being the key word. Sometimes there was no other way around it. When you went through this sort of grief, it was hard to hide the balder moments from each other.

"All good, kiddo?" I asked as I cut the engine.

"I'm not a kid anymore," Grant replied in a tight voice, the tension rolling off him. "Mom would never call me that. I wish she were here with us."

I swallowed down the acid in my throat. It was always this way with Grant. Either I said the wrong thing, or he complained I was overprotective. He wasn't wrong, but I still couldn't win where he was concerned. And I certainly didn't want to make a scene in front of family.

"Me too," I confessed in a softened tone. No truer words could be spoken. "Remember how she loved Aunt Jane's oatmeal-raisin cookies?"

"Yeah." The corner of his mouth lifted, the taut set of his shoulders easing. At least it wasn't a memory that stabbed us in the gut. "She always made an extra batch for Mom to take home."

"Then she'd sneak them after bed," I said, and he snickered, likely remembering how she was overly careful with her diet but couldn't help indulging every now and again. Her health was the one thing that always hung over our heads. The stroke had left her with a weakened right arm, and she sometimes wore a brace. But in the end, I wished she'd allowed herself to indulge more. "Which was fine by me because they're not my favorite."

"Mine neither. Who wants to eat healthy-sounding cookies when there's chocolate?"

I chuckled. It was always a family debate and one of the only times Grant sided with me.

"Exactly."

We stared at the lake for a few seconds more, both of us trying to get up the courage in our own ways. It felt serene being near the water again. In fact, Rebecca and I originally lived in a nearby neighborhood until we found our first home on the east side, closer to her parents and my father. Cleveland Heights was a distance from the lake, so the ride here was always a pleasant one, with the boats and the downtown skyline in view.

"What do you call a fish wearing a bow tie?" I asked with my hand on the door handle. It was showtime, and even if I wasn't feeling up to it, I needed to act the part. At least for my child.

He rolled his eyes. "What?"

"So*fish*ticated," I replied, pushing the door open.

He groaned, but I spotted the hint of a smile, which was just the effect I wanted. "You'll have to work on your dad jokes. That was pretty bad."

"Noted," I said as I rounded the car, and we inched toward the pavilion.

Rebecca would've said the same. It was a ridiculous thing I'd started when Grant was in sixth grade and being teased relentlessly by classmates, and apparently, it'd stuck. Middle school had been a challenge for him, so I was relieved when he'd found his stride in high school.

"Wait, I forgot my jacket," he said, handing me the plate and turning back.

Following behind him, I pointed the key fob at the car, unable to stop the words from forming. "It's really hot out. You sure you shouldn't leave that in the—"

"I'm sure," he said, yanking it from the back seat, then slamming the door. "*Mom* never cared what I wore."

His words delivered like a dagger, and I stepped back, my legs momentarily unsteady. "Watch your tone," I warned. "I know you miss Mom, and so do I. But like it or not, we still need to navigate through life together."

He grumbled under his breath as he slipped the heavy coat over his shoulders.

I was the overprotective and unreasonable one in the family. The one always worried that Grant would be bullied again. But somehow, my tone resembled my own father's disapproving one a little too well. Still, I wasn't going to allow Grant to call the shots. I was the parent.

Thankfully, my mother-in-law, Donna, flagged us over right then, and I could feel Grant relax as we greeted them with hugs. He loved his grandparents, and they'd been quite accommodating since Rebecca's passing, even though they were grieving too. They showed up at all of Grant's school events and made dinners when I was running late at work. They helped get us through the overwhelming moments. Between them and my monthly grief group, I was slowly coming out on the other side.

Speaking of the grief group, I didn't see Tristan anywhere and felt a bit disappointed. We'd immediately connected as outliers in the family, only related by marriage, and both having lost our significant others—Tristan's late husband was Rebecca's cousin. Tristan had referred me to the group at this event last year. Said it helped him not feel so alone when he was grieving Chris's death.

"How's work?" one of the great-aunts asked, taking the plate of brownies off my hands. Grant had gone off with his younger cousins, who asked him about his hat and begged him to play a game of cornhole. He'd rolled his eyes when his grandfather had nudged him in their direction, but I think he enjoyed helping them and being admired in return.

"Busy, as usual," I told her. I was an electrician for a well-known company, and there was plenty on my plate these days.

"Pete says the same," she replied, referring to her husband, who was a roofer. He'd mentioned once how busy he was in the warmer months. "I, on the other hand, feel refreshed after my summer break from teaching."

I smiled. "I'll bet."

As I moved closer to the cooler of beverages, I became reacquainted with the other family members and tried like hell to field all the questions and stories about Rebecca because I knew they meant well. Rebecca had always acted as a buffer and did most of the talking at these things, but in her absence, I was learning to hold my own.

I was able to escape one of the more involved conversations by volunteering to make a run for more ice. I nearly texted Marcus again on the way before remembering he had his own plans with family. We'd met in the grief group, had grown closer over the past year, and he would've totally understood how overwhelmed I was feeling in that moment.

Once I returned, I watched Grant and his cousins play a game of tag, then headed to the pavilion to load up on cheese and crackers while we waited for the food to be served. When the delicious scent of charred meat wafted toward me, I was pleasantly surprised to spot Tristan near Rebecca's uncles, who were manning the grill. I raised my hand in a wave, and he grinned.

Normally, he stayed close to Chris's mom and sister, using the opportunity to check in with them. But he'd obviously made other connections along the way, even five years after Chris's death. Tristan had shared once that he'd been raised in foster care, so it made sense he'd want to hold on to that sense of belonging with both hands.

I glanced over my shoulder to where Grant was sitting with his cousins, downing a glass of his grandmother's raspberry iced tea. The stitch in my chest intensified. It was definitely important to keep this connection for him as well. I felt lost without Rebecca, but this wasn't about me so much as about

Grant creating memories and spending as much time with this side of the family as he could.

He'd begun his junior year two weeks ago, and I prayed it was even better than the last. I certainly never imagined experiencing his first steps into adulthood, let alone high school, without Rebecca.

Once the food was served, I got Grant situated in line with a plate and utensils. His grandmother had done the rest, pointing out all the foods he should try. Along with the meat from the grill, there were all sorts of side dishes that had become staples for me after nearly two decades of marriage to the same person.

"Good to see you," Tristan said, stepping in line behind me. "You doing okay?"

"Getting there," I replied with a smile. I loaded some macaroni salad onto my plate before looking at who was nearby and lowering my voice. "Does coming to these things ever get easier?"

He frowned. "In a way, yes. The pain is still there, but it sort of settles into the cracks, if that makes sense." I nodded because it did. Totally. My heart was shattered, and I wasn't sure I'd ever be able to patch it up well enough to go on without her. But every day, I proved myself wrong.

"The way I see it, being here is a way to honor them," Tristan said closer to my ear. "I don't know how much longer I'll attend...maybe as long as they'll have me."

I felt that tightness in my throat again. "Makes sense."

He lifted a bun, then passed me the tongs to help myself to the cheese slices and tomatoes for my burger.

"And you?" I asked. "How's the dog-grooming business?"

Tristan and Chris had opened Doggie Styles together in Rocky River, and Tristan had continued the business solo after his passing, even expanding it and offering day care to their clientele. What a concept. But apparently, it was very popular.

"Busier than ever."

"That's good news." I winked. "Now get working on an east-side location so we can bring Ruby." Our golden retriever was eleven years old but still acted like a puppy sometimes, especially when we brought out the tennis ball. But she'd also slowed down in other ways the last couple of years, and I'd always wondered how an owner's death affected animals. She'd taken Rebecca's spot in our bed, almost like she wanted to comfort me at night, and I certainly wasn't complaining.

"Hell no. I'm stretched thin enough as it is," he replied. Likely because his boyfriend, West, took up any remaining time he had. I'd only met him once, and they made a nice couple. There was maybe a ten-year age difference between them, which wasn't obvious at all, and Tristan was very supportive of West's aspirations to be a chef.

I followed Tristan to the nearest picnic table to take the last couple of empty spots. Before getting situated, I checked to make sure Grant was still eating beside his grandparents at the next table.

I greeted Chris's mom and sister before finally taking a bite of my burger and savoring it. I'd slept in late and forgotten to eat breakfast and hadn't realized I was starving. Plus, I always enjoyed the food her family made. I missed Rebecca's cooking as well. But we made do, using Rebecca's recipes for Grant's favorite dishes, and over the past few months, we'd brought our own recipes into the mix.

"Still attending the group?" Tristan asked in a quieter voice, which I appreciated. No way I wanted to have that uncomfortable conversation with anyone else, about how someone grieved, or how long, for that matter. At least not today.

"Uh-huh." I wiped my mouth with a napkin. "I'll always be grateful for the referral. It's helping me work through my grief, and I've made some friends in the process."

"How *is* Marc, by the way?" he asked with a grin. Marcus had joined the group the year before me, and he remembered

Tristan from a few sessions before Tristan felt healthy enough to step away for good.

Before I could reply, Chris's mom asked Tristan a question about the restaurant where West worked. The conversation spun into other favorite places to eat in town, and I patted Tristan's shoulder as I stood to throw away my empty cup and plate.

I wandered back over to the pavilion, and after loading dessert on a new plate, I brought it over to Grant's table to share with him. He immediately reached for the peanut butter cookie while I went for chocolate chip.

"Your mother always loved my oatmeal raisin," Aunt Jane said to Grant from across the table, and I felt guilty that I didn't include any of her cookies on the plate.

"Yeah, she did." Grant's smile was sad, making my heart lodge in my throat.

"Maybe we can take some home?" I suggested, if only for nostalgia's sake. When Grant's gaze met mine, I couldn't exactly read his wavering emotions, but I thought maybe there was gratitude there.

Aunt Jane nodded enthusiastically. "I'll pack some up for you."

"*Thanks,*" I mouthed to her, and Rebecca's dad cleared his throat and looked away.

"I like your brownies," Donna said before taking another hearty bite of one, and it was the perfect transition. "You added nuts. I approve."

"It was Grant's idea," I replied, remembering how he'd made the suggestion tentatively, as if it would offend Rebecca. But it was another one of those little changes, nearly undetectable to outsiders, that showed we were moving forward.

We stayed for an hour more before we said our goodbyes and drove back to the east side, to the home where Grant had grown up. In my darker moments, I wanted to sell everything and move, to escape all the memories, but that was another thing the grief counselor didn't advise—making split-second decisions about huge things. Besides, I didn't want Grant to have too many changes in his young life. And most importantly, the house brought him solace, so we kept everything the same —except for Rebecca's clothing and the bedding in our room. While the latter had been comforting at first, it became painful soon after. It felt good to opt for fresh sheets that only smelled like detergent. I finally went through her closet around the one-year mark, and having Grant help me was one more step for both of us.

"Did you have fun?" I asked as we turned onto our street.

"I guess so," he replied with a shrug, keeping his eyes fixed out the window.

Our neighborhood was charming, and our house was too. As I pulled into our driveway, I noted the other Tudors and colonials surrounding us that were also over a hundred years old. They had aged well, along with the quaint businesses in the area. Rebecca and I liked it here and chose not to upgrade because we'd made plans, so many plans, for after Grant graduated from high school and went off to college. They mostly involved traveling and, of course, I could still go alone, but the idea had lost its appeal.

Time. Give yourself time.

"I know it's hard without Mom," I said as Grant balanced the plate of oatmeal-raisin cookies on his knee so he could remove his hat. His hair was sweaty underneath, but I resisted pointing it out. That would only lead to another argument. It was actually fitting that he wore the tricorn to Rebecca's family reunion because they'd bought it together from a thrift shop. Halloween was always interesting with the two of them.

Once inside, I fed Ruby, then let her out. Grant got on the computer with one of his two friends—Ellie, I thought, was the most likely option. Jeremy's time was more limited on the weekends because of his job at the local movie theater.

There were years when Grant didn't have any friends to speak of, not only because of his unique interests but because he was painfully awkward and shy. Kids developed differently, and though he was extremely smart, he'd suffered socially. And just as he'd finally found his footing, the rug was pulled from under his feet again with his mother's death.

Opening the cupboard where our mugs were stored, I started unloading the dishwasher, my eyes briefly focusing on the different-colored paint stains on the wall. It was the project I'd abandoned when Rebecca got sick. We had plans to modernize the kitchen—not that I knew what I was doing, but I would've at least made an attempt before asking for backup. Now the idea sat heavy in my gut. I supposed if I was going to stay here and have Grant visit often, I could still finish it.

I headed to the living room, sat down, and propped my feet on the coffee table. Flipping through the television channels, nothing held my interest. I considered working out or taking Ruby for another walk but just wasn't feeling it. She obviously wasn't either because she'd plopped down by my feet and snored contentedly.

I finally settled on a home-improvement show Rebecca had enjoyed watching. It was how she'd gotten the idea about the kitchen. She loved looking at all the different tiles and counter-tops, whereas I always noticed the shoddy electrical work.

Grant had apparently abandoned his computer game because he was suddenly in the room, holding the plate of goodies he'd brought home.

Settling down beside me, he handed me a cookie. "I'm sorry I snapped at you."

It was a peace offering, and hell if I wouldn't take the oppor-tunity to connect with him like this.

"I'm sorry too," I said after nibbling the edge of the cookie. "I'll work on not hovering so much."

"I know you mean well..." He sighed. "Sometimes I get frustrated about, well, *everything*."

His confession made my stomach tighten. I wanted to remind him to speak to his therapist about those feelings but didn't want to rock the boat. Besides, he was becoming more self-sufficient and didn't need any reminders from me. That was more obvious than ever.

"Suppose we both got stuff to work on," I murmured, and he nodded.

We watched and chewed as if it was the most natural thing in the world. And in some ways it was...except the cookie part.

"Not bad," I said, trying not to cringe at the sweetness of the raisins. Who in the hell thought this combination was a good idea?

He smirked, then burst into a full-on chuckle. "Yes, they are."

His laughter was contagious and felt so good, loosening my chest.

I held up what was left of my cookie and clanged it against his half-eaten one. "To Mom."

"To Mom," he replied before taking one more bite, then setting the unfinished portion on the plate.

I popped the last bite into my mouth and quickly chewed it down. "It sort of grows on you."

"Whatever you say." He cringed, then glanced back at the television. "Is this the show Mom always liked?"

"Yup." I stretched my arm behind his shoulder, and we settled in to watch. As he relaxed against me, I briefly buried my nose in his hair, memorizing his scent.

2

MARCUS

"I PUT YOUR HOSE AWAY, MA," I said through the screen door. "Thanks for dinner. Gonna head home."

She'd washed dishes while I watered her grass and pulled weeds from her flower beds. The summer heat wreaked havoc on our lawns, and if you didn't keep up with it, the grass would turn yellow. I used to care more about my own yard, but now I just went through the motions, pretty much like everything else the last two-plus years since Carmen died.

"Appreciate the help." Mom wiped her hands on a towel, her gaze softening like it always did lately. That same question hung from her lips, about how I was coming along, but she refrained from asking it too many days in a row.

I waved goodbye as I walked toward the sidewalk, then headed around the corner to my house. It was the reason we'd moved to Euclid, an east-side suburb of Cleveland, fifteen years ago. Well, one of the reasons. We wanted to be closer to my family—Mom's amazing cooking didn't hurt—but also to have a house we could afford. Even if it wasn't my dream home, nor Carmen's.

I stopped to help an elderly neighbor roll his garbage cans

to the curb before going home and jumping in the shower. I'd admit to feeling stir-crazy all day, but I'd refrained from heading into work lest my mother get on my case about not relaxing enough. Instead, I ran errands, did two loads of laundry, and accepted her dinner invitation. Especially since it involved the fresh perch she'd pulled from the freezer. She loved driving down to the 55th Street pier in the early morning hours for some *city fishing*, they called it. My grandfather—Mom's father—used to join her before he got too ill to get out of bed most days.

"Make sure you have a hobby," he used to tell me, *"or you'll spend your whole life working."*

But fishing was not my thing—all the sitting and waiting. Believe me, I tried.

Instead, I liked being more physical. I worked out with free weights and ran on the treadmill or in the Metropark most days of the week. But that didn't seem to do the trick today.

Once I was in a fresh pair of cotton shorts, I grabbed a beer from the fridge and headed to the porch, hoping to take advantage of the cool breeze coming off the lake. The kids across the street were running through the sprinkler, and I smiled to myself, remembering my own childhood. The local fire department would flush the hydrants, and the kids would take turns getting sopping wet in the flood of water they produced.

Though things had changed nowadays. Back then, I'd be gone for hours in the summer months without my mom knowing where in the hell I was, but now kids were rarely out of their parents' earshot anymore. When Carmen's nephew came to live with us one year, all he wanted to do was play video games and text his friends. She'd try to push him out the door to ride his bike, but I told her to let him be. I could see how his family issues were weighing heavily on him.

I tipped my head back and guzzled half the bottle, and the cool liquid felt good going down.

A dog started barking somewhere down the street, which only caused others to follow suit. It was a busy neighborhood, which didn't bother me the way it had Carmen. She'd always wanted to get away from the noise of the city and live someplace with more land. I actually didn't mind our small yard so much as our style of house. I wanted a place with more character, maybe something I could help restore or remodel, maybe near Shaker Heights. Hell, I'd even consider moving to Lakewood or Rocky River on the west side if the taxes didn't kill me. Except the joke in Cleveland was that once you were established, you didn't cross the Cuyahoga River. There was this ridiculous rivalry based on which side of town you lived on.

My stomach tightened as I remembered that Carmen had been driving on Dead Man's Curve heading west to meet a work friend when she was sideswiped by a truck and smashed into the concrete barrier. She died instantly. If that wasn't enough to keep my ass firmly on this side of town, I didn't know what was.

I'd live vicariously through my friend Delaney instead. He and his son, Grant, had some family thing at Edgewater Park today, and I remembered how pretty that drive on the Shoreway had been whenever I'd ventured that way.

When my phone buzzed with a message from the dating app I'd downloaded, I smiled even as my gut churned. **We could always meet somewhere halfway.**

Instead of responding, I decided to take more time to think my reply through. It was a big step. I'd originally joined out of curiosity, but I'd been too chicken to do anything about it. Until now. No one could replace Carmen. She'd been my everything. But someone different, with traits that didn't remind me of her, might help curb my loneliness.

The two-year anniversary of Carmen's passing had come and gone a few months back, and though it'd hurt like hell, at least I had family and friends, as well as my grief group, to cushion the blow. I'd joined it upon the recommendation from my doctor during a physical. I'd been suffering from chest pain, which turned out to be due to anxiety rather than a heart condition as I'd feared, and I'd been grateful for the advice ever since.

On the actual anniversary of her death, I'd met Carmen's parents at the cemetery, and we'd laid flowers on her grave. Afterward, I'd headed straight to a bar on Coventry, where I'd met Delaney, who'd become my closest friend from the grief group. Over a few drinks, he let me talk his ear off about Carmen and how much I'd enjoyed being married to her. I missed the intimacy most of all, which may be the reason I was feeling pretty pent up lately.

Fuck. I rubbed my hand over my stubble, enjoying the rough feel against my fingers. I'd let my beard grow since Carmen's death, a bit of a rebel move, I supposed, since she liked me clean-shaven. I wondered if Delaney would confess the same—his beard was shaggier than mine.

The truth was, the house was too quiet without her, which was why I worked way too much at Worthy's Salvage Shop, the business I'd inherited from my grandfather—Marcus Worthy II —who had inherited the place from my great-grandfather. It was the first Black-owned business in the neighborhood, and I'd vowed to keep it running for that reason alone, though I also loved it.

My dad had died from a sudden heart attack when my sister and I were preschoolers, and Mom worked two jobs to keep food on the table. When I was old enough, I'd ride my bike to Worthy's after school to help with anything Grandpa needed while my younger sister stayed with my cousins at my aunt's house. I loved working with my hands, and over the years, I'd learned to restore all kinds of stuff that had been passed down for generations, from upholstered chairs to music boxes and even church pews.

When my grandfather had gotten too weak to keep the business afloat, I took over. I kept it old-school while also making sure things were up-to-date, with a few exceptions like the rickety cash register I couldn't bear to part with or the shop sign that had to be a hundred years old but the customers seemed to like.

"Don't fix stuff that isn't broken," he used to say. *"Just give it a good shine."*

I clicked on a couple of my social media sites before finally responding to the dating app message and solidifying plans.

Sounds good. Fuck, my hands were shaking. I was really doing this.

Couldn't hurt. Besides, I didn't have anyone to take care of but myself. At least Delaney had Grant, though I couldn't imagine how difficult it must've been, raising him in the midst of so much grief. When the parents in the support group discussed their children, I vacillated between bitter resentment and relief. At least they had something to get them out of bed every morning. But I supposed it would also be a difficult reminder of the life you lost.

Carmen and I tried to have kids for years, but it never panned out. It was one of the ways she and Keisha connected, though for my sister, it was by choice. Same for marriage, and I respected her for it because she took a lot of flak for both.

Fostering Aaron, Carmen's nephew, had been both a challenge and a complete joy. He'd even invited us to his high school graduation before he went off to college. When he'd made an appearance at Carmen's funeral to offer condolences, I'd broken down in tears, and we'd promised to keep in touch. Now we texted each other every few weeks.

The sky was growing darker, so I went inside before the mosquitos got me. I turned on the lamp in the living room, glancing at the photo frame beside it. At Carmen's mahogany skin that was darker than my copper tone, the straightened hairstyle she'd worn the last year of her life. My natural waves were softer because I was a cross between my Black mother and white father, whom I'd unfortunately never gotten to know, being too young when he passed to remember much about him.

Truth be told, I had trouble figuring out where my biracial ass fit half the time—in school and sometimes in life. It was easier as an adult, and society had progressed, at least in bigger towns like Cleveland, though it was still far from perfect. I didn't know what it might've been like in the rural area where my dad was raised, and I didn't plan on finding out. City life suited me just fine.

I scrolled to my text thread with Delaney. Should I tell him about the dating thing? Honestly, I was afraid of what he would think. What a lot of people would think.

How was the reunion? I texted instead.

Just as you'd imagine. Awkward but also pretty okay.

And Grant? He'd said his son was close to Rebecca's parents.

He had fun with his cousins. Probably needed it more than me.

Maybe you both did.

Guess so.

I smiled to myself, glad it went well. I knew how tough it could be around family sometimes, especially those who thought it was time for you to move on. It was shortsighted but not surprising. Besides, lots of people did move on, some pretty quickly, and it was important not to pass judgment.

In fact, one man named Walter from our group got remarried to a woman who resembled his wife a little too closely only four months after her death. It was eerie, and we all knew it, given the looks around the room that day, but nobody said anything. Judy, our group therapist, had dived straight in, reiterating the stuff we were thinking. She asked what a new marriage meant to him, and he admitted he was crushingly lonely and wanted someone there to fill up the silence.

I got it. I really did.

But lo and behold, Walter announced a few months later that the marriage had fallen apart. He confessed he'd moved on too quickly and needed time to be alone. The therapist had worked with him through it, and each month he gave status updates on how his solo time was working for him. It was progress, and we all had a little of our own to share, no matter how small.

It was what made me return time and again—I felt like I belonged. But also because of Delaney. I felt connected to him most of all. Maybe because we were both around the same age, though he was three years older at forty-four, so I could make all the over-the-hill jokes I wanted.

But also, Delaney brought me relief in a way that surprised me. Sure, I had childhood friends, but this was someone who got it—got me. People could say they understood what a loss like ours was like, but they'd never lived it, and that had to be the reason why I connected so well with him.

Some people came into your life for reasons, or whatever that saying was, and I found it to be true. Whether we would stay in touch after either of us ended up being strong enough to leave the group was another question. But when I thought of not having contact with him anymore, it made me sad, maybe because it was hard to lose people, period.

Was Tristan there?

Yeah, it was nice to see him.

Cool. Always wonder if he's doing okay after leaving the group.

Yeah, think so. His boyfriend, West, wasn't there. But Tristan looked happy, settled...is that the right word? I just know I want to get to that place too.

You will.

You will too.

I swallowed roughly.

Thanks. So, what are you up to now?

Hanging with Grant.

I'll let you get back to it, old man.

I'll kick your ass.

I laughed, which felt good.

Only if you can catch me. Better get your butt on that treadmill.

Ugh, don't remind me. Been slacking.

I hear you. See you at group?

Definitely.

Awesome. Until then.

Night.

I ended up watching an action movie Carmen would've hated. And she would've still sat beside me with her glass of wine and one book or another... Fuck, I missed her. Missed feeling her warmth beside me. It was the exact reason I didn't wash her favorite sweater for months. It still smelled like her perfume.

When the scent began fading, it gutted me, so I knew it was time to move on. I cried when I put it in the washer. But the memory was still there, and I realized that was better than the torment the actual object caused. Instead of bringing comfort, it left this deep ache inside my soul.

And that wasn't healthy at all.

I headed to bed, turning on the fan to block out the silence then cutting the lights.

3

DELANEY

I CLOCKED out of work then headed home to shower and change. I'd spent way too much time threading wire through the wall in a crawl space today where it was stifling hot. If I were claustrophobic, I likely wouldn't have been able to complete the job.

"How was school?" I asked Grant, who was at the kitchen table with his laptop, completing a homework assignment.

"Fine," he said, and I bristled. The school could've caught fire, and his answer would've still been *fine* with little other added information, but I wasn't going to push it. Not today.

"I'll heat up the leftover lasagna while I shower," I said, noting that he was wearing a plain hoodie today as opposed to yesterday when he'd donned one of those Victorian-era ascots with a button-down shirt. "I'll need to head out after we eat."

"To your group?" he asked, though I'd already reminded him last night. But his nose had been stuck in his phone, so maybe he hadn't been paying attention. Except by now, he knew the group met the second Tuesday of every month. There was also one geared toward kids who'd lost parents, but he'd opted to see a therapist on his own instead, one his pediatrician had recommended after a particularly brutal night where he couldn't seem to stop shaking or crying. The therapy seemed to help provide him a safe space for his turbulent feelings. Much like I felt about my group, only there were more people with similar feelings, and that was a comfort all its own.

"Yep," I replied, opening the fridge and pulling out the pan of lasagna I made over the weekend. "I'll be home right after."

"I can do that," Grant said, pushing from his seat and reaching for the pan. He'd been ultra helpful in the kitchen, which seemed to be an outlet for him as well. "Ellie's gonna come over after dinner to work on our class project and stuff."

"Stuff? Like computer gaming?" I said, and he rolled his eyes.

"We're creating a really cool world," he replied in that animated tone he only used when discussing history or hobbies. Rebecca and I would share a secret smile whenever he was expounding on something, like the elaborate maps he enjoyed creating. "You know how absorbed we get."

"Of course I know. I was only teasing," I said, squeezing his shoulder. "Remember the rules: Stay downstairs when you're home alone. No bedroom."

"You don't need to keep reminding me," he replied, clearly exasperated. "Besides, we're only friends. You're so—"

"Don't even say it, Grant." I gripped the counter, my knuckles turning white. "All parents have rules. End of discussion."

"Fine," he bit out as I strode out of the room. There was that word again.

I'd admit that at one time, we wondered if Grant had a crush on Ellie and that was why he wanted to hang out with her so much. Thus, the beginning of rules for guests. Turned out, they were only friends with similar interests, which was nice to see. Recently, someone else from school began gaming online with them too. I'd only met Jeremy once, and he seemed like a nice kid, but the same rules applied, especially when they were home alone. It didn't seem unreasonable to anyone but Grant, and likely he would complain purely for the purpose of disagreeing with me. It'd gotten worse after Rebecca passed, as if he was taking out all his frustration and grief on me. I'd hoped we'd cross some threshold eventually, but then hormones and teen angst took over, so here we were.

I felt a bit of nervous energy as I showered and changed. Even though I looked forward to the group, it could leave me feeling raw and vulnerable, depending on the topics discussed on any given night. If anything good came out of this, besides befriending Marcus, it was realizing that people from all walks of life experienced grief and had the need to belong and feel heard.

While we ate, I prodded Grant a little about the physics project they were working on, which involved building a model rowboat using only cardboard, tape, and the teacher's calculations. It sounded interesting and was worth a lot of points, especially if they could make it float, and he thought they'd get a good grade if they put their heads together.

"I almost forgot," he said around a bite. "There's a college night for parents in a couple of weeks, and I'll be taking the SATs this year too. You were supposed to get an email."

"I'll make sure to pull it up and have a look." I tamed my reaction, but my stomach was going crazy from the idea of making all these decisions without Rebecca. "Have you given any more thought to where you'd like to apply? We can definitely tour some campuses in the spring."

"A school with a good history program, obviously," he replied with a shrug. He was so fucking smart. He could probably get in anywhere he applied. His statewide testing reflected that every year as well. I'll admit I was nervous for a while during his freshman year when his grades began slipping due to missed assignments. Some days he'd come home, lock himself in his room, and play computer games all night. His outfits had gone through a dark period as well, when everything he wore looked drab or stark like a Victorian Goth kid from the eighties. As if he was filled with so much sadness, it was reflected in every facet of his life, and I probably wasn't much better. But I'd reached out to his teachers and therapist, and somehow he'd pulled through.

I remembered the relief when he came downstairs dressed in the tie-dye hoodie I'd gotten him for Christmas, the one he'd initially pretended to hate. It felt like an earth-shattering moment, and in my world, it certainly was—like we'd rounded a corner. We'd pushed forward and created a new normal, which included more good days than sad lately. I supposed that was all I could hope for.

"I hear the University of Michigan has a good program, and maybe Oberlin too," I replied, having done a little research of my own over the summer. Though I'd admit the colleges I'd looked at had all been within a couple of hours' driving distance from home.

Any university would seem too far away, and before I knew it, I'd be an empty nester. Damn, that made me feel old, and Rebecca would tease that I had the creaking in my knees to prove it.

"I'll probably stick even closer to home," he said, not meeting my eyes. "Maybe Kent or Cleveland State?"

Fuck, I did not want him to feel like he was the one taking care of me.

"Grant," I said, tapping his wrist and waiting for him to look at me. "You're free to apply to any college you want. Even if it's a plane ride away. It's important for you to have dreams and live your life."

"But..." He lifted his hand and flapped his fingers like he couldn't get out the words.

"Do not make your decision based on me." I set my fork on

my plate. "I'll be okay. Besides, you'll visit often, and your room will always be yours to come home to, no matter what."

"It's not based on you," he scoffed, and my heart clanged against my rib cage. "Well, not really. Mom's here, her memory." He made a frustrated sound as he pushed his floppy bangs away from his forehead. "It's not a big deal."

"What do you think Mom would say?" I asked around a clogged throat.

"That she could picture me at some big university where I'd meet more people like me." Grant had always struggled to find people with similar hobbies, and in the right college environment, he would likely thrive. His high school years didn't look the same as mine, and that was okay. He'd gotten a late start in the friend department, and the last couple of years, he'd finally joined some clubs that catered to his interests.

"I'd have to agree." When our eyes met, his softened, and I felt instant relief that maybe I'd gotten through to him, no matter how unsettled it made me feel. Though I'd feel worse if he decided to stay for all the wrong reasons.

"She did always want me to visit her alma mater." His eyes lit up. "And hey, if I ended up at NYU, I wouldn't have to learn how to drive. Mom said she walked or took the subway everywhere."

I laughed and shook my head. He'd opted out of the program last year, and I'd let it slide, even though many of his peers were already driving by now. "You know it's an important skill to have. You don't want your old man carting your butt around all the time, do you?"

His eyes widened briefly in horror. "That's what my bike is for."

"Not in the winter months," I countered. The snow would be piling up before we knew it.

"You're right. I'll ask Ellie where she signed up for driving school." He sighed. "NYU is too far anyway."

I frowned. "A discussion for another time."

An hour later, I was in my car, driving to the community center in University Heights, where the grief group held its meetings. I parked, then entered the building, walking alongside an older gentleman who'd attended the meetings about as long as me. As usual, the chairs were already arranged in a circle so we could all see each other and interact when warranted.

I made small talk with a few of the attendees as we waited for Judy to pour herself a cup of coffee and begin the session. Marcus was running late, and by the time he arrived and sat in the empty seat across from me, Judy was already on her way to discussing tonight's topic, which was coping with grief through the holidays. I barely remembered the first season without Rebecca, except that it was awful and Grant had made me promise not to drag the tree out of the box. I had no idea how this year would go, but at least most of the fog had lifted. Marcus had shared a similar story with me about his first holiday without Carmen.

I glanced at him. He looked like he'd gone home to change after work because he didn't have any varnish stains on his shirt or dust on his jeans from sanding something or other. His hair looked a bit damp, especially where his dark locks curled near his ears. He was a handsome guy, getting plenty of admiring looks from ladies whenever we met in public.

His smile was dazzling, and when his light-brown eyes met mine across the room and that charming grin stretched his lips, I sat back, feeling a bit more settled. Like we were in fucking grade school and my best friend had just shown up to lunch, so I didn't have to go through it alone.

That line of thinking only reminded me of Grant's difficulties early on, some involving sitting solo with his lunchbox, which made my gut churn. I thrust it from my mind and tuned back into the conversation, even offering up the suggestion that it's all right to miss out on decorating or celebrations if it's too painful. Judy concurred and then transitioned to a different topic.

"Tonight is a special milestone for some of you," Judy said. It was strange to be on a first-name basis with the therapist, but that was how she ran the group, perhaps to give it a more intimate feel, given what we shared in here. "There are several in this group who've been attending consistently for a year. That means you've hung in there and worked through your grief. That deserves a round of applause."

The group erupted in noise as we clapped for one another. I blinked repeatedly, suddenly feeling emotional. It was surreal to think that I'd gotten to know the people in this room because they'd also lost a significant person in their lives. Whether they were spouses by law or in name only, we'd all shared our tears, gut-wrenching pain, and deep-seated fears about the future.

"Some of you might think my announcement means it's time to leave the group, that you've been here long enough," Judy said, making eye contact with each person in the circle. "But remember, no one can dictate how long or how much you're allowed to grieve. It's always all right to ask for more time or help."

A collective murmur went around the room, and when my gaze met Marcus's, he seemed a bit emotional and disconcerted as well.

"Let's share some of our small victories," she suggested. It was a phrase she used often to encourage us to point out the seemingly inconsequential things that helped in our growth. "One at a time, so we don't talk over each other."

One of the men admitted he'd stopped listening to his wife's last cell message on repeat, and a woman had finally cleaned out a closet and donated the clothes to the needy.

"Remember," Judy said, specifically looking to new group members, "those things are natural and make you feel closer to the person you lost. But, they might also hold you back, keep you from moving forward. You need to decide when the right time is for you to compartmentalize them. That doesn't mean you have to stop looking at or touching things that remind you of them. It just means you need to choose a dedicated time and a day for them, and stick to it so other things in your life aren't neglected."

It reminded me of when I'd spend way too much time watching home videos on the computer because it made Rebecca feel momentarily alive, like I could reach out and touch her. Eventually, I'd limited the reminiscing to the weekends, then to once a month. It was extremely difficult but necessary to take those small yet significant steps.

For Grant, I'd told myself. But for me too.

"Anyone else?" Judy asked, and I told the group about the college discussion I'd had with Grant earlier in the day. Marcus smiled across the way, and it made my stomach feel warm, like he cared, which, of course, he did. He was my friend. Other members of the group with college-age kids gave me advice on how to approach certain scenarios, which I appreciated.

Silence descended on the room, which generally meant attendees were finished sharing. But then Marcus hesitantly raised his hand. "I'm going on my first date."

I held in a gasp as a low murmur resonated around the room.

I'd spoken to him yesterday, and he hadn't told me. Not one inkling that he was even considering such a thing. Not that it was any of my business, but I thought we'd grown closer. And that was something huge, at least in my book.

Maybe he didn't consider me as close a friend as I did him.

Or maybe it was more of a struggle for him than I realized.

"How did you put yourself out there?" someone asked.

My heart was beating strangely, and I was trying to make sense of why. I should've been happy for him, but I felt blindsided by the information. Not that he was obligated to tell me what went on in his life. Except he always did, almost on a daily basis, as we rehashed our lives.

"I joined a dating site," he replied, and I held my breath. "So I was able to have some conversations first to weed people out."

Marcus briefly looked at me, then away, his cheeks clearly splotched red despite his copper skin tone.

Why was this so fucking weird?

"Congrats," Judy chimed in. "She'll be lucky to meet you."

"It's a he, actually," Marcus muttered, and the sound in the room blotted out as if I were stuck in some surreal dream.

Marcus had a date with a guy? In all the discussions we'd had over the past year, we'd never discussed our sexuality. Holy shit.

4

MARCUS

"Is this something you'd like to discuss further with the group?" Judy asked, effectively shushing those quieter murmurs in the group.

My stomach was going crazy, my hands were sweating, and I could barely look Delaney in the eye. Not that it mattered, because he seemed pretty thunderstruck, staring into space with his back rigid and lips parted as if I'd just announced I was flying to the moon or something.

"I...dunno. I'm bisexual, and it's been a long time since I've explored this side of myself." I lifted my chin with confidence—or at least I hoped it looked that way as I tried to take ownership of my words. "And before there are any misunderstandings, I was very happily married to Carmen, and I expected to be with her for the rest of my life."

"I hear you. I'm pansexual," a woman named Harmony said, and I breathed out in relief. "I would've been married to Marci for life too. But going forward, it would take someone special—male, female, enby...that doesn't matter to me—to even..." She trailed off, tears dotting her eyelashes, and I swallowed the lump in my throat.

"It's okay to not be ready," Judy said. "We're all on our own timelines."

Guilt poked at my gut for being ready—if *ready* was truly how I'd label it. It was more about loneliness and needing... human contact, other than from family and friends. I wanted to be flirted with, maybe even touched again, if only for one night.

"I'm not good with all these new terms," said John, an older gentleman who'd been attending about as long as me and had been married to his wife for forty years, if I wasn't mistaken. "What happened to just being gay or straight?"

"You've got to get with the times," replied Frank, another older gentleman. He was pretty outspoken on most topics, so this exchange didn't surprise me. "There are new terms for everything nowadays, and from what I read, these labels have really helped some of the younger generation come to terms with their sexuality."

"I'm too old to keep up," John complained with a wave of his hand. "What I want to know is, how can he be with a man when he's been married to a woman for—"

"Because being bisexual or pansexual means you are attracted to more than one gender," Harmony explained. "But that doesn't mean you can't fall in love and commit to one person. There are lots of misconceptions out there."

I probably should've added something more to the conversation, but I was too busy cursing myself for bringing up the topic in the first place. And preoccupied with how uncomfortable Delaney looked as he shifted in his seat across the room. What the hell was his problem, and why did I think his friendship with Tristan meant he'd be more open?

Maybe I'd been right not to mention it to him, though maybe I should've also felt guilty for not preparing him. In my defense, I hadn't planned on mentioning this with the group.

"This certainly took a turn," Judy said in an amused tone. "Are you all right with the group hashing this out?"

"Sure! They're normal questions people have, and I'd prefer to set the record straight, so to speak." I heard a chuckle from Delaney, which told me he was still alive. When our eyes met, he bit his lip and looked away, as if still working stuff out in his head. I tried to put myself in his place, imagined him telling the group something I was completely unaware of. For fuck's sake, I would at least let him know I still had his back.

"Any words of encouragement instead of questions?" Judy said. "Maybe you could look some of these terms up on your own time. We obviously have people in this group who fall somewhere on the LGBTQIA spectrum, so if you're curious, you can learn more about your fellow attendees."

"What for?" a woman who usually stayed quiet suddenly piped in. "They always throw it in our faces. Who cares if he's gay?"

"He said he's bisexual, and what the heck are you talking about? Isn't this a support group where we share with each other?" Harmony said. "Besides, we could turn the tables and say that straight people are always throwing it in our faces too. You're the default for everything in society. How do you think that feels?"

I tried keeping my expression neutral, but damn, it was hard to hear the bigotry. When I glanced in Delaney's direction, there was a scowl on his face, but I couldn't tell if it was for the insensitive comment or the response Harmony had lobbed back. It made me feel really unsettled about our friendship.

"The foundation of this group is empathy. We need to be able to share important, impactful things in a safe space. If you disagree that strongly, maybe allow him the dignity of your silence," Judy said pointedly to the woman.

"You're right. I apologize," she said to me, and I nodded. At least she appeared remorseful.

"Good for you, Marc," another woman in the group said. "You deserve a small victory."

I smiled. "It's only coffee. And maybe it feels easier because...it's a man. Not sure if that makes sense."

"It absolutely does," Delaney said, and I held in a gasp. There he was. Finally. The guy I'd come to call a friend.

"It's someone different," Harmony chimed in. "Maybe even feels safer emotionally in some regard."

"Yeah, maybe."

When my eyes met Delaney's, his were hesitant, and it made my stomach pitch all over again.

"I appreciate your sharing," Judy said. "I'll be curious to hear more next session if you're willing. Now I'm going to change gears a little and discuss..."

I barely heard anything she said after that, but it had something to do with older members helping newer members figure out how to talk to their children about the concept of death. Delaney remained silent throughout that portion as well, even though I'd heard him expound on the subject in the past. His son was an older teen, however, and the focus today was on younger kids. Maybe that was why he wasn't sharing. Or maybe because he was still reeling from my announcement. That seemed the better explanation since he made very little eye contact with me again.

As soon as the meeting ended, I forced my legs to move toward the exit because I had to get the hell out of there. People were still staring, and it felt uncomfortable. But I'd admit, now that it was out, it was sort of freeing. This was a group that shared a lot with each other, and I'd considered it a lifesaver these past months. Maybe it was time to walk away, but that felt wrong too. I wanted to be around to show others that you could go on. And for Delaney, too, since his grief was fresher than mine.

Should I rethink those reasons?

As soon as I made it to the parking lot, I sucked in the cooler air. It would be autumn soon, my favorite season because nothing could beat the changing leaves in the Northeast. They didn't last long enough, in my opinion, not when it was followed by the bitter winters blowing off the lake.

"Marc, hold up." It was Delaney, and I didn't know if I had it in me to face him right then, not when he'd acted so strangely after my announcement.

Still, I turned toward him, noting the others from the group walking to their cars. I wanted to thank Harmony for having my back right away—unlike Delaney—but I didn't see her anywhere. "Lane, I swear to God, if you're going to say something insensitive or—"

He blinked. "Are you kidding me?"

I aimed the key fob at my car to unlock it. "I don't want to feel disappointed, especially since you've always been supportive."

"And that's what I'm trying to be," he said, gripping my arm, "even if it did take me a minute to process that information. I apologize for that."

I scoffed. "Several minutes."

His eyebrows knitted together. "What?"

"You said it took you a minute, but it was several; believe me, I counted." I had no idea why this was bothering me so much, but I couldn't stop my frustration from pouring out. "I knew there might be a bevy of reactions just because I announced I had a date with another guy. But from you, I expected at least a thumbs-up or something that told me you were cool with it. I was worried that you—that our friendship—"

"Damn, I'm sorry." He pushed his fingers through his hair. "Guess I felt blindsided. I just wish you'd told me."

"Told you that I'm bisexual, screwed around with a couple of guys before I met Carmen, fell in love, and married her?" I replied, a little too forcefully. "That's not a topic that ever came up between us. In fact, the only reason I latched on to the idea was because watching straight porn was painful for me, so switching to gay porn was a refreshing change, and from there, I just...I don't know, let my imagination fly."

His eyes widened as he stared at me. I knew it wasn't because of the porn topic because we'd both admitted to doing it in the past with and without our wives. It was during a particularly late night at the bar over drinks, where the topic of being numb and not feeling much below the waist came up. Grief wrecked you not only emotionally but physically as well.

"You're right. And I *totally* get it..." He bit his lip as if to stop himself from saying anything further. It only served to unnerve me.

I crossed my arms. "Get what?"

"Nothing, just..." He breathed out. "That it must've felt strange saying it out loud."

"It was." I leaned my hip against my bumper. "Guess I thought you'd immediately be receptive because of...well, because of Tristan."

"Yeah, of course. Like I told you, I was taken aback. I'm sorry it took me so long to get my bearings. I completely support you."

"Fuck, okay, thanks." I was definitely riding him way too hard. What the hell had come over me? My shoulders relaxed. "You're right. I should've told you. I didn't even mean to blurt it out tonight. I don't know why I did."

He glanced toward the building. "Maybe because it's good to get it out there in front of people you've trusted with other information?"

"Yeah, maybe that's it." I shoved my hand in my pocket, toeing at a rock on the asphalt. "Plus, next meeting, I would've been asked how the date went. And I hate hiding shit. I mean, unless it's necessary."

"Understandable. So this guy you're meeting..." He gulped,

and I could tell something was off, no matter how much he tried to convince me it wasn't. "It sounds promising."

"Like I said, it's only coffee. Meeting someone two and a half years after my wife passed away." I swallowed the boulder in my throat. It still felt...surreal.

"It's a big step. The guy's lucky." He nudged my shoulder. "You're sort of all right to hang with."

He grinned, and I returned the gesture, feeling calmer than I had all night. And also weirdly flattered. To hear he enjoyed our friendship made me feel special. Mainly because he could've chosen to spend his time with anyone else. He had a hell of a lot on his plate.

He lightly rapped his knuckles on my trunk. "And I hope to be able to get there myself someday."

I nodded. "You will, in your own time."

I had joined the group six months before Delaney, and in some ways, I considered myself ahead in dealing with my grief. In others, I was behind. Delaney was better at being direct—except tonight, apparently. But damn, he'd been there for me when I'd only wanted to throw myself into work and hide.

And when he was ready, plenty of women would find him attractive. Not only because of his kindness and compassion but also...his dark hair and light-blue eyes were very appealing.

Nothing wrong with noticing any of those things about my friend.

I felt a spike of panic. "I hope this doesn't change—"

"Never," Delaney said, clapping me on the back, and for the first time tonight, I believed him. Maybe it did just take him longer for stuff to sink in.

I felt more settled getting in my car and driving off. I'd had a rough couple of years, but I was finding myself again, which was progress. At the same time, I was also irked because that discussion in group would've never gotten so sidetracked had I announced my date was with a woman.

On the other hand, I'd undoubtedly pushed the envelope and challenged people's misconceptions, so maybe I just felt empowered tonight. Might've been because I was biracial and definitely had moments when certain things about me were taken for granted, so it resonated with the unique hurt my own experience brought. Because my skin was lighter, I had more privilege in certain scenarios, something I've been reminded of by friends and family over the years.

The same could be said of being a cisgender male married to a cisgender female and appearing seemingly straight. The guilt that came with those scenarios was real. But so was the acute pain of never feeling like you belonged or fit well enough into any one box. Don't get me wrong, I'd had my share of racist comments thrown my way, but my feelings about it were more nuanced and mixed with the guilt of not having been dealt as hard a hand as others. So that was probably why I took it upon myself to change people's perceptions.

I didn't feel like going home, so I drove around a bit, heading through the older sections of Shaker Heights, where the architecture was charming. I ended up on Coventry in Cleveland Heights, where I parked, then walked the length of the busy, eclectic street, looking in shop windows, then entering the popular sandwich shop on the corner.

Delaney lived close, but I'd never been to his house. I considered texting to ask if he wanted to meet me at the local bar, but I was still smarting a bit from our conversation. I normally enjoyed the solitude my job provided, but tonight I wanted to be around people—even strangers who had no idea what I'd just confessed.

I paid for my turkey sandwich, then ate a couple of bites while walking back to my car. I placed my bag on the seat and slid behind the wheel. My heart panged as I passed by the cemetery on the way home. I barely remembered the day of the funeral, let alone the week leading up to it.

In the subsequent year, I frequently communicated with her family, but lately, the calls had dwindled—and yeah, there was guilt about that too. The last time I checked on her mom had been last month, but she'd seemed preoccupied with her grandchildren there, so the call was brief.

As soon as I pulled into my driveway, my phone buzzed with a text from Delaney.

What did the skeleton say when he walked into the bar?

I couldn't stop the grin stretching across my lips.

You and your cornball jokes. What?

I'll need a drink and a mop.

I laughed even though it was pretty bad. But that was him, always trying to keep the mood elevated, especially for his son. In this case, he was trying to reforge the connection between us after he'd confused me big-time.

Eh, could use some work, I teased.

There was an elongated pause as I watched the dots moving, indicating he was typing.

So, I just wanted to apologize again. I think...hearing you're moving on did something to me tonight, and I was in my own head a little too much. I'm sorry I confused you and didn't come through as a friend. Please know I'm here whenever you need me.

I felt instant relief. There was the person I'd gotten to know.

Thanks. All cool.

5

DELANEY

"I wanna kiss you, Lane," he said in my ear, and my entire body lit on fire. *"Wait for me after the game."*

I watched from the stands as he kicked the winning goal, and then I second-guessed myself the entire time I waited near the parking lot as it cleared of fans. There weren't as many for soccer as for football, which was unfortunate but just the way it was.

His smile split his face when he saw me, making the butterflies kick up in my stomach. He was so freaking cute, so when he pulled at my hand, encouraging me to follow him behind the now-empty stands, how could I refuse? My heart was beating out of my chest, and I was scared we'd get caught, but when our lips connected, the whole world melted away.

I woke up with a fucking hard-on, and that hadn't happened in a long time—outside of my normal morning wood, of course. But this was different. This was about desire. I'd been numb to any sort of sensation in my body except for my broken heart, so that memory from high school, after all this time, really tripped me up.

The only possible explanation was that Marcus's confession had gotten to me. And not only because it took me by surprise.

There had also been this prickle of something else in my gut, something I'd ignored for years, by choice, and I didn't know if I could make sense of it now.

After Marcus admitted to meeting a guy, it felt hot and stuffy in the room, and at one point, I considered getting up for fresh air. But that would've gone over worse than the idiotic reaction I had. I knew I needed to talk to Marcus afterward. To let him know I was supportive and to explain my reaction— even though I didn't think I'd done a very good job. And to hear him sound so bummed really affected me because, if anything, he'd become a lifeline this past year, and I hoped I was one for him too.

The admission was brave of him, braver than I could ever be. Or at least during this tumultuous time in my life where I was just trying to be a good parent and hold our family together with nothing more than a paperclip and old scotch tape. That was how it felt most of the time.

I rolled out of bed to jump in the shower before Grant's alarm went off for school. The problem was, even after taking a piss, my cock was still agonizingly stiff. I decided I could do something about it. It was too painful to think of Rebecca, no matter how pretty she was and how much we'd enjoyed each other's bodies over the years. It was still too fresh, and I'd only ache for her more.

Instead, I thought about my dream and what happened after that kiss. A few more meetups for sloppy handjobs and rushed blowjobs until we'd gotten our fill and parted as friends who'd experimented with each other. No chance either of us was ready for anything more, and certainly not going public, knowing my father's views on his gay cousin. My mom would've been stunned to learn I was attracted to boys *and* girls, but eventually would've come around. I would never know, though, because she'd passed the year after graduation. I'd met Rebecca during the Christmas holidays when I was twenty, and we'd married two years later, once she'd moved home after college and I was on my way to pursuing my electrician's license.

I gripped my cock in a tight fist and leaned my head against the tile, trying in earnest to jerk off before Grant pounded on the door to ask what was taking me so long. My brain transitioned from the guy in school to Marcus, remembering how he'd admitted to messing around with men before marrying Carmen. Would his date lead to a hookup, and why did that intrigue me so much? I'd always found Marcus attractive, but I'd never allowed myself to take my imagination further. Until now. I pictured his full lips kissing a faceless man, his strong, calloused hands gripping the man's shaft, then leaving marks on his hips as he roughly fucked into him, maybe at Marcus's place, in his bed or on his couch, not that I'd ever been there before. But hell, the picture I created was enough to make me groan deeply and shoot off. Panting, I quickly washed up and finished my shower, my legs feeling rubbery.

Good. Maybe I'd act more human around Marcus now. Besides, that hadn't been about him, only about the act of getting off. He just happened to crop up because of his recent admission, which obviously made me dream about my own experiences. I could admire beautiful men as well as women and always had. But the term *bisexual* wasn't something that had ever occurred to me, likely because I wasn't exposed to it enough back then for it to feel a real part of my identity.

So why couldn't I admit that to Marcus? That was something I was still trying to unpack. If I had, he wouldn't have felt so alone last night. Thank God for Harmony. But I also hadn't thought about that part of myself in a long time, and certainly not since Rebecca passed. It felt...*wrong* in the midst of my grief, but I didn't really know why.

Maybe because Rebecca didn't know I'd had experiences with men—nobody did, except the two guys I'd screwed around with. It wasn't that I thought she'd be angry, scared, or hold it against me. More that I'd known with great certainty that I'd found the person I wanted to spend my life with, and even if I fantasized over the years about attractive men, that part of me had simply faded into the background.

I toweled myself off then went to my room to get dressed. I pulled a T-shirt over my head—and my eyes snagged on her side of the bed. Over the years, in our more sobering conversations surrounding the topic of death, she'd begged me not to close myself off to others. To find happiness again. At the time, there was no way I could've possibly allowed myself to picture that scenario. Still, I'd promised her, if reluctantly. But looking back, I sometimes wondered if she knew this day would come.

Turned out, I wasn't the only one. Others in the group had shared similar stories of their partners giving them permission to move on or pleading with them not to be alone.

"It's drizzling outside," Grant said, shuffling into the kitchen while I was pouring myself a cup of coffee. "Can you drive me?"

"Of course," I replied, reaching for the cereal box. "How about getting home? I might be able to—"

"I have Scholastic Challenge after school, so Ellie's mom can drop me off." Scholastic Challenge was a club for kids like Grant who enjoyed geeking-out on trivia in different categories, including geography and world history. They competed against other schools until it was whittled down to the final competition in the spring.

I nodded. "Ah, that explains the jacket."

He looked down at himself. "Is something wrong with it?"

"No, you look sharp," I replied, setting a couple of bowls and spoons on the table.

When his shoulders relaxed, I breathed out, glad I'd said the right thing. Today he was dressed in what I would call business casual: black jeans, a button-down shirt, and a business jacket, which he'd gotten on sale at the local department store. If I had to guess, he'd probably whip out one of his ties too. He'd done it for his other club, Model UN, where they debated global politics with the history teacher who ran the club.

He'd also worked at the Natural History Museum the past two summers, which he enjoyed, so who knew what career awaited him. The world was wide open, and I couldn't be prouder. But I kept my opinion to myself because the last time I'd uttered such a thing, his cheeks flushed, and he later accused me of embarrassing him in front of his friend. How the hell was I supposed to know they were communicating on a chat right then?

By the time Grant and I were in the car and driving to school, I'd reconciled what I'd done in the shower that morning. It was bound to happen eventually. No way was I ready to date anyone, so why not let my imagination run wild?

"What's wrong? You seem distracted," Grant said, giving me major side-eye. He was good at that.

"Nothing." I turned on my blinker and merged into traffic. "I'm just thinking about my schedule."

"Liar," he replied because few things got by him. Even if it seemed like his nose was buried in his computer, he still somehow knew when stuff felt off or wrong. "It's definitely something else."

What harm could come from sharing some of my thoughts with him? I didn't want to place another wedge between us, so maybe a partial truth was in order.

"It's just...Marc announced something interesting last night."

It felt silly admitting it out loud. Why in the hell was I so affected by it?

His eyebrows knitted together. "What did he announce?" Grant knew he'd become a friend, had even spoken to him briefly on speakerphone once, and I certainly didn't want to alarm him.

"Just that he's going on his first date since..." I paused to clear my throat. "And I suppose I've been thinking about how strange that would be."

"Because you're not ready?"

Noting the panic in his gaze, I patted his arm. "Definitely not ready. Feels like I might never be."

He was quiet as we pulled into the school, and I regretted telling him. He had enough on his plate, and I was only adding to that by having him think about his dad dating someday.

"Mom was pretty great, so maybe that's supposed to be reassuring to me," he said hesitantly. "That you wouldn't want anyone other than Mom. But I worry."

My gut churned. "About what?"

"About when I'm off to college." He frowned. "You'll be lonely."

My stomach bottomed out at his vulnerable tone. "You don't need to worry about that. I've got plenty going on." I got in line behind the other cars in the school drop-off zone. "Besides, people can still have a full life without being in a relationship."

"I know." He sighed. "But I think you liked being married to Mom."

"I did. She was an incredible person, and I'll be eternally grateful she said yes when I asked her to marry me." My chest throbbed, thinking about the life we'd made together. Sure, there were ups and downs, but we hung in there. "And having you was the biggest joy of our lives."

"Okay, you can stop now," he said, rolling his eyes, but his cheeks had flushed bright pink. I wanted to laugh or tease him, but sometimes his emotions turned on a dime, still too close to the surface, and I didn't want to ruin this heart-to-heart, which felt so rare of late.

"I did like being in a committed relationship with someone.

I'd found my person...and that might only happen once in a lifetime."

He chewed on his lip. "Yeah, maybe."

Damn, it was hard to have this conversation with him. After Rebecca had the first stroke, she went through a fairly quick recovery, and though we knew she could potentially have another, I never thought we'd lose her this early. When she began having TIAs, which were considered smaller strokes and essentially a warning sign, she was checked into the hospital. Still, I thought she'd get some new meds and be okay. I didn't allow myself to think she'd never come home. She'd had the big one in the middle of the night, long after Grant and I had gone home to get some rest. The phone call I received at dawn still haunted me to this day. And telling Grant, well, fuck, that about did me in. I was forever changed after those first few harrowing days.

But I absolutely did not want Grant worrying about me. So it was time to put on a brave face. This conversation only solidified the notion that Grant needed stability right now, more than anything.

"Anyway, time to focus on school." I nodded toward the entrance. "Have a good day!"

I watched as he walked toward Ellie and Jeremy, who were waiting near the entrance, and I breathed out, glad he finally had a couple of friends he felt comfortable with and who accepted him.

I drove toward the exit, questioning again my decision to share that information with Grant. And also, I couldn't help wondering...if he'd known Marcus was bi, how would he have responded if he discovered I was like Marcus? That I found men attractive and had been intimate with a couple of guys? Obviously, I would never tell Marcus's business to anyone without his permission. He'd admitted it to the group, but that was as far as the information would go. I never shared with

Grant any details discussed in those meetings, much like he never told me what he spoke about with his therapist, not unless it was requested of him.

Regardless, there was no way in hell I was going to turn Grant's world upside down, no matter how grown-up he'd sounded lately. I needed to get him through high school and into college. Maybe then I'd be able to think about meeting my other needs with a man or a woman. For now, the idea left me feeling unsettled. I was definitely not ready for anything beyond what my imagination had conjured up this morning.

It wouldn't be easy to shake our conversation, so getting lost in work would help. It took me ten minutes to drive to the Lakeview Electric Company parking lot. I went to my locker and changed into the company shirt, then asked the office manager for my schedule, which included a handful of corporate offices. I'd always dreamed of working for myself someday, but relying on this steady stream of work had been exactly what I needed these past couple of years. I worked on my own in the field anyway, outside of doubling up on services with coworkers when warranted.

"Do you think you can add a residential stop at the end of your schedule today?" Connie asked.

"What do they need done?" I asked as I read through the paperwork affixed to the clipboard.

"Grounding a few outlets."

"Sure, that'll work," I replied with a smile, then was on my way out the door to the company truck I drove to my appointments.

After a long day of work, we ate pizza for dinner, and then Grant helped with the dishes before getting on his computer, this time to watch a movie.

But at bedtime, he lingered outside the bathroom door as I brushed my teeth, and I could tell he was gearing up to say something.

"What's up?" I asked.

"I just...I was thinking about our conversation this morning."

"Grant, I don't want you to—"

"Wait, let me get it out. No matter what happens, I'll be cool with it, eventually. I can't say it won't be hard for me to accept someone else, but..."

"No need to worry about that for a long time," I said, and I could see the relief in his gaze.

"Hey, you never know. Going out to dinner or whatever might be good for you."

"I've got you for that," I countered. "Or my coworkers, or...Marc."

"Marc is cool," he said to my utter surprise. "Especially since he gets what we've been through. You should hang out with him more often. Invite him over sometime."

"I'll take that under advisement. Now go to bed."

6

MARCUS

I WAS NERVOUS. Why was I so fucking nervous?

Once I left work, I went for a run in the park to work off some of the tension. I showered and changed into my nicest jeans—the pair Carmen always said were her favorite—and a button-down shirt. All while my pulse continued its erratic drumbeat.

I got myself together enough to drive to the destination we'd agreed upon and finally got out of my car. It was only coffee. I could make it through one coffee. I looked around the nearest tables and the booths along the back wall but didn't see him yet. I waited by the door for five minutes, wondering if I was being ghosted. Then I turned toward the counter to give myself something to do instead of obsessing about being stood up.

"A hazelnut iced coffee, please," I said to the barista, who was a friendly young adult with a bright smile. I wasn't a huge fan of coffee, except when it came to the benefits of caffeine, so I normally tried to add flavor.

"Name, please?" She lifted the cup.

"Marc."

My grandfather had preferred Marcus or Mr. Worthy. He considered it a sign of respect. But it'd never stuck for me. My family started calling me Little Marc for differentiation's sake, and Carmen had used the shortened version as well.

Once I'd gotten my coffee and added two sugars, my date still hadn't shown. I found a table near the window, feeling a bit miffed that the guy was either standing me up or running late. Tardiness was one of Carmen's biggest pet peeves, and I certainly wasn't perfect, especially when it came to work, but at least I'd learned to let people know with a quick text if something came up or the shop got too busy. *"It's important that people can take you at your word,"* my grandfather used to say, and I'd been trying to live up to that standard my whole life.

I pulled out my phone and scrolled through the app to see if he'd canceled, but there was no message. Instead, I noticed a text from Delaney. *Lane.* My grandfather would think his name was strong too. He'd also think it was admirable that Delaney had been his mother's maiden name. And it went well with his last name: Roberts.

Good luck tonight.

It was a nice gesture after he'd acted so weird at our last group session.

I wanted to complain that the guy was late, but I also wanted to keep it to myself. Not only because I was possibly on the verge of being ghosted, but because I needed time to process it.

I ignored Delaney's message for now and promised myself I'd only wait ten more minutes. That was when the bell above the door rang, and a guy with broad shoulders shuffled through the entrance.

I recognized James from his photo, so I lifted my hand to direct him my way, taking in his solid stature and chiseled jaw as he drew nearer. He was about ten years younger than me and very handsome in person, even more so than in the profile pic he'd posted.

"Sorry, I'm late. Traffic," he muttered, and I relaxed a little more. At least there was an apology, so I supposed I needed to cut him some slack.

"It's cool." I pasted a smile on my lips. "I would've ordered you something, but I wasn't sure what you liked."

"I actually hate coffee," he said with a wave of his hand.

My stomach tightened. "Well, shit. Why did you agree to meet at a coffee shop?"

"Because they sell other kinds of drinks here, and besides, it was a good halfway point for us." He looked over his shoulder toward the menu above the cash register. "I see they have hot chocolate. I'll be right back."

I couldn't help fidgeting as I watched him place his order at the counter. Something felt off, and I couldn't put my finger on what it was—other than my meeting someone for the first time after fifteen years of marriage. Our conversations leading up to this moment were perfectly pleasant, but maybe I wasn't paying close enough attention. I was likely amazed that he seemed nice, was attractive, and interested in meeting a couple of weeks after I'd joined the site.

But maybe thinking it was that simple had been my mistake. I was used to the old-school style of meeting someone, where you initially saw them face-to-face before asking them out. Of course, dating sites had been around back then, but they didn't really catch fire until after I was married. I'd heard a dozen stories over the years from friends or family who'd met their significant others online. I'd thought it was cool that there were easier ways of connecting with people, but it obviously came with its challenges—like not being able to read some-one's eyes or gestures, which left written dialogue up to inter-pretation.

And my gut ended up being right because when James

returned and got himself situated across from me, the conversation felt awkward. I might've chalked it up to nerves on my part, but once he got going, he enjoyed talking about himself a little too much. I literally could not get in a word edgewise. He only asked me briefly about my job, and just as I was going to explain how I'd inherited Worthy's, he launched into something about his friend who owned a gym. I drifted into my own thoughts, and when I heard him clear his throat, I realized he'd finished his story.

"So you work with old stuff?" he asked, so maybe I needed to cut him some slack for rounding back to his original question. "I'm more of a modern type of guy."

"Different tastes." I shrugged, feeling a prick of exasperation. "A lot of the stuff I restore is sentimental."

I thought about the shortwave radio someone had brought in today that stood about four feet tall and had been passed down in the family. I dove in as soon as the customer left, carefully cleaning it before opening the back to view the circuitry, losing myself completely in the task.

"Wanna get out of here?" he asked with a lift of an eyebrow.

Did I? If things had gone well, maybe I wouldn't have minded a hookup, or at least a make-out and groping session. But more so, I'd hoped my first time meeting someone would proceed more slowly. I wanted to ease into the idea, quite honestly. And it didn't help that the guy had rubbed me the wrong way.

"I...I don't know," I admitted. "The truth is, this is my first time since..."

Fuck, I didn't want to blow this by bringing up sad shit. But what did it matter? I didn't think there would even be a second time with this guy. There wasn't much of a connection, except maybe physically.

"Since what?" His eyebrows had drawn together.

I took a breath and then just got it out. "Since my wife passed away over two years ago."

His eyes grew comically wide. I hadn't told him that in any of our conversations. It was nice just to talk about myself without that topic being the focus. Now I wondered if James had ever lost someone dear to him, but I didn't want to sour the mood any more than it already was.

"Oh shit, have you been closeted this whole time?"

My gut tightened. Really? That was his first response? No compassion about losing someone?

"Closeted—no, I'm bi. It's just been years, and I thought... I don't know what I thought exactly." My fingers fiddled with my coffee-cup lid. "I'm sorry if I gave you the wrong impression."

He narrowed his eyes, a cross between amusement and impatience. "Were you only looking to experiment with someone? If so, we can still get out of here and—"

"No, been there, done that—before I was married. I was just hoping for a pleasant conversation, maybe a connection, and I figured I'd go from there."

"Yeah, okay." He looked away as if he didn't believe me. "For what it's worth, I've been with plenty of 'straight' guys who are closeted gays."

"I'm not..." I scoffed. What the actual fuck? "Thank you for meeting me. But I'm not looking for anything else, not tonight."

I reached behind me to throw out my cup in the nearby receptacle, feeling pretty frustrated. All I wanted was to get out of there.

"Looks like I ruined the evening," James said with a frown, which made me feel a bit guilty. Except, he was obviously expecting something physical to happen between us. Maybe *meeting for coffee* on an online dating site was just code for hooking up. What in the hell did I know? Damn, I was feeling my age.

"I'm gonna guess you have plenty of opportunities," I

replied, and the smirk on his face told me everything I needed to know. "Thanks for the coffee. It was nice to get my feet wet."

"Hope you figure it out." He stood with his empty cup, then bolted out of the shop. I waited several beats so it wouldn't get uncomfortable in the parking lot, and thankfully, I saw no sign of him as I slid into my front seat.

I felt unsettled the whole way home, wishing I hadn't mentioned any of that. Maybe I would've gotten into the guy, into the idea of leaving with him, if I'd just... No, I knew better than to force it. This was a date, not a hookup. It might've led to sex if we were both on the same page, but the messages between us all week only talked about grabbing coffee and meeting face-to-face. If he assumed something different, that was on him.

When I turned into my driveway, the house seemed as gloomy and empty as I felt right then. I considered walking over to my mom's place, but she'd probably ask a bunch of questions I wasn't ready to answer. My sister was good at the intrusive queries as well. Which was why I hadn't told either of them about the date, and even if I had, I wasn't sure I'd say it was with a guy.

My family knew I'd been with both men and women back in the day. But fifteen years had passed, being married to a woman I was deeply in love with, and the subject had never come up again. Just like James, they probably assumed I was only experimenting before "deciding" to be straight. Though I'd expected better from someone in the LGBTQIA community. Guess it only showed there were losers everywhere.

I winced as I got out of the car. I'd thought that of Delaney after the revealing group meeting and still felt like I was walking on eggshells where he was concerned, though he'd apologized and sent a supportive text tonight. It was hard to be disappointed by people you connected with, especially on a visceral level.

I turned on practically every light when I got inside, then some music to fill up the quiet—nineties R&B seemed to fit my mood. I changed into sweatpants, grabbed some water from the tap, then retreated to my living room, where I propped my feet on the coffee table and scrolled through my phone.

You around? I texted Delaney.

Absolutely. Wanna talk? he replied, likely figuring out I was home early.

Yeah.

"You okay?" he asked as soon as I answered my cell.

"Sure." I sighed. "It was a good experience, but it ended up being a bust."

He sucked in a breath. "What happened?"

"I just...I suppose dating is the same no matter what stage of life you're in." I pulled a pillow onto my lap. "You either vibe with the person, or you don't, remember?"

"Yeah. It's been so long," Delaney said with a laugh. "I wouldn't even know how to get on a dating app."

"It's easier than you think. But obviously, it's still hard, no matter how you meet someone. And it feels so fucking surreal, sitting across from a stranger you're trying to get to know. I was hoping I could just shut that other part of myself off, but it turns out I can't, so it got awkward."

He didn't even ask what I meant; he just knew. Grief. *Sorrow.* The person you loved no longer being in this world.

"I'm sorry." I could hear it in his voice—the empathy. The thing missing from the dude I'd just met. "Maybe that was a practice run, and from here, it gets easier."

"Maybe." I leaned my head back and closed my eyes.

"I was driving Grant to school the other day, and I told him you were going on a date," he said, and my eyes flew open. "I kept it general, no details about who it was with. I suppose I was curious about his reaction, and it was exactly what I expected."

"What do you mean?"

"He was a bit freaked. I could see it in his eyes. Which confirmed what I already knew. That my sole focus should be on getting him through high school. Know what I mean?"

"Yeah, I think I do. But I'm a bit confused. Were you considering dating too?"

"Hell no, and certainly not after listening to your experience," he said with a smile in his voice, and I snickered.

"It wasn't that bad," I replied as if I needed to defend the guy.

"Bad enough to keep me firmly single. Or should I say widowed?"

"That's gonna be up to you. This time around, I chose not to disclose anything before meeting him, but maybe I need to change my approach."

"Does that mean you're gonna put yourself out there again?" He sounded hesitant, and now it made a bit more sense. He wasn't ready, but maybe it was more about Grant than him, and I didn't know how to feel about that.

"I'm not really sure," I replied, and that was the truth. After a brief pause, I blurted, "So hey, do you ever find yourself doing things you know Rebecca would've never approved of?"

"What do you mean?"

"I don't know." I looked at my toes, which were dangerously close to knocking a candle to the floor. "Like, right now, I have my feet propped on the coffee table, and Carmen would've hated that."

"Ah, now I get it." He snickered. "I'll admit, I leave the kitchen a wreck sometimes, which would've driven her crazy. What do you think that's about—some sort of anger or rebellion?"

"I don't know. Maybe it's more about us figuring out who we are again without them?"

"I like that," Delaney said. "Not sure anything is truer."

We stayed on the phone for another hour, talking about random shit. From the very first meeting in the grief group, it had always been easy with Delaney. We'd exchanged numbers at the second meeting, after we'd stayed in the parking lot, talking for far too long. After the next one, we'd gone out for a drink, and the rest was history.

But even after we got off the phone, I was still a bit worked up.

So I looked up some gay porn and got myself off to two average guys fucking. They were grunting and sweating and evenly matched in size and age, and hell, it was beautiful to watch. I'd also admit to wondering the whole time what it might've been like tonight if James had been more like Delaney. Not just how attractive he was, but his personality too.

Dangerous territory...

7

DELANEY

I WATCHED through the window as Grant wheeled his bike out of the garage. The weather had held up through most of September, but today called for rain. Grant had insisted he could make it to school and back unscathed, and instead of arguing, I'd decided to let it go. *Natural consequence* was what Rebecca would call it whenever I'd freak about any of Grant's decisions, and she was right. If he got rained on this time, he might decide to proceed differently next time the forecast looked iffy. As a parent, you needed to pick your battles, but it was harder in practice than it looked. At least it was for me.

Today he wore a graphic tee that read: *Burr Shot First*, referring to the infamous duel between Aaron Burr and Alexander Hamilton. Rebecca had taken him to see the *Hamilton* musical a couple of times, and he owned the soundtrack. It made me smile when he finally started playing it again about a year after she died. As if it'd been too painful to relive it before then. It offered me reassurance that we'd eventually be okay.

I raised my hand in a wave as he rode off down the driveway, thankful he hadn't put on his felt top hat for the ride. It was sure to be distracting to some drivers, and I was always worried about close calls when he rode in the bike lane.

Or...that's what I told myself. Deep down, it was about not wanting to lose him. And okay, I also never wanted my child to be ridiculed the way I was as a kid—which for me had been mostly by my own father. He was a hard man to live with and, obviously, the effects were long-reaching.

After finishing my coffee, I rinsed the mug, gave Ruby a new bone to chew, then locked the door behind me to start my day. Marcus's date night hadn't been far from my thoughts all week. He'd sounded so raw and vulnerable afterward, and had I been with him, I would've tried my best to make him laugh. Maybe told him one of my corny jokes. Because when he smiled, it was dazzling and lit up his whole face.

The part I couldn't quite wrap my brain around was the sudden relief I felt once he'd told me his date hadn't turned into anything more. Was it because I didn't want him to move on and leave me behind? Ridiculous. We'd be friends regardless. At least, I hoped so.

So why hadn't I told him yet about my history with guys? Truth be told, it still felt like a quiet part of myself that had only perked up when Marcus announced his date in group.

Of course, the dream only served to remind me of my past, and I felt like I was viewing the world around me through a different lens. Which didn't make a ton of sense because being bisexual was a part of me, even if I'd never put a name to it back then or understood it better. But maybe that was no excuse.

Still, I wanted to think on it a bit longer.

Once I got to the office, changed into my work shirt, and slid into the truck with my roster for the day, the sky had turned gloomy. It sprinkled on and off all morning and afternoon, with rumbles of thunder in the distance.

My last appointment was canceled, and by the time I was back in the parking lot, the rain was hard and steady, accompanied by lightning. I planned to go inside and complete the paperwork from my appointments, but I was trapped in the truck for a long spell, waiting for a break in the weather. I used the time to check on Grant, who assured me he could get a ride home after club.

"Hope we don't lose power," the office manager grumbled, fiddling with the transistor radio she kept on her desk as I slipped inside.

"No kidding. It's wicked out there." It was rare that we lost power in our neighborhood, but a storm like this hadn't come through in a few months, so anything was possible.

Once I changed back into my regular clothes and made sure the invoices were accurate, I scrolled to Marcus's number, curious how he was fairing at his shop.

Has the storm blown through already?

Not yet, but already lost power. Sitting in the dark with a flashlight, finishing my sanding job.

That sucks. No generator?

No, but every time this happens, I wonder why I've never invested in one.

Well, I can help with that. I am an electrician, after all. My last appointment got canceled, so how about I stop by to see if there's anything I can do to help?

I certainly couldn't restore his electricity because that was up to the city and its power grid. But I knew a few linemen, and they were sure to already be working around the clock.

My heart was beating a little strangely as I waited for his response. I'd never met Marcus for lunch or even seen his place of employment, let alone where he lived. This seemed like the perfect excuse.

Sure. Come on by.

Once I plugged in the address, I got on the road and headed to his business. As I pulled into a space in front of the redbrick

building, it dawned on me that I'd driven past this area at least
a dozen times and it had never registered.

I'm here. It's pouring, so I'm gonna make a run for it.

Rain pelted me as I stepped out with my toolbox, but then
Marcus was there, holding the door open for me with a smile.
Despite the chill, it warmed me instantly.

I stepped inside to a mid-century time warp. There was stuff
everywhere. So much so that I didn't even notice the front desk
until I trailed behind him to the back room. In my defense, the
shop was dim, the only light coming through the narrow
windows, the back door, which he'd propped open, likely to
allow cooler air to filter through, and from a few candles he'd
lit around the space.

I'd heard countless stories about his business, including the
origins and different projects he seemed excited about, but
actually being there was on a whole other level. Worthy's was
like a cross between an antique shop and a junkyard, and it was
hard not to want to take in everything all at once.

"Your shop is pretty awesome," I said, turning in a circle,
noticing all the stuff lining each surface and crammed into
every nook and cranny. "I've passed by this place so many
times, but the outside looks pretty inconspicuous."

"True," he said, glancing out one of the tall windows, the
view obscured by the rain. "I could change the sign to something brighter and more noticeable, but it's the original, and I
can't seem to part with it."

"No, you should keep it." My gaze snagged on a couple of
wooden cabinets lining the far wall. I had so many questions.
"And all this stuff is..."

"A wreck. But it's my wreck." He laughed as he led us to a
back corner, where a flashlight highlighted something he was
working on. "It's either stuff people dropped off for me to refur-
bish or endless projects I've been dabbling in for years."

"Damn, no wonder you're always here."

Marcus grinned. "I could sleep here and still never get everything done."

"I believe it." My gaze caught on a standing radio that had to be from the forties or fifties. "Okay, that's pretty darn cool."

"My newest project." He motioned me closer. "A 1946 Philco. Tricky, though. Been at it for hours."

My fingers brushed over the sanded wood, noticing the buttons and dial at the top and the accordion-style slats below that covered the vertical speaker. "What's tricky about it?"

"The circuitry." He turned it around so I could see the open back portion, where he'd removed the panel to expose the ancient board. "I don't have the skills to actually fix it, but I can make it look nice."

"Damn, I'd love to take a stab at it sometime." And I meant it. I missed dabbling in the kind of stuff I used to when I was a kid and had gotten one of those circuitry kits for Christmas. And Christ, now I remembered how I'd try a little too hard to impress my father by rewiring stuff to light up or make sounds.

"I've got it for the next couple of months since the customer is traveling abroad. So have at it. In fact, most of the things I'm taxed with are last-ditch efforts to save something sentimental, so the timeline is pretty lax."

As I walked around to check out more of his shop, I thought about his offer. The idea of fiddling with stuff made excitement course through me. Maybe I'd stop by on a weekend when Grant had other plans.

"Now I'm curious about your house if this is what your business is like." There was a little of everything there, from the smallest trinket boxes to tall bookcases. "You must have some interesting decor."

"Not really." He frowned. "We've never been that enthusiastic about our house. As I told you, we had plans to move one day."

"I remember." It was during one of our drinks-at-the-bar

evenings after group. "So this place holds more sentimental value than your house?"

"Exactly."

"I can see why," I said, noticing an interesting set of wooden salt and pepper shakers. "It belonged to your grandfather. Your great-grandfather too, right?"

"Yep." He stared out the window as if remembering something. "I used to help Grandpa Worthy when I was a kid. I'd ride my bike here after school. It's one of my best childhood memories."

I smiled. "I like that and can totally see the appeal."

He walked me through some of the more interesting projects, like a school desk from the turn of the century and, honestly, it was great. I could tell how much it meant to him, and I felt privileged to have been invited here.

When the lights flickered on and off, he stopped in his tracks. "What does that mean? Is there hope I'll get electricity back?"

"Let me test an outlet," I said, though I already knew this outage had to do with the city's power lines. But right then, I wanted to somehow seem useful to him.

I walked to the entrance, where I'd left the toolbox I'd carried inside from my car. Opening it, I reached for the multimeter, then tested the voltage in the outlet near the front desk. "Just like I thought. Nothing registers. It might be a while."

"That sucks." He sighed. "I wonder if I've got power at home. Thought my mom could tell me, but I forgot she's visiting my sister in Mentor today. Their electricity is still on."

My thumbs were already crafting a text, first to Grant, who should've arrived home by now, then to a friend who worked for the city. "Hang on, let me ask one of my contacts."

I sent off the message and was surprised when I could already see him responding, so maybe he was on a break.

"It's a huge outage, but he thinks some parts of Euclid might still have power," I said, glancing at the return text. "My friend will be working into the night."

"Imagine having that kind of job," Marcus said, shutting the back door, then blowing out one by one the candles he'd lit. I could see through the window that the rain had momentarily abated.

"At least they get paid double time." I shrugged. "I'm a union guy, so been there, done that."

"Guess I gotta stay closer to you when there are outages."

For some reason, my stomach tightened at his statement.

"Suppose I'm useful for something." I cleared my throat. "But I can totally set you up with a generator for times like this."

"I might just take you up on that."

I felt my ears grow warm. It was good to feel valuable.

"I live close by, only a few streets over." Marcus reached for his keys behind the front desk. "So I'm going to head out, see if my neighborhood has electricity."

"Fingers crossed for both of us. I texted Grant to see how we're faring too." Right then, my cell chimed with a response from Grant. "Speak of the devil."

The storm's cleared, we didn't lose power, and I'm home safe and sound.

Awesome. Be home soon.

I thought about my conversation with Grant from the other morning.

"Here's an idea," I said to Marcus as I followed him out the door. "If your power's out, come have dinner with me and Grant."

I held my breath as I waited for his reply. I didn't know why I needed this so much. But maybe Grant had been right about spending more time with friends.

"Would you mind following me home to check on the

lights?" he asked in a hesitant tone. "If I'm out of luck, I'll totally take you up on your offer."

"Sounds like a plan."

I slid behind the wheel of my car and quickly texted Grant. **Just FYI, if Marc's neighborhood doesn't have power, I invited him to have dinner with us.**

Cool.

I smiled.

My pulse was beating erratically the entire time I followed him home, which didn't make a ton of sense. Marcus was my friend, and I had extended an invitation. No big deal. Except, not only had I never seen his workplace until today, I was about to see where he lived, and if the power was out, he would be meeting my son. That was likely the reason I was feeling out of sorts.

He lived in a neighborhood of small bungalows, and when we pulled into his driveway, I could see what he meant about his house—not that I'd admit it out loud. It didn't feel like him, not after visiting his shop. I could see him living in something with more charm and character.

"See what I mean?" he said when I followed him up the steps to his porch, as if he could read my mind. Hopefully it wasn't written all over my face.

I shook my head. "It's a nice house."

"I noticed you didn't call it a home." He glanced over his shoulder as he placed the key in the front door. "You're just being kind."

"Absolutely not."

He pushed it open, and I waited on the landing as he tried a lamp. When it didn't turn on, he told me to wait as he stepped farther inside. I could actually picture him living here with Carmen and making future plans. Too bad they were never able to come to fruition.

"You're right that it doesn't feel like you, but it's a cozy place," I said as he returned, wearing a clean shirt. "Your furniture is nice."

"Guess it'll do for now." He locked up the house behind him. "Thanks again for the offer. I would've boiled in here from the humidity alone."

"You were gonna boil in that store too, Mr. Workaholic."

"Yeah, suppose I can ignore shit around me when I'm working."

I nudged his shoulder. "I like it. How dedicated you are."

His cheeks colored as we stared at each other a bit too long.

A crack of lightning broke up the moment.

"C'mon, let me feed you," I said, suddenly feeling unsure of the menu I'd planned this week.

"Not cooking for one always sounds good to me," he said with a laugh, but I heard the tension in his voice. If I didn't have Grant to care for, would I even make an effort?

By the time he followed me back to my neighborhood, the weather was beginning to clear, with the sun peeking through the clouds.

8

MARCUS

ALL IT TOOK WAS one storm and a chance text exchange for me to finally see where Delaney lived. It was a quaint neighborhood, and by the looks of the outside of his Tudor-style house, I'd probably love the interior too.

I parked behind him in the driveway, and as I turned off the ignition, I surmised that his square footage certainly beat my small bungalow's as well. I couldn't help being immediately envious because Delaney's house had the kind of charm I wished mine had. It was older than other houses in this area but in good shape, and the exact reason I liked driving through this part of town whenever I had the opportunity.

Not that I was knocking my neighborhood. Everyone I'd encountered was friendly, and it was cool to live right around the corner from my mom. But this was the type of house I'd always aspired to own, even if it was different from Carmen's idea of living on a ranch away from the city. I'd always hoped we'd reach a compromise, and I was gutted that I never had the opportunity to find out.

Delaney waited for me on the generous front porch. As I walked up the steps, I noticed the solid wicker furniture that resembled my own. I wondered if he sat out here as often as I did on mine. The backdrop of the fall leaves would make it totally worth using on a regular basis.

Inside, the place was just as impressive, and I took in the living room with the built-in bookcases, likely original to the house, and the dining area with its lovely crown molding. But before I could ask how old this structure was, I was assaulted by a blur of reddish-blond, fluffy fur.

"Hey, girl." I squatted down to the dog's level and petted her. When she licked my face, I laughed. "Ruby, isn't it?"

"Don't maul him," a voice said from the other room, and then I saw him, his son, Grant. His dark hair was the only feature on him that resembled his dad, and from the photos we'd exchanged after group one night, I thought maybe his eyes and face shape favored Rebecca more.

No doubt, it was surreal to be a guest in their home after hearing about their lives for the past year. But maybe it was time. After all, he'd let me cry on his shoulder enough times since we met.

"Grant, this is my friend Marc," Delaney said as Grant stepped fully into the room.

I lifted my hand in a wave. "Nice to finally meet you in person."

"Yeah," he replied, dipping his head in an awkward way, and it reminded me of how I'd respond as a kid getting introduced to adults. "Uh, Dad said your electricity went out?"

"Yep." I glanced out the window, noting it was sunny. "How was the storm here?"

"It got pretty bad while I was in school." He bent down to pet Ruby's head. "The lights flashed a couple of times."

"I'm just glad no trees went down around here," Delaney said. "We've got some large maples."

"It's one of the things I like best about this part of town," I said. "Guess it also has its drawbacks."

"Totally. We hold our breath every storm," he said, and Grant nodded. "Suppose we're lucky our house is still standing."

"I'm gonna guess this house was built pretty solidly, though," I pointed out. "What year was that?"

"1908," Grant piped in, and I smiled.

"Don't get him started," Delaney said. "He'll tell you the history of the whole neighborhood."

"*Dad,*" Grant muttered in a strained voice, his cheeks dotting pink, and I could see the tension between them. Delaney had mentioned it a couple of times, but I'd chalked it up to Grant being a moody, hormonal teenager. I certainly was no angel during that time of my life.

"Is that right?" I replied. "Well, I'm a bit of a history buff myself. Maybe not an expert like you, but I've had some cool stuff brought into my shop. Discovering the origin is always a treat."

"Really?" Grant's eyes lit up. "Any wardrobe pieces?"

"Unfortunately not. It's not that kind of business." I toed the hardwood floor, which looked to be original to the house as well. "But Cleveland definitely has its share of vintage clothing shops."

"Oh, he's well aware," Delaney said. "Grant will have to show you some of the period pieces he likes to wear."

"Yeah, I collect stuff like that," Grant replied in that same mortified tone as if Delaney was embarrassing him simply by pointing out his interests. Ah, teenagers.

"Speaking of clothing, I like your shirt," I said, noticing the historical reference. *Burr Shot First.* "Some say Burr shouted the word *wait* before he killed Hamilton. That he apparently noticed too late that Hamilton had his gun raised toward the sky."

"Uh-huh," Grant replied. "Do you think he had any regrets?"

"I don't know." I folded my arms and thought about it. "Not that it's historically accurate, but in the musical *Hamilton*—"

"He went about his business as if he hadn't just killed someone he once considered a friend."

"Right. Though he likely believed Hamilton had slandered him, and that was the last straw." I shrugged. "I'm just glad we don't honor that tradition anymore. I have horrible aim."

"Same." He smirked. "Though it might solve some disagreements more efficiently."

I snickered. "You've got a point."

Delaney listened with an amused expression on his face. "Uh-oh, looks like I'm the odd guy out."

I raised an eyebrow. "Are you saying you never saw *Hamilton*?"

"Oh, I did. *Once. Grant* and Rebecca let me tag along the second time."

Grant turned his head to try and hide his eye roll. "I also have the soundtrack."

"Me too." I raised my hand to high-five him. How could I not? The first successful hip-hop musical and witnessing the diverse cast was heartening. "What's your favorite song?"

He chewed on his lip, considering my question. "Maybe a tie between 'Alexander Hamilton' and when King George sings 'You'll Be Back.'"

I grinned at the memory. "He is a pretty amusing character."

"Okay, you two," Delaney said with a smirk. "I'll start dinner. You're free to follow me into the kitchen."

"Sounds good. Thanks again for inviting me." I paused to take in the wood-burning fireplace as well as the family photos lining the mantel. They definitely seemed happy in all of them. Damn, life was harsh sometimes. "Hopefully I'll get out of your hair soon enough."

"It's no problem at all," Delaney said over his shoulder.

When I followed Grant through the dining room to the

kitchen, I was pleasantly surprised. Usually, these century homes had small kitchens and closets and too many walls that acted as barriers, but this was a decent size. And okay, I knew a little too much about this style of architecture.

"Have a seat." Delaney pointed at the table, then turned to Grant. "Did you get your homework done?"

"Yep," he said, heading to the fridge. "I can help you chop the broccoli."

"Hope you like broccoli cheese soup?" Delaney asked hesitantly. "Suppose I didn't exactly tell you what was on the menu."

"That actually sounds perfect. What doesn't sound perfect is me sitting here watching you two cook. Let me help?"

"I should've expected as much from you." He smirked. "Want to chop some onions and carrots?"

"Absolutely," I replied, pushing from the table to stand.

I'd admit, chopping vegetables beside Grant at the counter while Delaney stood over the stove, making a roux, was not something I'd ever pictured. As I listened to Grant tell Delaney about his club, it felt...strange but good. And way less quiet than my place.

When Grant had a snarky response to something Delaney asked, I quipped, "So I guess teenagers haven't changed much since our generation?"

Delaney grinned over his shoulder, and I was relieved we were on the same page. He'd told me once that his mom had passed and that he and his dad didn't get along.

"Whatever," Grant scoffed. "I'd probably never even survive growing up in that decade. How did you go all day without cell phones and computers?"

"You'd be surprised," I replied as I blinked repeatedly from the scent of the onions. "We had to rely on our imagination."

"Did you and your wife have children?" Grant asked, and Delaney shot him an uncomfortable look.

"It's okay, Lane," I said before turning back to Grant. "We were never able to. Not for lack of trying. But we did help raise her teenage nephew for about a year."

"Where is he now?" he asked, seeming genuinely curious. That was surprising because sometimes kids just weren't that inquisitive.

"Aaron graduated from college and moved to take a job in California."

"Cool." Grant glanced at Delaney, who stood ramrod straight for a moment before placing the broccoli in the large bowl beside the cutting board.

I wondered if I'd touched on a tricky subject for them, like college.

"Should we set the table?" I asked to change the subject as I rinsed the knife in the sink.

Grant nodded, then helped me retrieve bowls, napkins, and utensils.

By the time the soup was bubbling and ready to be served, I was starving. The smell must've enticed Ruby as well, and the golden retriever was now lying underneath the table, possibly hoping for scraps.

"This is delicious," I said after we sat down and I dug into my bowl. "Has your dad always been this good a cook?"

"No," Grant said with a laugh. "But after my mom..." He trailed off, looking remorseful for bringing it up.

"It's okay, you can talk about her," Delaney said, reaching for his drink. "It's important that we normalize saying her name and remembering all the good things."

It was something Judy had said once in the grief group, and while I understood the sentiment, it was still fucking tough.

Grant swallowed a bite of soup, then nodded. "Anyway, Dad started using Mom's recipes after she passed. He's still not as good a cook as she was, but he's getting there."

"Thanks for the compliment," he said to Grant, and I could

tell it was heartfelt. I wondered if I'd just witnessed one of their more sincere moments.

"What is the best thing you make?" I asked, adding oyster crackers to my soup.

"Probably her chicken paprikash?" He looked at Grant, who nodded in agreement.

"I bet it's fantastic. I'm not very good in the kitchen, so I can be bribed with home-cooked meals—just ask my mom. There's a reason I live right around the corner from her."

Grant leaned toward Delaney. "You should invite Marc when you make it again."

"I'd love that," I replied, feeling a warmth flood my stomach.

I met Delaney's eyes, and he nodded, seeming tempted by the idea.

When Grant's phone buzzed with a text, he looked down and smiled. "Dad, can I—"

"Go up and play *Crusader Kings* with Ellie?" He said it like it was a regular occurrence, and from what he'd told me, it absolutely was.

Grant wiped his mouth with his napkin. "Jeremy too."

"Sounds fun. Don't stay up too late."

Grant stood and rinsed his bowl in the sink. "I'm practically an adult," he replied as he opened the dishwasher.

"Nope, you're still my teen until you're official."

"Whatever. C'mon, Ruby." He headed toward the stairs to the second floor, and Ruby trailed behind. I was going to guess that she provided them much comfort in these difficult months. "Bye, Marc, hope your power comes back on soon."

"Me too. Thanks for having me."

9

DELANEY

I watched Grant head upstairs to his computer. I was relieved the dinner had gone pretty well. Grant certainly seemed to find a connection with Marcus, and it was a nice reprieve from his usual grumpiness whenever I interacted with him. Maybe Marcus provided the levity we needed after trying for so long to find common ground.

"He's just as you described," Marcus said, pushing back from the table. "Whip-smart and a history buff to boot."

"Yeah, he definitely takes after Rebecca in that department," I replied, remembering how their heads would be bent toward each other as they shared relatable memes or videos.

"Hey, don't do that. You're just as smart," he said as if recognizing the stab of frustration in me that I'd never measure up.

"It's not..." I shook my head, trying to find the right words. "They shared a special, palpable connection. It was...beautiful to see. She loved science, he loved history, and they would nerd-out together."

He nodded, then folded his arms. "And what do you love?" he asked, and my gaze snapped to his.

I was taken aback by his question. Not that we hadn't

discussed common interests every now and again, but honestly, we mostly discussed our grief. "I...I dunno, exactly."

"Sure you do," he insisted. "Take your time."

"All right." I swallowed thickly. "Uh, well, some of it you probably already know."

"Refresh my memory."

Damn, why was he being so insistent?

"Christ, is this what it felt like going on that first date?" I teased. "*Tell me everything about yourself.*"

He laughed. "Unfortunately, yes, and it sucks."

"I hope that doesn't mean you've deleted the app and given up?"

"Not yet," he admitted, then motioned between us. "Sometimes I think it might be better to just make a new friend."

"We're not exactly new."

"No, but maybe this is our transition from being deep in our grief to thinking about what's next and who we are without them."

Fuck, that hurt, but he was right.

"Does your family know you're dating again?"

"No." He winced. "We're celebrating my mom's birthday next weekend, and I might just tell them."

"That hard, huh?" I teased.

"What do you think?" He raised an eyebrow. "Now stop changing the subject and answer my question. What does Lane enjoy?"

"Crime shows, obscure documentaries, working out." I smirked. "This old man finally got back on the treadmill. Plus, I've got a weight machine upstairs, and that helps me blow off steam." I patted my belly, which had grown soft in the past few years. "And to keep my paunch from becoming a bigger one."

"Tell me about it. That whole metabolism and age thing," he said, though I didn't note an ounce of fat on him. "But cut yourself some slack. You have a nice physique. And the weight machine explains why you've got some good guns."

"Thanks," I muttered, flushing, and felt that same prick of something in my gut. Something I didn't want to name.

"I like crime shows too, by the way. Every Friday night I watch *Dateline* because they feature—"

"Real-life mysteries," I supplied, being all too familiar with the show.

Marcus smiled. "Yep. Carmen liked to read, so she'd leave me to it."

"Same with Rebecca," I mused. "Though she'd look up from her book from time to time to add one comment or another."

He chuckled. "They might've made good friends."

"You might be right," I said as Marcus stood and began collecting our bowls. "Hey, you don't have to do that."

"Of course I do. You invited me over, and you cooked." Marcus brought our dishes to the sink. "We had a thing in our house—whoever made the meal didn't have to do the dishes. And before you complain, I like to wash dishes by hand."

"Okay, fine." When I sat back down, it was like taking a load off, which was such an unexpected sensation. Like I'd been running on all cylinders for the past couple of years. Still, it was a foreign feeling, and I needed to do something with my hands. "I'll pull up the website for the power company to see if there are any updates in your area."

"Good idea." He turned the faucet on and reached for the sponge.

"It looks like your area is still down," I said once I'd punched in his zip code. "But they have an alert system now. If I key your number in, they'll send a text alert when your electricity has been restored."

"Sounds good," Marcus said absently, and when I looked

up, he was staring at the wall beside the dishwasher. "Are these paint samples?"

"Yeah." I sighed. "We'd planned to update the kitchen, but then the worst happened, and I just *couldn't*, though it definitely needs it."

"Understandable." Marcus reached for a towel to dry his hands. "What was your vision?"

"To paint the walls, maybe save money by refinishing the cabinets." I pulled out a large Tupperware container to store the soup leftovers. "Rebecca wanted a large kitchen island to replace this table." I slid the container of soup on a shelf in the refrigerator.

"Why not let me help?" He poured water into the pot to let it soak.

"How so?"

"Your cabinets. In case you didn't notice, I own a business where I've gotten pretty good with refurbishing old stuff." He threw me a pointed look, and my face heated. I felt like a dope as he stood back and scoped out the space. "I also have the perfect cabinet you could use as a kitchen island. It's been in my shop collecting dust for years, and I've been looking for a good home for it."

"I couldn't..." I sputtered, feeling overwhelmed by the offer. "Besides, when would you have time?"

"I dunno, weekends? What else do I have going on? Okay, that made me sound pathetic. You know what I mean."

I nodded because I absolutely did. Staying busy, hoping that it somehow helped fill up the hole in your heart.

"Sorry," Marcus said, "not trying to overstep. It was only an idea. Just ignore me."

"No way. Now you've got me thinking." I looked more closely at the paint colors I'd tried on the walls. Rebecca hadn't liked any of them. "I'd pay you, of course."

"You could pay for the materials, but otherwise, I'd actually enjoy it." He cleared his throat and stepped back as if he'd gone in too hard on the idea. "Talk it over with Grant. It's just...these older homes need to be preserved. My grandpa used to like this quote that went something like, *Our future relies on preserving our past.* And I like to think that applies to restoring old things too."

"I like that. I feel guilty that I haven't gotten around to it. Not that I'd be any good, except with the electrical."

"Hey, that's absolutely something I'd never be able to solve," he pointed out. "And we both know that when life throws you shitty curveballs, you have to readjust your plans."

"True," I admitted. "Even if it takes us a while."

Our eyes met and held for a brief moment, and it felt so damned good to be around someone who really got it.

"It looks like another storm is rolling through," Marcus said, glancing out the window. "Any chance we can head to your porch? I love sitting on mine when it rains, and yours looks way cozier."

"A man after my own heart," I said, and his eyes lit up. I opened the fridge and grabbed two beers. "Let's go."

It felt peaceful out on the porch as we watched the clouds pour water on the world around us. The cool air felt good, and so did the cold beers going down. I tried to stifle a yawn. I was tired, but I also didn't want him to feel like he was imposing.

The truth was, I was enjoying myself. We didn't have many guests outside of family, and ever since Rebecca passed, it felt awkward around the married couples we'd hung out with. Besides, they were mostly Rebecca's work friends from her real-estate office. Not that they hadn't been gracious and extended invitations, but I just couldn't bear to be around all that...togetherness.

"I might head home after the storm passes. I don't want you to feel like—"

"I don't. And you have an alert on your phone now. Wait it out a bit more. You don't want to sleep in this stifling heat."

"Are you sure?" He reached forward to tap my knee, which produced a buzz over my skin that matched the electrical energy in the air.

"Of course I'm sure." I motioned toward the door, trying to shake that strange feeling that had come over me. "Want to head back inside and watch something?"

"A crime show?" He winked.

My stomach tightened. "*Law and Order SVU?*"

"Perfect."

We got ourselves settled on the couch, and I chose an episode. Marcus admitted he wasn't as far into the series as I was but urged me to hit Play.

I couldn't stop yawning, though, and it seemed to be contagious because the next time I glanced at Marcus, he'd fallen asleep with his head leaned back against the cushion.

I found myself watching him—his soft mouth with slightly parted lips, his fluttering eyelashes, which had fanned against his cheeks. He was a handsome guy, and I felt guilty for staring. But maybe it was more that I was allowing myself to notice things again. And people. *Attractive* people.

It was as if I was suddenly coming up for air after choking for so long on the heaviness of the grief inside me, and maybe Marcus had everything to do with it. Maybe he'd opened my eyes to future possibilities just by being honest in a roomful of people who were grieving too. And maybe he'd put a name to this thing I'd kept hidden inside me.

Suddenly his phone buzzed with a text, startling us both.

His eyes sprang open. "Shit, sorry." He ran his hand over his face and sat up, trying to get his bearings.

"No worries," I replied as Marcus lifted his cell. "Maybe it's the electric company."

"Yep." He offered a sleepy smile. "Looks like my power is restored."

"Great news," I replied, my face still feeling flushed from all my confusing thoughts. "Take your time getting your stuff together...and then I'll walk you out."

Afterward, I cleaned up the kitchen in a daze, then headed upstairs to bed.

"Grant?" I said at his door, which was propped partially open.

"Yeah, Dad?"

As I stepped inside, I saw he was no longer on his computer. Instead, he was in front of his fish tank, changing the filter. He'd had the tank in his room for years and was pretty responsible with it.

"Just letting you know Marc went home. His power's back on."

I glanced at Ruby, asleep in his bed. It was a mutual love affair between them, and I knew she'd brought him as much comfort these past months as she had me.

"That's good news," he said absently, watching the fish. "I'm glad you're friends."

"Yeah, he's a good guy," I replied, then cleared my throat. "So listen, we were talking about updating the kitchen and, well, Marc offered to refinish our kitchen cabinets. I haven't given him an answer yet because it would uproot our lives a bit and I don't want..."

His eyes briefly met mine. "Why do you think he wants to help?"

"He knows how to do all sorts of stuff because of his business." I thought back on our conversation about it. "Or maybe he likes to keep busy."

"Because his wife died too?"

I nodded, not meeting his eyes because I felt vulnerable right then. Like he could see right through me. How I did much the same because if I stopped long enough to think about how our lives had been turned upside down, I might just come apart at the seams. And I wouldn't be much good to anyone. Not that Grant thought I was good at much. Though his remark at dinner seemed genuine.

"Might be a good idea," he said. "Wasn't it something Mom wanted to do for a long time?"

"Yeah. So maybe that's part of the reason."

"Too bad she'll never see it," he grumbled.

Fuck.

"How do you know? People believe all sorts of things. What if she checks up on us every now and again and can see what we're up to?"

He rolled his eyes. "Those are just things people believe to give them hope."

Damn, he sounded so much like Rebecca. She was skeptical of everything, including the afterlife. But she never imposed her views on him, instead encouraging him to ask questions and find his own answers. I always liked that we'd given him that freedom, but when it came to explaining death and suffering, there were no simple answers, no matter what you believed.

I straightened and met his gaze head-on. "What's wrong with having a little hope?"

"Nothing, I suppose." His computer had been abandoned on the edge of the bed, and he glanced back at it as if remembering something. I wanted to ask what, but I kept myself in check. If he wanted to share, he eventually would. There was that hope thing again.

"Well, good night."

"Night, Dad."

10

MARCUS

"COME HERE and give your auntie a hug," Mom's sister, Sherry, said as soon as I stepped inside the door. "I hear you've been working yourself to the bone. Just like my father did."

Not like I have much else going on, I wanted to say. I adored my family, but they loved sticking their nose in my business. It was born of concern, of course, but sometimes I wondered how anything got by them. "It's been busy, customers dropping off stuff to be salvaged left and right."

She clucked her tongue. "Be sure you make time for other things as well."

When my gaze met Keisha's, she smirked, likely happy that it was me under the spotlight rather than her. She loved teasing me or joining in on the grilling I received from family members, and I gave it back good. Still, I didn't dare pass up this cherished family time. Today it was only my mom, aunt, sister, and her boyfriend, Jeff. But I'd grown up with my cousins because Mom and Aunt Sherry remained tight despite their differences. One of my most vivid memories from childhood was the phone cord stretching across the room as Mom talked to her sister, sometimes for hours, while cooking or cleaning.

"I hope you're hungry because we have plenty of food," Mom said as I kissed her cheek. Mom always insisted on cooking for everyone, even though it was her birthday. I'd made sure to stop at her favorite bakery for a Black Forest cake and then at the store for vanilla ice cream.

"I definitely am." I patted my stomach. "Besides, how could I refuse my mother's amazing cooking?"

"That would be the day," she said, raising her spatula at me. She was making her famous lasagna, and the smell had drawn me inside as I came up the walk. Aunt Sherry was in charge of the garlic bread, Keisha made a salad, and Jeff, who was a really nice white guy completely smitten with my sister, had gone out to buy candles because I'd forgotten. Again.

In fact, we were a pretty diverse family. Aunt Sherry's second husband was from Colombia, and two of my cousins had what would be considered biracial marriages, just like my parents. Of course, back then, it was shocking for a white man to marry a Black woman, and up until the 1960s, it wasn't even legal. I wished I could ask my dad questions about that time of his life because apparently, his parents had practically disowned him. But he was steadfast in his love for my mother, and the way she'd described it, despite those external hardships, she wouldn't have it any other way.

Once we'd all gathered around the table to eat, I dug into my lasagna, wondering how Delaney and Grant might've fared here with my family. Why it even crossed my mind, I didn't know. Maybe because meeting Grant reminded me of helping raise our nephew and how vulnerable he'd been as a teen. What would I have done if he'd been living with us at the time of Carmen's passing? I felt for Delaney in that regard. And based on what he'd shared in the grief group, he felt like Rebecca had been the better parent, and that bummed me out because he didn't give himself enough credit. He was a good human being.

Sure, our friendship had turned awkward for a minute because of the way he'd initially responded to my dating news. But he'd more than made up for it since then, so I could forgive him for that. Besides, I got this feeling he was working through his own stuff regarding meeting anyone new, especially since he'd tried to gauge Grant's reaction to the idea.

Speaking of dating, Aunt Sherry was already up to her shenanigans, pushing me to get out more. "Any new friends in your life?"

"Will you stop pushing him?" Mom scoffed. It was a point of contention with Aunt Sherry, likely because Mom had lost a spouse too and had never remarried.

"Actually," I said because it was the perfect opportunity— and honestly, this was my family, and they were a huge support in my life, "I went on a date, but it didn't go very well."

"What?" Aunt Sherry said and looked accusingly at Mom. "And you didn't tell me?"

"I had no idea," she said, narrowing her eyes. "And I can see why. He didn't want his nosy auntie meddling."

Aunt Sherry rolled her eyes, and Mom patted my hand reassuringly.

"No one could replace Carmen, anyway," Keisha said with a sniff. She and Carmen had been tight, and I didn't expect her to easily accept anyone who came into my life.

"True. Which was probably why..." I trailed off, wondering if getting into the details now was the right decision.

"What was she like?" Mom asked, still looking shell-shocked about my announcement. "The woman you met?"

I winced, already regretting the decision to share. But also hoping to get it over with so it wouldn't be hanging over my head. "Actually, my date was with a man."

I heard Keisha whistle as I took in my Aunt Sherry's stunned expression. "Say what?"

"I'd been with a couple of guys back in the day. You already know that," I said, waving my hand dismissively, hoping this didn't turn into a thing. I could see Jeff shifting uncomfortably in his seat. He'd been witness to plenty of family discussions by now, but I supposed not quite like this.

"It's been so long, I'd forgotten," Mom said in a near whisper. "I thought maybe it was a phase."

Keisha snorted. "It's really not a phase if you're actively hooking up with dudes."

Good God. I could feel the blood rush to my cheeks, and I couldn't even look at Mom, let alone Aunt Sherry. It made me feel like a teenager all over again. Keisha's crude response didn't exactly surprise me, and she normally always had my back. Though she was sure to get on my case later about not telling her or seeking her advice. The truth was, I hadn't really needed it.

"Are you saying you're gay?" Aunt Sherry asked with raised eyebrows, and I noticed how Jeff's face had turned a bright tomato red like he wanted the floor to open and swallow him.

I squared my shoulders. Time to act my age and help my family understand. "I'm bisexual. I've dated both men and women, but when I met Carmen, it was all over. I knew she was the person I wanted to spend my life with. It doesn't mean I'm less bisexual just because I was married to a woman. It's part of my identity. I was monogamous and devoted to Carmen, who just so happened to be a woman."

"I won't say I completely understand," Aunt Sherry replied, "but I will always support you."

Keisha smiled, and so did Jeff, which made me breathe out in relief. Mom's eyes softened, and she reached for my hand to briefly squeeze my fingers. "So this gentleman wasn't up to your standards?"

I winced, remembering the awkwardness of the coffee date. "He seemed...self-absorbed."

"So it was a perfect match!" Keisha declared, and I

pretended to throw my napkin at her. She always thought I was too quiet and introspective, even when Carmen was alive, whereas Keisha could be outspoken and brash, which was why we fought like cats and dogs as kids.

They went on to discuss how Keisha was doing at her job in medical sales—she always kicked ass—as well as her and Jeff's recent beach trip to Puerto Rico with his two adult children, whom Keisha had grown close to as well.

"Did you at least use sunscreen?" Mom asked Jeff teasingly, and we all laughed because he'd admitted in the past how easily he burned. Apparently, it had also been an inside joke between my parents because my dad would get red in the face if they spent any amount of time in the sun. My skin sometimes got blotchy too from being outdoors too long, so I felt like I had something in common with my father, some little connection that soothed that twinge in my chest every time I saw an old photo or heard a story and wished I'd known him.

After Carmen died, Mom was a constant comfort, promising I'd get through it despite the immense heartbreak. She'd always said my father was the love of her life, to the dismay of her family, who'd always had the worry about the escalating racial tensions back in their day and had been witness to the Hough riots. And don't even get me started on Dad's closed-minded family in rural Ohio.

But Mom had been modern for her time and even hyphenated her name when they married. She carried on the tradition with my sister and me, and though I was proud of the Davis part of my name, I mostly went by Worthy because of my grandfather's business. Mom had never even dated anyone else, at least not that I knew of. But I'd always wished she'd find a bit of happiness again—not that a relationship defined you.

Mom was a force to be reckoned with. I'd married someone similar in Carmen, and had it been me who'd gone early, I'd want the same for my wife. We'd discussed it in our more tender moments, and I knew she'd encourage me to date again, even though I hadn't had much of a desire to seek anyone else out since the date gone astray. Maybe because it reminded me just how difficult it could be to find someone you connected with. I'd probably try again, but for now, I'd stopped opening the app.

When my phone buzzed with a text from Delaney, I grinned at the message.

I swear, if Grant plays the *Hamilton* soundtrack one more time, I might go mad. I blame you for making him remember it existed.

Sorry, not sorry.

"What are you smiling about?" Aunt Sherry asked. "A new dating prospect?"

"No, just a friend." Though the idea of him being any sort of prospect made my stomach clench in a strange way. "Delaney. *Lane.* I met him at my grief group."

"I remember," Mom said. "Sounds like he's been a good friend to you."

"He has." I nodded. "He lives in this century home in Cleveland Heights, and I'll tell you what—"

"You fell in love as soon as you walked inside?" Keisha teased, knowing my proclivity for old, charming things.

"Okay, I wouldn't go that far," I replied, almost wincing as I remembered how I did actually fawn over each room once I stepped inside. "But I did offer to help him refinish the cabinets in his kitchen and some other stuff."

Though I probably freaked him out even mentioning it. Likely, he thought it would disrupt Grant's life too much. And that was understandable.

"That's right up your alley," Mom said. "But don't you have enough on your plate?"

I shrugged. "This would be in my spare time. For fun."

Jeff laughed. "Only you would think something like that was fun."

"Right?" Keisha said, and I rolled my eyes.

"Your grandfather used to do some dabbling on the side too," Aunt Sherry said. "He loved fixing up their house. Drove your grandmother crazy."

"He sure did," Mom added. I smiled at the memories, thankful again that I'd been able to work with my grandfather and inherit his store.

After dinner, we sang happy birthday and passed around slices of cake. I wasn't a big fan of Black Forest, but I ate it anyway so Mom wouldn't get on my case about not finishing my plate.

We retired to the living room, where Jeff turned on the Browns and Steelers game, which was on Primetime tonight, obviously due to their decades-old rivalry. I wondered if the television was on in Delaney's house and if that was something he and Grant shared. I was going to guess not.

Instead of trying to guess, I lifted my cell to ask him.

Does Grant enjoy sports?

I looked up to watch the Steelers run the ball into the end zone as I waited for his reply. Jeff threw up his hands and grumbled about the defense. The usual.

No. Neither of us really do. Why?

Because I'm at my mom's and the Browns game is on.

See? I totally forget. LOL. I'll turn it on now.

Don't bother. They're already losing.

Ugh. Figures. How was dinner? Did she like your cake?

Good. And yes.

Glad to hear it.

My thumbs hovered over the keys as I wondered if I should tell him more while my nosy sister was seated right beside me. But she seemed as into the game as Jeff.

I also told them about my date, but only after my auntie drilled me about my love life.

That's always fun, isn't it? So how did it go?

Surprisingly well. I know some won't truly understand, but I feel supported nonetheless.

That's important.

Yeah, it is. Thanks. So how was your day?

Busy with errands. We also visited Rebecca's grave. Grant wore his Lafayette coat with the brass buttons in her honor, which is likely why he's been blaring *Hamilton* all evening.

Damn, that got to me. It was so symbolic and sentimental, and he probably didn't even realize it.

Ah, that makes a ton of sense. Damn, your kid is something else. Cooler and braver than I've ever been.

My confession to my family paled in comparison.

Yeah...yeah, he is.

When I pushed my phone back into my pocket, I could feel Aunt Sherry watching me, but I pretended not to notice.

11

DELANEY

I PULLED down my street after a stressful workday. It was late
September, and I felt like a heavy cloud was hanging over me,
due in part to it being our twentieth wedding anniversary. I'd
mentioned it at grief group a couple of months ago when
important dates had been the topic of conversation, and I'd
been deep in the sorrow and shock of it being two years since
her passing. I planned to take some of the advice Judy had
offered, including indulging in memories even if they were too
painful. It was better than ignoring them and allowing them to
fester.

Marcus had been supportive as well, walking out with me to
the parking lot that night to discuss it and then texting me
today.

Thinking of you.

How in the hell did you remember?

I'm good with dates.

Well, shit, teach me your ways.

Ha-ha, maybe someday. For now, be gentle with yourself.

Thanks. I'll definitely try.

I didn't think it would hit me as hard as it did, but this

morning I considered calling in sick, queuing up the video from our wedding day, and then wallowing in the melancholy.

But I'd needed to send Grant off to school, which forced me out of bed. Always did. He was well aware of the date—I'd said as much during our visit to her grave last weekend. He'd glared at me as he slid in the front seat, wearing full revolutionary garb, the costume Rebecca had helped him find, as if daring me to say something. The visit was sentimental for both of us, and no way was I going to ruin that.

I met Grant as he was about to head out the door. Apparently, I'd forgotten he was invited to dinner at Ellie's house tonight—which solved my having to cook something. Plus, I wasn't feeling very hungry. Probably something to do with the tension in my stomach all day. I threw my keys on the counter and slipped out of my shoes.

"You sure you don't want me to stay?" Grant asked after taking one look at me. My mood must've been written all over my face, no matter how much I tried to hide it.

"Absolutely not. I'm good." I squeezed his shoulder. "Besides, I didn't have any dinner ideas anyway."

"Okay. I'm gonna ride my bike over. Be home in a few hours." Ellie's parents were cool, and since she only lived three streets away, he was fine to walk or ride his bike—they'd likely play video games after dinner, and he'd lose track of time. But he was mostly good about curfew.

"Don't forget to honor their rule about bedroom doors staying open," I said in a rush before I could stop myself. He was well aware of their rules, which mirrored my own, but I certainly didn't want him to jeopardize their trust. Not when it'd taken him so long to find such a good friend. Rebecca would've given me *the look*, the one that told me when to back off if I was acting too overprotective, and I supposed I was no good on my own without that sobering reminder.

Grant stood stiffly with his back to me. "Do you really have to remind me every single time? Nothing is gonna happen with Ellie and me except playing video games. I'm not like you!"

"What the heck does that mean?" I replied, utterly confused.

"I..." He shook his head. "I don't know why I said that. It didn't come out the way I wanted. I was just pointing out that she's my friend. Nothing more."

"Got it, loud and clear." I was perplexed and a bit hurt by his tone, but I let it go. There was nothing I hated more than arguing with Grant. "You should get going. See you later."

He stood there a moment longer, as if wanting to say something more, but I didn't have it in me to drag it out of him. I got busy unloading the dishwasher, and when I heard the door shut behind him, I breathed a sigh of relief.

"I'm not like you."

Way to rub it in, kid.

Once the dishes were put away, I changed into sweats, then sank down near an old chest in the living room, where we stored our photo albums. I considered texting Marcus something silly instead of going down memory lane, then recalled how Judy had encouraged me to be indulgent.

Pulling out the first album, I scooted backward to rest against the couch and began paging through our wedding photos, remembering how excited and sure of myself I felt that day, marrying my best friend, tearing up at the first glimpse of her walking down the aisle. We looked so young and happy, and I almost didn't recognize myself without the scruff I'd begun sporting shortly after she passed, too emotional to care about facial hair, let alone any other forms of grooming. I'd eventually gotten it together but kept the beard, maybe as a marker of sorts.

Before I knew it, an hour had passed as I smiled and blinked back tears, and went through a hundred other emotions. Ruby must've sensed I was going through something because she lay down beside me and propped her head on my knee.

"Such a good girl," I said, brushing my fingers down her coat.

I packed the albums away and stood, glad I'd followed Judy's advice. I felt a bit worse for wear but okay. Better but not perfect. Sometimes I thought I might never experience that buoyant, happy feeling again.

When the doorbell rang, Ruby barked, startling me. Hopefully it wasn't a door-to-door salesman.

I opened the door to find Marcus standing on my porch. "Marc. What are you doing here?"

"I'm sorry I didn't call first. I was sort of in the neighborhood." He grimaced as if reconsidering his decision. "I don't want to intrude. I thought maybe you'd want company. Or just this."

He produced a bottle of bourbon from a paper bag. It was the same brand we'd sipped during one of the evenings we'd met at a bar and had agreed it'd become a favorite. It was smooth and bold, with other complex notes, and suddenly it felt like the perfect idea for a night like this.

"I...uh..." I opened my mouth to speak, feeling a bit thunderstruck, not only because Marcus had shown up but also because it was such a kind gesture.

"It's just...you sounded so down when I messaged you earlier."

"You can tell that from a text?" I teased, finally finding my voice.

"We've gotten to know each other pretty well, right?" He shrugged. "And I know firsthand how hard these kinds of days can be."

My heart throbbed. "Thanks. You're a good friend."

"You are too." He handed me the bottle as our gazes

clashed. "Anyway, here you go. I know how much you enjoyed this when we were at the bar."

When he turned to leave, panic seized my chest. "*Wait.* Come inside for a drink?"

He shook his head. "It's okay to say no. You're not obligated to invite me inside just because I showed up uninvited."

"I..." I looked down at my bare toes. "I didn't realize until you were actually here how much I needed the company."

When our eyes met again, his softened a fraction. "Okay, but only if you're sure."

Once I let him inside, he followed me to the kitchen.

"Is Grant here?" he asked, glancing toward the staircase.

"He's at Ellie's tonight." I reached for two whiskey glasses from the cupboard, trying to remember the last time they were even used. "How did you and Carmen celebrate anniversaries?"

"It was a big deal in the beginning of our marriage, but then it became just us being together, doing any little thing we enjoyed." He twisted open the whiskey. "How about you?"

"Pretty much the same, outside of this big one, where we considered traveling somewhere. The details were never hammered out." In hindsight, maybe that was for the best, or else I'd be lamenting some sort of trip abroad or to the West Coast. I held the glasses steady while he poured us three fingers each. "We definitely enjoyed going out to dinner."

"Same." Marcus smiled. "Do you have a favorite restaurant?"

"Yeah, the Asian one on Coventry."

"The one that's been there forever?" he asked, squinting as if trying to picture it.

"Hunan's," I replied, finally remembering the name.

"That's it. They make the best brown—"

"Sauce," I said at the same time as him.

"No way. You too?" he asked, his eyes alight in wonder.

"Damn, that sounds good." I patted my stomach, remembering right then that I hadn't eaten dinner. "Sometimes I crave it."

"Wanna order delivery?" Marcus asked hesitantly, still apparently feeling like he was imposing. "Unless you already—"

"I could eat."

"Yeah?"

I nodded. It would feel nice to share another meal with him.

"Okay, pulling up the site..." He lifted his cell and punched in the web address. "Chicken or shrimp?"

"How about both, and we can mix and match?" I suggested.

"Perfect," he replied, raising the phone to his ear and placing the order.

I felt lighter than I had in hours.

"Done," he said once off the phone. He lifted his glass and clinked it to mine. "To twenty years of loving someone with your whole heart."

"Absolutely," I said around the boulder in my throat. Fuck, that'd made me emotional. "Hey, you never know...maybe they're out there somewhere, cracking jokes about us. Rebecca telling Carmen how she hated the way I left my socks laying around."

Marcus snickered. "Or Carmen complaining that I was a terrible cook but tried anyway."

"Really?" I said around another sip. It felt warm going down. "Have you improved at all?"

He frowned. "I don't really know. I'm the only one eating it."

Wasn't that the fucking truth?

We sipped and talked about random stuff and set the table. Before we knew it, the doorbell rang and our dinner arrived.

We carried the brown bags to the counter, then set the containers in the middle of the table. We opened the chicken and shrimp with the delicious brown sauce, which was a bit tangy and a little spicy, and the smell made my stomach grumble. We loaded some of each on our plates, then dug in. I briefly considered saving some for Grant until I remembered he wasn't a fan, preferring plain sticky rice with salt and butter. Rebecca was a fan of their garlic sauce and didn't like to mix and match, instead savoring her favorites all on her own.

I didn't know why I was making a comparison right then, except that it was a reminder of what I could expect in the future. If I ever dated someone again, there would be different things to get used to about a person. It seemed too much to consider, though, too painful as well. I prayed it went smoothly just like it did now with Marcus. He was easy to get along with, and I was grateful he'd made the effort to stop by.

"God, I missed this," I said around another bite. "It's been too long."

"Same here," he replied before relishing a forkful. "Glad I thought of it."

After two helpings, we cleaned up our dishes, then went to enjoy the cooler night on the front porch. Marcus poured more whiskey into our glasses, and I brought the bottle along, just in case. But I was already feeling the effects, and soon enough, it was bound to loosen my inhibitions, something I was all right with tonight. It had been an emotional day.

We clinked glasses again, and Marcus said, "At least we were lucky enough to have successful marriages. Many of my friends didn't even make it past five years."

"I hear you. A committed relationship is hard but rewarding."

"I think the key is communication because as the years go by, you both change and grow and can sort of lose track of each other if you don't check in regularly," Marcus said, staring at a fixed point near the street.

"True." I was suddenly feeling a bit ill. "And there were things I never told her...about me. About when I was a teen."

"We all have stuff we keep private. You've been carrying this guilt around this whole time?" he asked, concern in his tone.

"Yeah, maybe. Maybe not. I just...she was a good woman, and I always thought, *Damn, I'm lucky to have her* and never wanted to rock the boat." I blamed the whiskey for my loose tongue. "Grant loved her so much, and sometimes I felt like a third wheel... Fuck, why am I saying this to you?"

"I'm glad to be here for you." He patted my knee. "Don't feel bad about it."

"I guess the whiskey doesn't help," I mused. "Thanks for... being here. For making me feel comfortable."

"Of course." He cleared his throat. "And damn, the guilt can swallow you whole."

"What kind of guilt are you carrying around?" I swung my glass toward him, and some sloshed on my wrist.

"About going on a date, for one."

"We all have needs. Emotional and physical."

"I didn't for a long time," he admitted, making me recall one of our earlier conversations.

"Same. I haven't until..." I clamped my mouth shut. Holy shit, what was I saying?

"Until what?" he asked, leaning forward a little.

My heart thumped in a staccato rhythm. I was dying to get it off my chest, to finally say it out loud to someone. I inhaled a sharp breath, then went for it. "Until recently when...well, actually when you announced your date in group." There, I'd said it. I held my breath, waiting for his reaction.

"I don't understand."

Fuck, I so didn't want to look at him. But this was important. Maybe it would help him understand better my behavior that day.

"You asked why I was acting so strange in group...I was a jerk for not snapping out of it sooner," I explained, "but it wasn't because I was being insensitive. It was because you brought forth something in me that'd been buried for a long time."

"Your physical needs?" he asked, clearly confused.

I almost laughed because I was probably making little sense. I wouldn't have understood my weak-ass explanation either.

"In a way, yes." I swallowed. "That same night, I dreamed of someone I hadn't in a long time."

"Who was it?"

"My first crush in high school." I could feel my face heating. "It was a guy."

He gasped, his hand covering his mouth, but waited me out.

"We experimented with each other, then went our separate ways," I said, my stomach warming at the memory of those first times. It was after I'd already lost my virginity to my first girl-friend, and it had felt different but good. So fucking good. "I went on to crush on other guys...and girls. No way I wanted to be found out because my dad was—is—a super homophobe."

And I hadn't wanted to make waves at home, just like I never did in my own marriage. Christ, that sudden awareness took my breath away. I was too careful with everything.

"Are you telling me you're bisexual?"

"I honestly never had a name for it until...well, until your confession. Rebecca never knew. Nobody did. Every now and again, I'd fantasize while jacking off, but it's been so damned long. And if Grant knew... We're already on such shaky ground."

"Hey, your secret is safe with me," he said, and I knew he meant it. "But I'm curious about that dream. Why do you think you had it?"

"Probably because I've been numb for so long...and it felt like being shocked awake to hear you'd taken that leap with someone. Does that make sense?"

"Yeah, of course."

"Again, I'm sorry I reacted that way. I would take it back if I could."

"Don't waste another precious minute worrying about it. Okay?"

I sighed. "Yeah, okay."

We stayed silent, each processing while sipping the rest of the bourbon in our glasses.

"Does this mean you're ready to get out there?" Marcus asked hesitantly.

"Hell no. I'll just live vicariously through you. I'll consider it —*maybe*—once Grant has graduated and is well into college."

"But you have needs too." He sat up. "And there would be nothing wrong with you—"

"No way. Even discussing it makes me feel sick to my stomach and guilty as hell."

"Understood."

I unscrewed the top on the whiskey and poured a bit more into my glass. When I motioned to him, he waved me away, which made sense because he had to drive home.

"Do you ever wonder...?" Marcus began, then looked at me. "Would we have become friends had it not been for the grief group?"

"Maybe not," I admitted, my stomach feeling unsettled. "Which sucks because I enjoy our friendship."

Marcus clinked his glass to mine, then said, "I'd like to think that in the right circumstances, we'd still somehow become friends through some shared experience."

"Yeah, maybe. We may have both been at the restaurant without knowing it. I might've even seen you across the room and thought, *That is a very handsome man. I'd like to be friends with him.*"

He laughed. "Are you trying to say you find me attractive?"

"Sure. Why not? I find a lot of people attractive."

Our eyes met, and there was this bright energy there—that

was the only way to describe it. It made my pulse tick up in a throbbing tempo.

"I find you attractive too," Marcus said, clearing his throat and shifting in his seat.

"Why, thank you." I lifted my hand and started fanning myself, my skin feeling on fire. "Did someone raise the temperature out here?"

"This is the perfect opportunity for one of your corny jokes. The ones you use to change the subject or lighten the mood."

Well, damn. "Busted."

12

MARCUS

"HOW ABOUT WE HEAD INSIDE?" I said because the conversation had gotten a bit...heavy and personal and *heated*. I didn't know why I liked hearing he found me appealing, but I did, and that was dangerous territory, mostly because he'd placed strict parameters around his needs. Not that being attracted to someone meant that it had to lead someplace else, only that I didn't want to make him uncomfortable about his admission. Feeling attractive would be a good boost of confidence for anyone, period.

"Good idea," he slurred as he stood with his glass, then reached for the half-empty bottle.

As he lumbered through the door, I trailed behind him, making sure he didn't bump into anything. In the living room, he sank down on the couch and patted the seat beside him. I probably should've taken off by now since this visit had only been on a whim, but I was enjoying his company, and going home to an empty house wasn't so enticing right then.

So I took a load off and talked about random shit with him for a bit longer.

Besides, Delaney was tipsy, and it might be a good idea to

keep an eye on him. He'd made some unexpected admissions that completely threw me for a loop, and I needed to tread carefully so he didn't have any regrets. It was important he felt safe enough to express himself, especially since he tried to hold it together around Grant like most parents probably did. Getting those feelings out was healthy and helped with the grieving process, as I'd come to learn. Not that he was done suffering—and his heart might feel as irreparable as mine—but milestones were important. It meant there was a path forward to a new sort of normal.

"What time is it?" he asked, sitting straighter as if he'd get in trouble for slouching. "I should probably check on Grant."

"I thought you said he was at Ellie's house," I replied, noting how freaked he looked. Was it because of the drinking or because he'd let it all hang out? "Does she live around here?"

"Yeah, but earlier..." He glanced toward the window, then allowed his shoulders to unwind again. "I said the wrong thing to Grant before he left, and we got in an argument."

"Don't be so hard on yourself." I hated that he tensed up so much when he was in parent mode, seeming so unsure of himself.

"In case you haven't noticed, I suck at this on my own." He sighed. "Rebecca always knew how to level with Grant, to appeal to his sweeter side. She was the perfect buffer between us."

I'd noticed some tension between Grant and Delaney during my last visit, but I thought it was normal teen stuff. When Aaron came to live with us, he would get mouthy sometimes about our curfew or rules, but in the end, he knew we were right.

Still, what did I know? That was only one year of my life. This was an entire lifetime. I couldn't begin to imagine.

I wondered if I should stop him from having one more sip, but I also thought it was okay to get shit-faced every now and again as long as someone was there to keep you safe. Hell, I'd even wait up for Grant if he passed out and I needed to help him to bed. Grant would have to understand.

Suddenly Ruby was there, sniffing at Delaney's hands, and I knew animals could sense when people were upset.

"It's okay, girl," he said, petting her. "I'm just being emotional."

Once she seemed satisfied that he wasn't dying, she lay down by the fireplace. I felt a pang in my gut, wondering if I shouldn't get a dog or a cat to keep me company. We always thought we were too busy and didn't want to have to leave an animal alone all day. I spent late hours at the store some nights, and Carmen had a busy job as a consultant in the IT industry. Which meant she traveled as well, and damn, just thinking about seeing her tired smile after a long trip made my chest ache. After she died, some nights I pretended she was on the road and would come rushing through the door any minute.

"I'm sorry this is so hard," I told Delaney. "I don't know Grant, but I suppose he's going through his own stuff too."

"Definitely. His person died too. Grant always loved Rebecca best," he murmured as he stared at a family photo on the fireplace mantel, one where they were all smiling and looking happy.

"There's no chance that boy doesn't love you."

"He may love me, but I bet he wishes—" He screwed his eyes shut as if holding back tears. "There I go, trying to say the quiet part out loud. Why the fuck am I getting emotional about this? Goddamn it. Sorry."

"It's not like we've never cried in front of each other before." I tried to comfort him by patting his knee. Hell, in group, everyone cried at one time or another. And one night, we both teared up at the bar and were afraid to bring attention to ourselves, so he told one of his corny jokes instead. "If only you could see me blubbering privately."

"Yeah, but that's privately," Delaney said, frantically swiping at his tears.

"Hey, don't try to hide from me. We've been to hell and back together," I said, leaning forward and swiping my thumb under his eye. He gasped as if my touch had burned him, and it only made the emotion in his eyes grow more complex.

"Ah, shit, I'm drunk. It's probably better if you let me snot all over myself alone."

"No way," I replied adamantly. I had the urge to touch him, to comfort him in a more tangible way. "Can I...give you a hug?"

His lips trembled as he nodded, and I didn't waste any time, just scooted forward and pulled him into an embrace.

He was rigid at first, and I thought I'd made a mistake, but then he relented, winding his arms around my waist and melting into me. And fuck, I didn't realize how good it would be to hold him—to hold anyone. Flesh and blood and heavy bones. Damn, it got me all emotional too, but one of us had to hold it together.

It wasn't like I hadn't been hugged since Carmen's passing —by family, friends, and even a couple of customers. But somehow, this felt different. Like we'd crossed into new territory that could easily become addicting.

"Thanks for...for this," he said against my neck, and fuck if feeling that whisper of lips, along with the scrape of his scruff against my skin, didn't make me shiver. I didn't want to let go. The tantalizing scent of his woodsy cologne or soap or whatever it was didn't help either. Damn.

We stayed that way for another long moment before he had the sense to finally pull away. His cheeks were flushed, and he wouldn't look at me, and I supposed I wasn't much better because my pulse was throbbing and my ears were hot. All because I'd held another man. Another attractive man, who was also my friend.

If I was being honest, I'd felt the flicker of attraction from the very beginning when he'd first sat across from me in group. But that was a quiet and muted sort of awareness like it would be with any other guy. Tonight, when Delaney pulled open the door, wearing gray sweatpants, his feet bare, my immediate thought was how striking he was. He filled out his white T-shirt very nicely too.

"You all right?" My gut twisted as I wondered whether I'd crossed some imaginary line. Weren't friends allowed to comfort each other when one of them was hurting? Just because we'd both admitted to being bisexual didn't mean we weren't still human beings offering comfort to each other. Just that there was an extra layer to that connection.

"I don't know," Delaney replied, pushing back to sit a few inches away from me on the couch.

Christ. Maybe I should've left.

"If this is about me hugging you...I just thought..." I swallowed the growl of frustration in my throat. "You were in pain, and I wanted to make you feel better. But maybe I should've..."

"I liked it a little too much, okay?" he admitted, his gaze fleetingly meeting mine.

"I don't understand. I liked it too, but that doesn't mean—"

"It's been so fucking long, and being held by someone I care about felt too damned good." He forked his fingers through his hair, then twisted the strands as if what he'd confessed was a bad thing.

"Why is that wrong? I'll hold you anytime you ask me to. It doesn't have to mean anything more than human contact." I bit my lip, thinking it through another second. "We should be able to do that for each other after what we've been through."

"I guess you're right," he murmured. "I might just...*hold you to that.* No pun intended."

I chuckled, but *damn.* I liked that idea a little too much as well. Before I could get my thoughts together for a proper response, we heard the kitchen door open and then Grant's tentative voice. "Dad? Is someone here?"

"Ah shit, I'm a fucking mess. I need to get it together." Delaney stood and swiped his hands over his clothes and through his hair. It sucked that he had to hold it together all the time. "In here, Grant."

"Marc!" Grant said as he walked into the living room. "You're here."

"Yep, just came by to keep your dad company," I said hesitantly, realizing that it might not have sounded like the best reason. But I had nothing to hide.

"Did he need that?" He turned to his dad. "You told me you were okay and that I—"

"*Grant.*" I saw the frustration in his expression that he'd messed up yet again.

"No big deal," I said. "I was just in the neighborhood and decided to stop by."

"Then why does my dad look...I don't know." His eyebrows knitted in confusion.

"It's all good. Just let me use the bathroom. I'll be right back," he said, lurching toward the stairs, and I could tell how hard he was trying to walk normally.

"Is he okay?" Grant asked me. "Or is he just putting on a good face like he always does?"

Instead of answering him, I asked a question of my own. "Why do you suppose he does that?"

"Obviously to make things easier for me." He balled his hands. "But I'm almost an adult. I wish he'd—never mind."

I shouldn't have gotten involved, but still, I asked, "Wish he'd what?"

He sighed. "I wish he'd just stop being so uptight about things, but I also get why he is. He's trying to keep me safe or whatever," he said with a flap of his hand. "Mom was always more chill about stuff, but Dad and I butt heads a lot."

"Your lives have changed dramatically, and you're just trying to find your way. I get it." I glanced toward the stairs. "He worries a lot."

"I know. Sometimes I don't want to tell him things because he has so much on his plate."

My chest squeezed because I knew he was a good kid and was just trying to navigate his newfound relationship with his father. "Ever think he feels the same way?"

He blinked. "Yeah, I guess so. Hey, you're easy to talk to. I bet you were good with your nephew."

"Thanks. I tried." I could feel my cheeks burning. "Just like your dad, and I probably made as many mistakes."

When I heard a noise near the stairs, I turned to see Delaney standing there, looking much more awake and sober. Guess a cold splash of water to the face helped.

"You want anything to eat before bed?" Delaney asked Grant in that same faltering voice, like he was walking on eggshells. "Cookies and milk?"

Grant rolled his eyes, pretending to be irritated, except a smile broke across his face, and he nodded. Guess Delaney was able to appeal to the little kid in him after all.

"I'm gonna head out and leave you to it," I said, suddenly feeling out of place. I wasn't part of this family, no matter how cozy it had felt tonight.

"I'll walk you out," Delaney said, and when our eyes met, his crinkled at the corners, making me feel warm inside all over again.

"See you later, Grant," I said, and he waved as he knelt down to pet Ruby, whose tail was wagging frantically.

"Hey, Marc?" Grant called from his perch near the fireplace.

I spun toward him. "What's up?"

"Dad said you'd want to help us with our kitchen?"

"Yep, but only if it's cool with you." I glanced quickly at

Delaney. "I can't help loving the charm of these old Tudors, so I'd totally enjoy it."

"These houses are all prewar era," Grant said. "In fact, this used to be known as one of the rich parts of the city."

Delaney shook his head and smiled, likely marveling at his child's penchant for collecting random facts. I'd admit to nerding-out on architecture magazines and artifact websites. It not only helped with my business, but with my other interests as well.

"Don't I know it," I replied. "Unfortunately, there is plenty of redlining around here too."

"Yep, mostly in Shaker Heights." He tipped his chin toward the window. "It's the reason there's no easy access to the freeway from this side of town."

I whistled. "Man, you sure know your stuff."

"That's the same thing Dad always says."

"We're obviously right," I teased, and Grant scoffed, but his eyes were alight with humor. "So would you be okay...with me helping?"

"Uh-huh," he replied as Ruby licked his hand. "It would be cool."

"Awesome. Your dad and I will work out the details." I turned toward the door again. "See you soon."

At the door, Delaney said in a hushed tone, "Thanks, again. For coming here and letting me...well, you know."

"No problem." I squeezed his shoulder. "I know you'd do the same for me."

Resisting the urge to hug him again, especially in front of Grant, I said my goodbyes instead.

I smiled nearly the whole way home as I turned up the radio and sang along to the music. Being around them had done my heart good. Plus, I felt ridiculously excited about helping them update the kitchen and couldn't wait to discuss the ideas running around in my brain.

And not just because it involved Delaney.

Okay, maybe that *was* part of it. I couldn't stop thinking about how vulnerable he looked...and how warm and solid he felt in my arms. I kept telling myself anyone would, except maybe the guy from the coffee shop. He would've just felt wrong. Which only proved that the person and the connection mattered. Delaney had come to mean something to me, so it only made sense.

"I might just hold you to that."

Fuck, I hoped he would.

I pulled into my driveway, glad I'd left a light on in the living room so it wasn't so dark and empty. Maybe I'd have some milk and cookies of my own while relishing the memory of that warm embrace. Might sound pathetic, but it was all I had right now.

13

DELANEY
OCTOBER

I⊤ WAS the first weekend of the month, and we were on our way to see my father at the assisted-living center in Mayfield Village. Grant was fidgeting beside me. Today he was wearing a T-shirt that read: *You Had Me at Napoleon Bonaparte,* along with his French Revolution bicorne hat.

I thought Marcus would get a kick out of that shirt, but I'd resisted texting him—mainly because I was still working through what had happened between us the other night. I'd been a blubbering mess, and I hoped he didn't hold it against me, though I felt safe enough with him and was pretty sure he wouldn't give it another thought.

At least not the crying part, but maybe the other. I smiled to myself like a hormonal teen. And maybe I was, in that regard. To have a guy hold me again. Offering physical comfort was new between us, and not something I would've ever expected, but it felt good.

I also resisted asking Grant what he and Marcus had been discussing when I'd walked in on their conversation after splashing cold water on my face. I'd admit I immediately felt envious that Marcus seemed to get along better with my own son than I did.

"Why are you so restless?" I asked Grant as he straightened his hat for the umpteenth time. My father was used to his costumes, and so was the nursing staff, though today's outfit was tamer than most.

But my father could also be pretty biting with his remarks, which was one of the many reasons I'd always been so tense around him, though I'd also grown pretty numb to it, or at least that's what I told myself. But by now, I'd made my peace. We'd never have a close relationship, and I was okay with that. He wasn't an easy man to be around. I just hoped I hadn't transferred my anxiety to my son. So much for breaking out of the mold.

"I don't know," Grant replied, staring out the window. "It worries me to see Papa like this."

Grant had definitely become more sensitive about lots of things since Rebecca's death. But mostly about medical stuff, and who could blame him. "You mean getting up in age?"

"Yeah, that." He glanced briefly at me. "And whatever is going on with his heart that you mentioned before."

"Congestive heart failure," I said, supplying the term that had eluded him. "Which means his heart isn't pumping blood as efficiently as it could be. That's why I'm grateful we got him into assisted living when we did. He'll have access to around-the-clock care if anything should happen." Though he might have to level up to skilled nursing as his disease progressed. We'd cross that bridge when we got there.

"True," he said absently as if we hadn't really touched on what was bugging him.

"What are you not saying?" I asked, but he ignored me. "Grant?"

"Okay, fine." He scowled. "I know Papa loves me, but sometimes he's a jerk."

"I know. He's always been that way." There was no reason to deny the truth. Grant and I were well past sugarcoating stuff, not when life had been so brutally honest with us.

"When you were a kid too, right?" he asked, and my gut tightened. I wished he'd been exposed to my mother's kindness instead. But at least he had Rebecca's parents for that.

"Yep," I admitted. "I didn't go to him for many things. I had my mother for that. She was awesome."

An uncomfortable silence descended in the car. "Grant, I know—"

"No, Dad, don't. You're not like Papa." I held in my gasp as my heart rose to my throat. "I know we butt heads all the time. But he's like, cranky, and sort of cold. You're just annoying."

I barked out a laugh. "Thanks a lot. Well, hey, you are too, so I guess we're even."

We shared a smile, and it felt so fucking good. Just one smile from my kid could make my whole damned day.

"We'll just check up on him, visit for a while, and then we'll be back on the road in no time," I said as I turned onto Mayfield.

Grant nodded, staring at the storefronts we passed. It was busy this time of day, and it had taken us longer to get here than expected. "I feel bad for him sometimes too. Do you think he has any friends?"

"I'm sure he does. He's surrounded by other residents, and they have group activities all the time," I replied as I pulled into the parking garage. "It would be worse if he were living alone."

That prickly stillness ensued again, and I wondered if Grant was thinking about the same thing I was—him going off to college. Or maybe I was projecting. Why did life's themes mimic each other so much? Maybe so you learned not to repeat them...

"What's an astronaut's favorite part of a computer?" I asked once we'd gotten out of the car and walked toward the entrance.

Grant groaned. "What?"

"The space bar."

"Oh my God, *stop*." Grant turned away as he fought a smile. My work here was done.

We went inside to check in and were greeted by the front-desk receptionist.

"I like your hat," she said with a smile.

"Thanks," Grant replied, his cheeks tinging pink, and it hit me again how brave he was to be unapologetically himself. Apparently, I needed to take some pointers from my own kid.

Once we were handed our visitor badges, we walked down to his room. My father was sitting in his favorite chair near the window, with the television blaring an old John Wayne Western. He barely blinked when we stepped inside, and a ball of tension hardened in my stomach. In a lot of ways, my father was my first bully and pretty much shaped my worldview. The bastard.

If only Grant could see that all I ever wanted was to protect him from the bullies of the world.

"Hey, Dad," I said at the same time Grant greeted his grandfather.

He did a double-take at Grant's hat, frowned a little, but held his tongue. No doubt he would've lit into me as a kid, calling me any number of names, maybe even queer, so it was a relief he'd softened a bit for his grandchild.

It wasn't without help. The first time I'd stood up to him regarding Grant was during the time he was being teased in school for being different. I warned my father to butt out, and he finally saw me as an adult who wouldn't put up with his bullshit. Threatening to cut contact with him might've helped too. He loved Rebecca, and though he never admitted it, he enjoyed visits with Grant, so he toed the line, mostly. He never bullied my kid, but Grant was right; he wasn't very friendly.

"What brings you here?" he asked in a grumpy tone, barely looking away from the movie.

"We wanted to visit you," I said as we stepped closer.

He scowled. "You mean you felt you had to."

"Of course not." I felt frustrated all over again, like that little boy always trying to please him.

He rolled his eyes. "Your wife was more honest, at least."

"Rebecca could always charm you," I said, and he knew I was right. "She was good at smoothing everything over, just like Mom."

His gaze shot to mine, and I saw a flicker of vulnerability there. Dad was lost when Mom passed, much like I was now. I couldn't look at Grant right then, but I could feel him shift uncomfortably beside me.

Dad pointed at Grant's T-shirt. "Wasn't Napoleon the short general?"

"No, well, *yes*," Grant sputtered, "but it was only propaganda put out by the British in order to delegitimize him. They said he was five foot two, but in reality, he was more like five foot six, which is pretty average height. Plus, he was always surrounded by the tall soldiers in his Imperial Guard."

"Five foot six is still considered short for a man," he said with a wave of his hand, and I bristled. He'd always had that air of machismo that rubbed me the wrong way—especially when I'd been making out with a boy on the regular after soccer games. "And wasn't Napoleon a loser anyway with all his wars?"

"Actually, no. His average was pretty good."

Grant launched into the history of the wars Napoleon fought, and I was glad for the reprieve. I looked around the room, making sure everything seemed in order and that he was receiving decent care. I'd heard any number of horror stories from customers and coworkers who had parents in care in one facility or another, but so far, we'd been satisfied. Besides, there was no way he'd keep quiet about anything he found unsatisfactory, except perhaps the abundance of vegetables they served with every meal.

"How are you feeling, Dad?" I asked, noting the pill sorter sitting on his bedside table. They allowed their residents lots of independence until more assistance became necessary.

"You worry too much," he replied flippantly. "You always have. I'm fine."

"How about your last doctor's appointment? Did he increase your blood pressu—"

"How's school, Grant?" he asked, anything to avoid the conversation about his health. I'd just have to ask the nurses on the way out. Or email. I swear, this man and his pride.

Grant sat down near him and went on about his classes and friends and video games. My father lectured him about getting outside more, much like he did with me when he realized I wasn't very interested in sports. When I joined shop class in high school, where I thrived with the circuitry lessons instead of the woodworking ones, he seemed more satisfied, possibly because he'd been a machinist in a tool factory his whole life. Mom once shared that his own father, who'd died when Dad was twelve, had been toxic and ruthless, so maybe Dad was still living in the past or something.

I must've zoned out for a minute because the next thing I heard was Grant talking about our kitchen. "And his friend Marc is gonna help since that was what Mom wanted."

Dad looked at me then. "Who is this Marc person?"

I made big eyes at Grant before replying, "He's a friend from my grief group."

"Grief group? Such mumbo-jumbo. When your mother died, I didn't need anyone to help me grieve," he said mockingly, pushing all my usual buttons, and I felt a spike of anger in my gut.

"Yeah? Well, maybe if you did, you wouldn't have been such a—" *Jackass my whole life.* I cut myself off, not wanting the visit to go to hell. Besides, it wasn't worth it. We'd had that argument before, and nothing had changed. He never apologized for how he made me feel as a kid, and he never would. Same shit, different day, and I certainly didn't want Grant to witness me losing my cool with my father. Life was not like the movies, where everything was wrapped up perfectly at the end. Some things just remained as they were, and you developed a thicker skin and found other people to help quench your soul. Maybe in our next lives, we'd be friends. "Anyway, Marc owns a salvage business and has an affinity for older homes, so why not?"

"I suppose," Dad said. "Might've been too much work for you anyway."

I shrugged, ignoring the thinly veiled insult because he was right. I had no idea how this was going to go down with Marcus and our kitchen, but he looked so earnest about it, so maybe it was worth a shot? If it ended up being too much work, we could always bag the idea.

Grant asked about activities at the center, and Dad told him about bingo night and the one evening a month when they brought animals in to visit the residents. Grant seemed satisfied that his papa was active enough, and before I knew it, we were back in the car, another visit behind us.

Grant must've known the visit had taken a lot out of me— maybe out of him too—because he was quiet on the way home, and I was grateful for it. It'd always been hard to be around my dad, and I certainly missed my mother's laugh and easy smile.

I likely took after my dad more than my mom, and that sat heavy in my stomach. Except I would never want to make Grant feel ashamed of himself. And yet...wasn't that what I was doing by questioning his every move? Where was the line drawn between concern and interference? I needed to find it soon, before my relationship with my son went to shit. Before he went off to college and communication became strained. Before I moved into assisted living and my son reluctantly visited me out of a sense of obligation.

I was going down that dark road again, and I needed to cut it out.

"Wanna stop for some burgers?" I asked to get myself out of this funk.

His eyes lit up. "Five Guys?"

"Is there any place else?"

I headed toward Cedar Road, where the popular hamburger chain was located. Their burgers were good, and I was plenty hungry. And no, I wasn't trying to bribe my child. I was trying to build a connection. It was a start, at least.

Once we parked in the busy lot, I turned off the ignition. Grant hesitated a moment as he reached for his hat, which he'd placed on the dashboard. Was he waiting for my usual suggestion of leaving it in the car? I hated that he second-guessed himself around me. I reached for the hat and plopped it on his head. "What year were these invented anyway?"

His eyebrows drew together. "I think the early 1800s."

"Tell me more about which militaries adopted them while we stand in line."

And he did, with much animation, as we stepped inside the busy restaurant. Once our burgers, fries, and shakes were ordered, we found a table near the window. As usual, Grant received some gawks from nosy adults, but this time I stared back until they looked away. Maybe because being around my father had driven the point home that Grant was mine. I'd helped create him and shape him, the job was sacred and precious, and I needed to remember that more often. I wouldn't trade him for the world, and maybe he needed to hear that more too.

At grief group the following week, there was a certain buzz in the air when Marcus entered the room, everyone undoubtedly anticipating the details about his date with a guy. I'd admit, it felt like ages ago since he'd met that dude for coffee, and I was curious if he had anything else on the horizon. The idea of Marcus holding or comforting another guy made my gut tighten uncomfortably, but I knew it was selfish to want to hoard more of his time.

That wasn't the only reason, though, and I knew it. Ever since the night I'd gotten tipsy, there was a different vibe between us, our text conversations striking a bit deeper in tone. Like my visit with my father, for example. I'd told him everything that night, including some childhood crap, and even about my dinner afterward with Grant.

"All right, everyone," Judy said loudly, and all the side conversations became muted. "Let's address the elephant in the room. But it'll be Marc's decision to share anything."

When our eyes met, his crinkled in amusement. Judy likely knew that little would get done if she didn't address it head-on.

"It depends," Marcus replied, folding his arms across his chest, and I found myself mapping the prominent veins along his muscled forearms. "Do they want to know the details so it helps them in some way, or for pure titillation?"

"What do you think?" Harmony asked with an eye roll.

"Not true. I want to know what it's like to move forward," Frank said. "Not that I'd be any good on the dating sites. I'm not young and virile any longer, but I'd like to think there's a possibility of me finding companionship again."

"It depends what you mean by companionship. A true courtship, or something to scratch the itch?" John piped in, and the group laughed uneasily.

"Both are valid," Judy said. "As long as you're on the same page with the person and there's mutual consent."

"True," John said. "Though this consent thing they talk

about nowadays isn't something my generation discussed. A man had his place, but he should never put his hands on a woman."

"Well, you're actually saying the same thing. That's how we referred to it back then," Frank said. "Now, can you be quiet long enough to let Marc speak? I want to hear how his date went."

"Sorry to disappoint you, but it didn't actually go so well. We weren't a good fit." Marcus winced. "What I realized is that typing messages into a phone is different from figuring out if you're compatible in person. That's not to say people can't meet and find their person that way. It's just not a perfect system."

"Because there's no sarcasm font?" I teased.

"Exactly," he replied with a laugh. "I also can't tell if their dad joke is cute or corny."

I shrugged. "Cute, obviously."

"I sense an inside joke." Harmony winked at me, which made me blush. "Do you plan on deleting the app—or maybe you already have?"

"I haven't, and I don't have any plans to delete it, not yet," Marcus replied, and I felt my gut pinch again. "It was a good experience regardless of the outcome. My advice is to go for it, even if the end result feels like a waste of time. It's good to make connections with people so we don't feel so alone."

"Hear, hear!" Frank said, and I blew out a breath, wondering why I was feeling so strange and overheated.

"Great advice," Judy said. "Anyone else want to share their dating experiences?"

When others jumped in to share, I only half-listened, not because I couldn't relate, at least not yet, but because I remembered how I'd confessed my sexuality to Marcus. In his own way, he'd helped me find myself—a part of myself that had been buried for years. Maybe that saying was true that people came into your life for various reasons and to help you find different versions of yourself. But not all of them stuck around, and you had to find a way to live with that.

After the meeting ended, we walked together toward the parking lot.

"So, I'll see you this weekend?" Marcus asked. "To discuss a plan for the kitchen and take measurements?"

"Looking forward to it," I replied as I got to my car.

"Me too." Marcus smiled, and I felt light as air again. "See you soon."

14

MARCUS

"I COULD WORK on the cabinets one section at a time, so you're not totally uprooted," I said as the three of us stood in the kitchen. I had worked that Saturday morning as usual. Over the past couple of years, I'd sometimes lose track of time, staying until dusk, but today I was home by noon, and after mowing my mother's lawn, I headed over to Delaney's.

I'd admit I was surprised that Grant had wandered away from his computer to listen to our plans. Maybe Delaney had told him he needed to be involved? He was wearing a T-shirt that said: *Don't Believe Everything You Read on the Internet. Signed, Abraham Lincoln*, and when I told him it was cool, he blushed in an endearing way.

"That's a good idea," Delaney said, one arm crossed with the other hand beneath his chin as he considered the options. "We can load our dishes into boxes and swap them out as stuff is finished. What do you think, Grant?"

"Yep, that'll work." He seemed to be taking in the sunny-yellow color on the walls, which was a bit dated and didn't seem to match Delaney in the least, let alone Grant.

"I'll haul the cabinets to my shop for refinishing."

The sample colors I'd spotted near the dishwasher a couple of weeks back were a mix of muted and bright colors, so it was hard to tell what direction they were headed with the design. If I had to guess, Rebecca enjoyed bolder choices, whereas Delaney's were understated.

"Do you have to take them to your shop?" Grant asked. "Couldn't you work on them in our backyard or the garage if it rains?"

"That's not a bad idea." I glanced out the window at the fluffy clouds. So far, the autumn weather was cooperating. "But I don't want to put you out."

"You wouldn't be." Delaney squeezed Grant's shoulder. "And that way you can keep work separate from your side project."

"I promise to play cool music while you work," Grant said with a grin, no doubt referring to a certain musical we'd recently discussed.

"Well, that seals the deal." I held out my fist, and Grant bumped it. "Will you also promise to show me your hat collection? Your dad told me how cool they are."

He dipped his head, but I could tell he was pleased by my request. "I could do that."

When I glanced at Delaney, his eyes had softened. He'd actually never used those exact words, so maybe I was embellishing. Or maybe I was trying to help bridge the gap between them.

I cleared my throat. "How about we head to the paint store to look at swatches and other supplies? We can take my truck." I had driven the vehicle I used for Worthy's Salvage Shop and made sure to clear the front seat for Delaney, knowing we'd likely run some errands to prep for the job.

"Sounds good," Delaney said, reaching for his house keys.

"Can I tag along?" Grant asked, and I noticed Delaney stiffened briefly, likely more stunned than me.

"Did you finish studying for driver's ed?" he asked, and now it made more sense why Grant was so interested in tagging along. Did any kid enjoy studying, even if it was to eventually get behind the wheel? I remembered Delaney telling me in passing that Grant was trying to earn his temporary license since he'd bowed out last year, and once he did, Delaney could teach him how to drive. I could practically see it—the tension in the car between them, much like when my mom tried to teach me years ago before my uncle stepped in to help.

Grant stopped short of rolling his eyes. "Yep. I've been at it for hours."

"Okay. You can absolutely come," Delaney replied, and I was surprised he didn't ask to see the evidence of his efforts like my mom would've. "I'll let Ruby out before we take off. C'mon, girl."

Grant slipped into his shoes while Delaney opened the door for Ruby to take a bathroom break. She was obviously getting up in age because she seemed stiff whenever she rose from the floor, and there were little white hairs around her muzzle. No way I'd mention it, though, because that was sure to be a sore subject for both. It was a cruel reality that animals only brightened your life for a handful of years. Might've been another reason I'd resisted the idea.

"Can we stop at your salvage shop too?" Grant asked expectantly.

"I suppose we can." I glanced at Delaney, who shrugged. "I have supplies I can retrieve from there too."

The three of us squeezed into the front seat of my truck, with Grant between Delaney and me, but neither seemed to mind. The radio was playing a classic rock song, and Grant's enthusiasm seemed to spur Delaney on. He turned up the music, and Grant didn't even complain. When I sang the refrain and Delaney joined in, Grant laughed but hummed along too, which made it feel like we were on a fun little field trip.

They clashed over colors at the paint store, but when I pointed out their similarities, they settled on two samples of softer grays for the walls.

"Still want to head to Worthy's?" I asked when we got back in the truck.

"Let's do it," Grant replied enthusiastically, and Delaney laughed.

The closer to the store we got, the more fidgety Grant became. Delaney held his tongue, despite the tic in his jaw, but it only seemed like pure anticipation to me.

"This is it?" Grant asked as I parked in front of the store. "I would've never guessed."

"That's what I thought at first too." Delaney smiled at me across the seat. "Wait until you get inside."

I unlocked the door, and they followed me in.

"Whoa," Grant said as I hit the lights, and he stepped beyond the front entrance.

"Told you," Delaney said with a smile. "And this time, I'm not here in the dark. Which reminds me to bug you about purchasing a generator."

I smiled and shook my head. "Feel free to look around while I consider what supplies I'll need."

Grant took his time perusing the various projects lining every surface as if they were sacred, commenting here and there about time periods while Delaney and I rounded up drop cloths and sanding tools to store in his garage.

"This is the radio I was telling you about," Delaney said to Grant as he stepped toward the Philco project. I had finished staining it since he was here last. "I still want to fiddle with the circuit board."

"And I still think you should," I replied, but he was already stepping behind it, inspecting it as if in a trance or on a mission. I recognized that look, so I left him to it and summoned Grant farther into the larger room.

"Wait, I recognize this." Grant stepped up to a vintage box on a table. "Is this...this is a type of spyglass from the British Royal Navy."

"That's right." Holy shit, this kid was so fucking smart. And impressive. "It's antique brass with a nineteen-inch telescope and in darn good condition."

He was completely mesmerized by it. "Can I touch it?"

"Absolutely. I know you'll be careful."

He gently lifted the spyglass, his fingers shaking, his lips parting in awe. I so appreciated his reverence for vintage collectibles.

"My customer had a relative who served in World War I overseas."

"What's the country of origin?" he asked, looking down at the design carved into the brass.

"India, if I'm not mistaken."

"Yeah, that makes sense." He carefully placed it back in the wooden storage box, then turned to view the store as a whole. There didn't appear to be any rhyme or reason to how things were stored, but I knew exactly where everything was located. "I think this is the coolest place I've ever been."

My chest constricted, and I struggled for a proper response.

"And the store itself has a history," Delaney said, coming up behind him. "Right, Marc?"

"Yep." I smiled at him. "Worthy's was founded by my great-grandfather and was the first Black-owned business in the area."

Grant's eyebrows lifted to his hairline. "Is that why you kept it going?"

I nodded. "And because I can't picture myself doing anything else."

"Cool," he replied, and then his gaze landed on something across the room, and his feet followed.

"Thank you," Delaney said as we watched him look through

a table of vintage maps of the city. They actually belonged to me. I was a collector of sorts too.

"Of course. Had I known he'd respond like this, I would've brought him over sooner."

Delaney smiled. "So, hey, I think I know how to fix that radio if you want me to give it a shot. It just needs a couple of new coils, and I can get those."

"Seriously?" When he nodded, I said, "That would be great. In the meantime, let me show you something."

He followed me to the back of the room, toward a rectangular cabinet.

"I was thinking about this for your kitchen island," I said, moving some of the larger items stored on top. "The height is right. We could choose a countertop, there's plenty of storage, and there would even be room for stools."

"This is cool." Grant wandered over and ran his hand over the finish. "Who did it belong to?"

"It came from a turn-of-the-century farmhouse, which is why it's so rustic-looking. But I'll sand and stain it to match your cupboards."

Grant threw up his arms. "Awesome!"

"I guess that's a yes," Delaney said with a laugh. "But only if you're ready to part with it. Wouldn't you want—"

"I am," I replied, cutting off that line of thinking. I knew he meant well, but I didn't want to go there. "And besides, I know you'll make good use of it."

It felt right to use the sturdy piece in Delaney's home, and I'd get to visit it whenever I was invited over. The way things were going, I hoped that would be often.

"I'm hungry," Grant said to Delaney as we were heading out to the truck, carrying the supplies I'd gathered.

"We can make something when we get home. Maybe sandwiches?"

"Unless you're up for some pizza?" I said, not trying to

insert myself into their plans, though it didn't really seem like they had any.

"What do you have in mind?" Delaney asked as he placed the drop cloths in the bed of my truck.

"How about Geraci's?" I was thinking about the small, old-school pizzeria in University Heights that'd been in business since the fifties.

Delaney's eyes lit up. "We haven't been there in years. What do you say, Grant?"

"Let's do it."

So we did, Grant chattering animatedly on the way there, mostly about my shop and the British Royal Navy. We ordered two pies and stuffed our faces with the pizza that reminded me of childhood. On the way back to their house, Delaney turned up the music again, and we all sang the refrain to an overplayed pop song. It was cheesy and fun, and given the satisfied grin on Delaney's face, he thought so too.

15

DELANEY

THE NEXT WEEKEND brought fantastic autumn weather, though the leaves wouldn't reach their peak color until the beginning of November. Fall was always a relief from the blistering-hot summer months, and Marcus would no doubt enjoy the mild temperatures and sunny weekends as he used our backyard to sand and paint.

When I glanced out the window, I noted the vivid blue sky, so the weather would likely cooperate all afternoon. I smiled, watching Marcus don eye protection before firing up his electric sander. There was something so attractive about how sure he was of himself when it came to his work—and I needed to stop staring, or he was liable to accuse me of stalker behavior.

I made my way around the boxes and drop cloths to the refrigerator. It was less daunting to do the kitchen update in stages, and we already had a system going. I painted and updated the electrical boxes in the spaces where the cabinets were missing so that Marcus could do his thing outside.

"Send Grant over anytime," my mother-in-law, Donna, had said when I'd told her of our kitchen renovation plans. I'd also noted the melancholy in her voice, which was why I'd nearly

avoided the subject, but I didn't want her to be surprised on their next visit. I might've been projecting again, but it was as if she thought we were moving on and leaving Rebecca behind, and that wasn't the case at all.

Grant had decided to stick around this weekend and take his grandmother up on the offer another time, likely because he was solidifying plans with his friends.

When I walked outside to hand Marcus a soda, he said, "I was thinking white for the cabinets and a charcoal for the island, to complement the pearl-gray wall color you chose."

For the lower cabinets surrounding the sink, Marcus would have to complete the work indoors, and an errand to choose new countertops and stainless-steel fixtures was on the horizon.

"Let's ask Grant because he's the one who—"

Suddenly, a familiar tune drifted through Grant's upstairs bedroom window, and Marcus grinned because it was from *Hamilton*. Grant *had* promised him music. When Grant slid the window open farther, I spotted his revolutionary jacket with the brass buttons along with the tricorn hat.

Marcus hooted his approval and clapped his hands, and I felt guilty about all the times I'd worried my child would be ostracized in public. If Marcus could embrace his uniqueness so easily, why couldn't I? Grant's cheeks were flushed, his smile bright and beautiful, and I felt a sharp stitch in my chest that I didn't appreciate him fully.

"We were just talking about the paint colors," I called up to him. "Want to come down?"

"I will in a minute. Is it okay if I bike over to Ellie's house? She finally passed her driver's exam and wants to take her mom's car to the movies."

"Sure," I replied, though I bristled a little inside. It was always hard to imagine teenagers on the road, and Grant wouldn't be far behind. "Which theater?"

"The Cedar Lee. Jeremy said we can use his employee discount for our tickets."

"What about dinner?"

"Popcorn and soft pretzels?" Grant teased.

"A guy after my own heart," Marcus said with a laugh.

I stopped myself from asking if he was going to wear that outfit. Of course he was, and it would be fine. Even if it wasn't, he was old enough to take care of himself.

When Grant walked out a few minutes later to retrieve his bike from the garage, Marcus asked about his outfit, then sought his advice on the paint colors.

"I think the island should be stained a dark wood so the natural grain shows through," Grant said.

"Look at you, knowing your stuff," Marcus replied, and I'd admit I was pleasantly surprised.

"I don't really. I sort of...looked it up," Grant said, his cheeks pink. "It's just that it's old and cool and should be shown off."

"I like that idea," I said, and Marcus agreed.

"Don't worry, I'll text you when I'm coming home." Grant got on his bike and headed down the driveway toward Ellie's house.

"Have fun," Marcus said with a wave, then turned to me. "Good job, Dad."

"What do you mean?"

"Not freaking out about the car thing. Or maybe it's just me who'd have a hard time with my teen on the road." He winced. "That might have to do with Carmen's accident, though."

Fuck, I'd forgotten about her car accident. He hadn't mentioned it in a while.

"I'm sorry. That totally makes sense." When I squeezed his shoulder, I could feel him shiver, either from my warm hand or the memory. "And don't let me fool you. I'm *always* freaking out about Grant's safety. But I've been trying not to make him feel like a little kid."

Marcus playfully elbowed me. "I say it's working."

"Thanks," I muttered, my ears feeling hot.

We stared at each other for an elongated moment, and I couldn't help thinking how appealing he was even in his paint-stained work clothes. I cleared my throat. "So, I'm gonna go finish prepping that wall."

"Sounds good."

I headed inside to update the electrical socket and put tape around the trim and baseboards. Then I got lost in the motion of the paint roller, which I'd always felt was somehow soothing. Before I knew it, another couple of hours had passed. I stored away the paint supplies and my tool kit, then scrubbed my hands in the sink.

"All set for today," Marcus said, startling me out of my thoughts as he came through the door. "Looks good in here. Okay if I use your bathroom to wash up?"

"Of course. You have plans to get to?"

"Not really. Just hate the dust from the sander."

"I hear you." I hesitated a moment, then said, "You wanna grab dinner? I have some leftover chicken paprikash, or we could order—"

"I would love some," Marcus said, and my stomach felt all funny, though I wasn't sure why. Maybe because I enjoyed his company so much. He turned toward the hallway with the bag he'd brought in. "Be right back."

I pulled out the leftovers, then set the table while it was reheating.

"Smells amazing," Marcus said when he rejoined me in the kitchen. He'd changed into clean jeans and a T-shirt.

There was too much clutter around, so we took our plates and a couple of beers into the living room. We ate on the couch while watching an action movie that was already in progress.

"So good," Marcus said as he shoveled in another bite, and I smiled, pleased at the compliment. A comfortable silence descended while we enjoyed our food and relaxed.

"Has Grant ever dated anyone?" he asked, his gaze transfixed on a photo of the three of us on the end table. It was of us downtown in front of the Playhouse Theatre, the *Hamilton* marquee lit above our heads. Grant had been so happy that night, had even dressed for the occasion.

"No. We did wonder about Ellie at one time, but I think they're just tight, and Jeremy rounds out their trio. Why do you ask?"

"I don't really know. Just curious, I guess." He glanced over at me. "He's a good kid and would certainly make for an interesting date."

"He would," I replied, then winced. "Though it's hard to imagine your kid flirting with anyone."

Marcus laughed. "Just like it was for us to imagine our own parents."

"True," I mused. "Grant would shield his eyes whenever I'd hug or kiss Rebecca. Just like I did when my dad would give my mom those eyes. You know the ones I'm talking about."

"Oh yeah, I'm well aware." Marcus placed his empty plate on the coffee table. "Would you consider yourself an affectionate person?"

I thought about it a second, but the answer came almost immediately. "Definitely. It feels nice to be touched. How about you?"

Marcus nodded. "I miss that. Which is why the offer from the other night still stands."

Our eyes met and held. I could feel myself trembling, so I placed my empty dish atop his. I nearly got up to take them to the sink to avoid the conversation but then stayed put to face it head-on. I thought about it at least once a day, after all. "I wouldn't mind another one of your hugs."

Without a word, he pulled me against him as if he'd only

been waiting for permission. I wound my arms around his neck, my head landing at his throat as I took in his spicy scent and the warmth of his skin.

"Fuck, why does this feel so good?" I murmured against his skin, making him shiver.

"Because it's human contact?"

"Suppose so." *And because it's you—your warmth and scent and how they put me at ease.*

"What else do you miss about having close contact with someone?" Marcus asked.

"I don't know. Everything, I guess. Even the intimacy from a simple kiss."

"Yeah, I hear you." His arms tightened briefly. "After being married so long, you tend to take those things for granted."

"It's true," I replied. "You can fall into the trap of being too tired or busy. Carving out time is crucial."

"I never want to take it for granted again." He sighed. "I can still remember how exciting that first kiss was."

"I remember too." We'd gone to a movie, where we'd held hands the entire time, and as soon as we got outside to the car, it was hard to hold back after so much anticipation.

"You'll have that again someday...with someone new."

"Yeah, but I don't want to kiss just anyone." It was so much easier to say these things with my head buried in his shoulder and not looking him in the eye. "It means even more to me now —who I allow close. Does that make sense?"

"Definitely. But it's also okay to simply crave touch and close contact, even if it's only for one night. Neither way is invalid."

"Agree. No shame at all." When my phone buzzed with a text, I stiffened. "It might be Grant."

When he let me go, I instantly missed the contact.

I sat up and reached for my phone, noting the time.

The movie is about to start. I'll be home by curfew.

Thanks for letting me know.

The moment between us seemed over, and to avoid any awkwardness, I reached for our plates. "Let me clear these dishes."

I breathed out when I got to the kitchen, reminding myself that what we were doing didn't have to change anything. That first time certainly hadn't.

As I headed back to the living room, I heard his laughter ring out, and soon enough, I saw why. Ruby had not only jumped onto the couch but had toppled Marcus and positioned her front paws on his chest, straddling him as she licked his cheek.

"*Ruby.*"

"It's cool," he said with a bright smile that instantly warmed my stomach. "She's a good girl. Probably smells our dinner."

"You silly dog," I said, reaching for her collar and helping her down from the couch and to her pillow in the corner of the room.

Marcus was still lying prone, and I allowed my gaze to slide over him, enjoying the view. The sliver of bronzed skin between his waistband and shirt was enticing all on its own, but it was the bulge in his pants that kept me riveted—and wondering so many things. *Wanting* too. My pulse spiked when I felt his penetrating gaze roaming over me as well.

"I bet it's nice to sleep with an animal," he rasped out. "Lying beside something alive and warm."

The words felt too fresh, the deep ache almost visceral as I rubbed at a spot on my chest.

"It definitely is. Ruby takes turns between my bed and Grant's." My voice sounded hoarse as I attempted to thwart the image of Marcus feeling so utterly lonely. "Um, let me grab the remote. Maybe we can—"

"*Wait.*" When his rough fingers curled against my wrist, my breath caught, the rawer emotions coiling around my lungs. "Would it be too much to ask if you'd...lie with me for a bit?"

"It wouldn't be too much. I'd like that." His eyes softened a fraction. Fuck, my heart was pounding. "But...do you think it's a good idea?"

"It's whatever we want it to be. No judgment here, remember?" His expression morphed as he looked away. He was just as vulnerable, just as afraid. But I also detected a spike of anticipation, as well as desire, which was flattering, quite honestly. Unless I was mistaken. It had been so long. "It's just you and me," Marcus said. "Two friends who've been through a lot."

Right then, I wanted to wipe all his doubt away. To let him know he wasn't alone. That's what he'd done for me—provided me moments of peace where, for a time, I could forget myself and all that'd happened. I wouldn't trade that for anything in the world. To have found such a good friend.

And friends did this for each other, didn't they?

He shuffled over to lie on his side so that when I slid down on the couch, we were facing each other. It was a tight fit, and I almost joked about it, but he looked so serious.

"Fuck, thanks," he said, and we were so close, I could feel his breath against my cheek. "I needed this."

"To feel connected to someone?" I asked, and he nodded. "Yeah, me too. I mean, I already feel close to you, but this is a whole other level."

"Okay, less talking, more hugging," he said, likely to get me out of my own head.

So I allowed instinct to take over, my fingers winding around his neck and hauling him into a tight hug. So tight, in fact, that my dick was on board with it, and from what I could tell, so was his. It felt foreign, yet so achingly familiar that my chest throbbed.

"Shit." I pulled away. "I'm not trying to poke you or anything. It's just—"

"Natural," he murmured. "Especially after so long."

"Exactly." I sighed. "You're good at this. Making me feel comfortable."

"Not like it's a hardship," Marcus said as our eyes met.

"I just appreciate it, is all." I leaned forward and kissed his cheek. I didn't know what made me do that. That whole *natural thing*, I supposed.

Marcus's eyebrows rose as he stared at me, his fingers squeezing my hip. His hand was warm and heavy, and I liked how it anchored me. His lips parted as if he was searching for the right words, and I imagined what it would be like to inch my mouth closer and fit our lips together. To steal his breath, to surprise him even more.

Instead, I held myself still and went for honesty. Bravery too. "I always thought you had nice eyes—warm and kind. Your lips are nice too."

The corners of his eyes crinkled at my admission. "If we're complimenting each other...I like your hair and your body."

My hand again found my gut, which had seen better days. "I don't know about all that, but thank—"

"Hey," he said, his fingers covering my hand. "Don't sell yourself short. I guarantee that I like everything I see. You're a good-looking man, Lane."

"Well, fuck." I averted my gaze as my skin flushed. "I haven't heard that in a long time. Let alone from another guy."

He arched an eyebrow. "Does it matter if it's another guy?"

"Obviously not. Except to certain people in my life, and that's not something I'm ready to face. Not with Grant—"

"No other people are here," he replied, his hand sliding up my chest to my neck, making shivers travel the length of my spine. "This stays between us. No one knows our needs like we do. It's nobody's business anyway."

Before I could respond, he tugged me back into his arms, kissed a sensitive spot right below my ear, and sighed against my shoulder. Pinpricks lined my skin, the sensation so close to the surface, everything felt magnified. When a whimper escaped my throat, Marcus drew back, concern in his gaze.

"Lane?" He cupped my chin, forcing me to look at him.

"Do you think our needs are similar?" I asked just above a whisper.

He shrugged as his hand dropped to my hip. "Possibly. Maybe we should find out."

I looked at his eyes, his mouth, and felt electric energy spark between us. I angled my mouth closer to his, banishing all thoughts from my head and relying solely on instinct. "Is this okay?"

He nodded, his eyes closing briefly on a sigh.

When my lips brushed against his, Marcus shivered. One more gentle pass before my mouth settled against his, resting there as I took in the different sensations. His lips were plumper and a little chapped. There was no aftertaste of balm or gloss, and it was hard to reconcile that at first. But I just closed my eyes, tuned out all that other shit, and let myself enjoy it. Feel safety in it. *In him.*

When Marcus hummed, pressing his lips lightly against mine, I sighed, finally pushing the doubt and guilt aside. Instead, I focused on the prickliness of his beard, his brusque movements and sounds, and the solid bulk of his muscles as our bodies inched even closer.

Marcus kissed me gently, then more gruffly, his desperation obvious, and I gave back in kind, my tongue slipping out to brush across the seam of his lips. He moaned low in his throat when our tongues finally met, flicking against each other hesitantly, then more bravely, tangling, exploring as we ate each other's groans.

It was almost too much and not enough as my heart galloped in my chest like a dozen wild stallions, breaking free and feeling too reckless all at once. I could feel his stiff length aligning with my own, providing solid friction as my fingers gripped the small of his back, then his waist, his shoulders, finally settling in his hair as the kiss went on for who knew how long.

My stomach filled with a warmth I hadn't felt in ages, and I was liable to come in my pants if we didn't cool it. But I also couldn't find it in me to care.

My lips felt tender, but the steady pressure of his mouth against mine was wholly satisfying and filled me with over-whelming relief, momentarily appeasing the desperate loneli-ness gnawing at my insides.

Marcus pulled away to catch his breath, his expression open and vulnerable.

And so fucking beautiful.

Winding my hands in his hair, I hauled his face closer, pouring all my longing and frustration into another kiss and smelling the spicy, musky scent on his skin. I was overcome with a sentiment that pulled at my very core. I knew in that instant that if the situation had played out differently, in another time and place, I would've gone for it, taken my chances, and asked to date him.

I didn't know why I was feeling so emotional in the middle of all this. But kissing Marcus was so intense and heady, so *incredible*, that I didn't know what to do with all the sensations and feelings pelting my senses. They ended up spilling over and out of me in different ways. Marcus noticed right away that something had changed. He drew back to look at me, his thumb swiping at a stray tear that'd escaped my eye.

"I...I'm sorry, Marc. I don't know what's come—"

"Shh," he cooed, kissing my lips, then each of my cheeks. "Turn over onto your other side."

I didn't question it, just flipped to face the television, the long-forgotten action movie still in progress.

Marcus tugged at the cream-colored throw from the back of the couch and draped it over us. "Let me hold you."

Sighing contentedly, I relaxed against his chest, reveling in the strength and warmth of his arms. After a few long moments of feeling his shallow breaths against my neck, the steady patter of his heartbeat, I shut my eyes and fell into the twilight of sleep.

"Want me to leave?" he whispered against my ear, however many minutes later, and my eyes flew open.

"Only if you want," I said over my shoulder. "But I'd rather have the opportunity to hold you too."

"Fuck. I'd like that," he said into the crook of my neck, and we shuffled around, now facing the other direction, his back to my chest.

"Feels so good," he said around a yawn, and I couldn't have agreed more.

After I set the timer on my cell, I rearranged the throw and wound my forearm against his stomach. Soon enough, his breaths evened out, and we both drifted into dreamland.

I jerked awake at the trilling sound on my phone, immediately noting the time. "Hey, sleepyhead. Grant will be home soon." I steadied my tone, concealing my frustration that we didn't have all night.

"Shit." He sat up, thankfully understanding the sensitivity of the situation.

Once he had his belongings in hand, I walked him to the door, where he thanked me and kissed my forehead. It made me want to pull him back inside and finish what we'd started.

As I watched him walk to his car, I rubbed my fingers over my swollen lips, already reliving being kissed like that—so desperate and needy, like he was trying to climb inside me and live there for a while. And I was certainly no better.

Damn, it had been a good night.

16

MARCUS

"I LET Mrs. Smythe know she can pick up her chairs on Monday," Marian said before she left for the day. Thankfully, I had a good office assistant who kept track of all the invoices and answered the phone to field questions and set appointments. She was only part-time, but that worked well because even though I enjoyed interacting with the customers, it gave me time to get stuff done.

The chairs were a set of six that needed to be caned, which was a weaving method using rattan palm I'd learned from my grandfather early on. It was tedious work, but the customer only cared that they were ready by Thanksgiving dinner to seat her family. I'd stained them a deeper teakwood as well to match the new table she'd ordered.

"Great. I should finish them up tomorrow morning."

It was Friday afternoon, and it had been a busy week. Not that I didn't think about what happened between Delaney and me every spare moment. I was nervous at first that he'd start acting differently around me, especially since he'd made it clear he was not ready for anything. But he couldn't pass up human contact any more than I could. And even if I was interested in further exploration, I knew this was not the right moment in time for him, and that was okay. As long as my arms around him brought him as much comfort as his did me. It didn't even matter that I was so fucking hard nearly the entire time we were in proximity and then needed to jerk off as soon as I got home.

But based on our evening text conversations, so far, we seemed okay.

Of course, the first text from him had been a terrible dad joke that made me grin like a damned fool. He was a goofball—a gorgeous one. Damn, the way his lips and body felt against mine...that was hard to shake.

Why do melons have to get married?

Why?

Because they cantaloupe.

I groaned to myself. **Good God. I guess this is your way of saying everything is cool between us?**

I sure hope so.

I smiled in relief. **I didn't want you to have any regrets because I don't. It felt good. Really good.**

It did feel good. Really good.

Goofball. Glad to hear it. Don't overthink it, okay?

Easier said than done. Do you even know me?

LOL. It was worth a shot. See you this weekend?

Absolutely.

Saturday morning, I finished repairing the dining chairs for the customer's pickup on Monday, stopped home briefly, then headed over to my mom's on foot to cut her lawn. The weather was mild and sunny, and it would make for a good afternoon to sand more cabinets.

"Ma?" I called as I walked through the front door.

"In here, Marc," she replied from the kitchen.

The first person I saw was Keisha, sitting at the table. "Hey, big brother."

"How's it going?" I noticed that my mom was busy making some of the sweet tea we all loved.

"It's all good." When Keisha smiled, I knew her reply was genuine. She had really come into her own in her career and relationship. "Just getting off work?"

"Uh-huh." I swiped at the dust on my jeans. I didn't bother changing since the whole day consisted of one form of getting dirty or another. "Here to do the lawn and anything else Mom needs."

"Mom and I are going shopping at the outlet mall this afternoon."

"Sounds fun," I replied, even though it didn't at all. But they were tight like that and loved to hunt for bargains together. Sometimes they'd rope Carmen in too and stay out all day, having a load of fun.

"I don't think the lawn needs cutting yet, Marc."

I glanced out the window. She was right. The growth slowed in the fall before picking up in the spring, and since there'd been little rain, there wasn't much difference compared to the last time I'd cut it.

"Soon enough, I'll need to rake the leaves." Though it would never be like the piles Delaney's street would have with all those trees. "Let's give it another week."

"Okay, sweetie." She handed me a glass of tea. Grateful, I took a sip, knowing it would be refreshing. "Want to tag along with us? We'll be getting lunch too."

"Actually, I'll be heading over to Delaney's." I lifted my thumb over my shoulder. "I'm helping with his kitchen, remember?"

"How's that going?" Keisha asked, looking up from her phone.

"Pretty good. We're going slow, refinishing one section at a time," I explained, and I realized right then that it was a metaphor in a way, for our lives, or maybe for our hearts. "While I sand the cabinets in his backyard, Delaney, and sometimes his son, Grant, paint inside."

When they looked at each other instead of saying anything, I was confused. "What?"

"Nothing, just..." Keisha cocked an eyebrow. "That smile on your face."

"Huh? I wasn't—" Had I smiled? I didn't even realize it.

"Oh yes, you did." Mom winked. "So either you really like that side job you got going for yourself, or you really like that man and his son."

"Of course I do." I gulped and looked away. "Lane is my friend, and I enjoy being around him and Grant. Plus, I enjoy keeping busy. You know that."

"Uh-huh." When Keisha threw me a knowing look, I scoffed. I was going to kill her. But the truth was, I was already looking forward to my Saturdays with Delaney, and not only because of what happened between us, but because I really loved the work. And okay, their company.

"The two of you together are a pain in my ass."

Keisha lifted a hand to high-five our mom as they laughed at my expense.

I shook my head as I placed my empty glass in the sink, then headed toward the door, waving my goodbyes. "Enjoy yourselves, but not too much."

After speaking to an elderly neighbor on my way home, I made myself a sandwich, then headed over to Delaney's.

It was our first time seeing each other since our make-out session last week. He was in the backyard, playing with Ruby, and as I made my way toward him, his skin flushed as soon as our gazes clashed.

"Can you make sure the latch catches?" he asked, and I

pulled on it to verify that the gate was secure. "Thanks. It can be temperamental, and I don't want Ruby getting lost out there."

We took turns throwing her the tennis ball as we caught up on the plan for the day. But I'd admit, I couldn't help noticing how well he filled out his flannel shirt and those muscled arms that had been wound around my neck, his strong fingers gripping my scalp. I'd get myself in trouble if I didn't stop thinking about that passionate side of him and where it could've led. But also the heartrending, tender side too.

Thankfully, we heard the gate open and firmly close as Grant walked his bike to the garage. He was wearing jeans, a black vest over a white T-shirt, and a newsboy cap as if he'd just returned from selling newspapers on the street in the early 1900s.

"Hey, Grant!" I waved. "Nice hat. Were you hanging out with friends?"

"No, I, uh..." His eyes flashed to Delaney as if he would disapprove of what he was about to tell me. "I went to this vintage clothing shop on Coventry."

"Did you find anything?" Delaney asked, and Grant shook his head.

"You've still got time," he said, then looked at me. "Grant is trying to put together his Halloween costume."

"Ooh, will you be trick-or-treating with friends?" I asked as he parked his bike in the garage.

"Nah, I'm a little too old for that," he muttered, red dotting his cheeks, and I felt stupid because I should've known that. But I remembered trying to make the tradition last as long as possible as a kid. I still wanted all the candy and hoped the neighbors didn't notice my age.

"Grant is going to pass out Halloween candy this year, in costume."

"Ah, that makes sense," I replied, and why wouldn't it?

Grant loved to dress up, and I'd bet Halloween felt like the perfect opportunity to showcase some of his looks. "Do you get a lot of trick-or-treaters on your street?"

"Tons," Delaney said, reaching down for the ball as Ruby's tail wagged excitedly. "How about you?"

I shrugged. "To be honest, the last few years, Carmen and I kept the porch lights off and hid inside the house with our own stash of candy. Guess we'd become old and bitter."

Grant and Delaney chuckled at my confession. I supposed we would've kept it up if we'd had children. Though you wouldn't have known my sister and I were adults given how much candy our mom stocked up on, including full-size Hershey bars, but she loved handing them out every Halloween. Even tried getting us to help her, and I finally relented last year, just for something to pass the time.

"No pressure, but you can come hang with us on our porch that night," Delaney said, and of course, the idea immediately appealed to me because of how much I already enjoyed the cool night air, along with a cold beer. The company too.

Grant's eyes lit up. "You totally should."

My chest felt tight as I met Grant's gaze. "Only if I can help with your costume. What are you gonna be?"

"I was thinking of dressing as King George." He kicked the tennis ball in Ruby's direction. She was panting openly but still going strong.

"That's a cool idea." I could picture him answering the door in his opulent clothing, playing the part with a patronizing gaze.

"Thanks, but..." He frowned. "I haven't been able to find the right kind of crown or scepter, which is why I tried the place on Coventry."

"Wouldn't a costume shop—" I began, but Grant winced as if I'd said a horrible word.

"Grant likes his pieces to be more authentic," Delaney said with an edge to his voice. "So finding them can be challenging."

"Ah, I see." They both looked away. "That's what makes all your looks unique."

I could feel the tension between Delaney and Grant tightening like a screw, and I was going to guess that this had been a point of contention between them before. Grant was picky, which wasn't necessarily a bad thing unless that meant Delaney had to constantly field his disappointment or disapproval.

Delaney steered Ruby toward a water bowl he'd filled near the garage while Grant pulled out his phone. I made myself busy setting up the sander and drop cloths.

"How did the Vikings secretly communicate?" Delaney asked, obviously trying to cut through the tension in his own corny way.

Grant shrugged grumpily at the same time as I said, "How?"

"By Norse code."

I snorted and shook my head.

"That was a better one, at least," Grant said, trying hard not to smile.

"Only because it has a historical spin," Delaney replied.

"True." Their silent feud seemingly ended, Grant asked, "Is it okay if Ellie and Jeremy hang out here tonight?"

"Of course," Delaney said. "Let me know if you want me to order pizza or anything."

"Okay, I will."

We watched him and Ruby walk inside through the back door, Ruby still trying to catch her breath.

"You all right?" I asked after another silent beat.

He nodded. "Grant and Rebecca always had so much fun with Halloween. This is the first time since she...that he wanted to participate again."

I swallowed past the lump in my throat. "That's good news. And I'll keep an eye out for any King George memorabilia."

"He'll figure it out, don't worry." He grimaced. "But thanks. I can tell Grant likes when you ask him about his costumes. You would've probably fit right in with them."

When he turned toward the back door, I reached for his arm. "Hey...don't do that."

His eyebrows knitted together. "Do what?"

"Exclude yourself like that," I replied with more conviction. "Sure, Grant and Rebecca were close, but I bet he needed you just as much, if maybe in a different way."

"I...I'm not sure..." He seemed at a loss for words.

"Well, I am. Grant loves you. And I won't pretend to understand the dynamics of your family. But I can take a good guess that you were the one who brought a bit of reality into the mix. Some levity and security too." He stared at me wide-eyed. Why the hell had I said all that? "You can tell me to fuck off if I overstepped."

"No, I...*you*...thank you. For always being a good friend." He turned toward the house. "I'm gonna get to work."

Shit. I hoped I hadn't soured the mood even further.

I got started on a new row of cabinets, and before I knew it, hours had passed. I was startled when Delaney called me inside to have pizza with Grant and his friend Jeremy, who scarfed their pieces down before getting back to their grand strategy game or whatever it was called. I watched them nerd-out for a while, smiling to myself about the geography and historical facts being thrown around between these super-brainy teens. They were totally cool and didn't even realize it.

I wasn't sure what their interactions were like with Ellie in the mix because she had a last-minute thing come up, apparently. But Jeremy and Grant seemed to feed off each other's energy, giggling like little kids instead of nearly young adults.

When I looked over at Delaney, he was smiling about it too,

and I had the urge to close the distance between us and crash my lips against his. I distracted myself by asking if the crown molding was original to the house, something I'd wondered about every visit.

"I think so, yes," Delaney said. "It's in every room upstairs and even in the attic."

"Is your attic finished?" I asked, nerding-out in my own way.

"Yep. And I just realized you've never seen our second or third floor." He motioned to me as he turned toward the stairs. "Follow me."

"Doors need to remain open," Grant said in a teasing tone. "It can only lead to trouble." Both of us froze on the steps, Grant obviously not realizing how close to the truth he'd come.

"Very funny," Delaney lobbed back in a stern tone, but there was no way to hide his flushed cheeks.

He first showed me the three bedrooms on the second floor and how, in the master, the molding was a bit more ornate, giving me a clue that it was early twentieth century. I couldn't help noticing the king-size bed and wondering if he'd done any updates like I had after Carmen passed.

As if reading my mind, Delaney said, "I changed all the bedding about a year later. Cleaned out the closets too. It just felt like it was time. How about you?"

"Same," I replied with a frown, remembering how incredibly difficult it had been to pack away someone's life, someone who was no longer of your world. I could only pray she would approve. It was strange and yet so natural to be having this sort of conversation with Delaney...but then I remembered it was how we'd initially connected.

Next, he led me to another stairway. He clicked the light switch near the banister, and I followed him up to the finished attic.

"Damn, this is nice," I said, noting how it was angled on

both sides with rafters, even if it did make for a bit of a tight fit for anything wider than a queen-size bed.

"This was Grant's playroom when he was younger, thus all the boxes." He motioned with his hand. "I installed electric baseboard heaters so we could use it in the winter, but haven't done anything with it since. I'm actually surprised Grant hasn't asked to move up here for more privacy."

"That might give the whole doors-open policy new meaning," I said, looking over my shoulder to the staircase.

When Delaney made a sound in the back of his throat—part groan, part frustration—our gazes clashed, and the tension in the room thickened. Just three long strides and I could hold him again, away from any prying eyes.

My shaft plumped at the thought of skin-to-skin contact, and when he shifted and adjusted himself in his jeans, it was obvious he was having the same issue.

"Fuck," he grunted, and that bolstered my confidence enough to close the distance.

I cupped his face in my hands and wasted no time planting a kiss on him, even as I worried I'd overstepped. I felt dizzy from his woodsy scent as I broke away. "Sorry, I couldn't resist. I know this is not the—"

He gripped the front of my shirt and pulled me to him. "Stop talking, and do that again."

Our bodies slid together, our mouths connecting in a deep, bruising kiss that felt like it lasted hours when clearly it was only minutes.

"Fucking hell, I'm so turned on," Delaney said in between kisses, his hands rounding my hips to my ass. When he dug his fingers into my flesh, our stiff shafts aligned, making me shudder.

"Any more of that, and I'll come in my pants," I groaned, burying my face in his shoulder. Damn it. I wanted him so much right then, wished we had more than a few stolen minutes.

"*Please.*" It was a desperate sort of plea that resonated in my bones as he rubbed our groins together in a slow, hypnotic pattern.

My lips found his ear as my fingers slid to his waistline. "Let me make you feel good."

He trembled as his eyes met mine. "Only if I can do the same."

"Hell yes," I replied, and then it became a mad rush of our fingers warring, clumsily unbuttoning the other's pants, sliding down zippers, freeing our cocks from the tight confines of our jeans.

I reached for his red-tipped cock first, which poked from the top of his briefs. He was warm and thick in my hand as I stroked him from root to tip and watched him pant openly.

"Damn. I've been dying to see you, and I am not disappointed." His stomach might not have been as flat as those of buff guys at the gym, but he was sexy as hell.

"Fuck." His fingers connected with my nape, and he hauled me into a deep kiss. "I'm definitely not gonna last."

"Neither will I, which is good because we don't have much time."

"Don't remind me." As soon as his long fingers curled around my shaft, I knew I was close. My cock felt overly sensitive to his touch, and besides, this was too much of a late-night fantasy come true.

"You feel so good." His eyes were fixed on my shaft as his thumb circled my slit. Like no time at all had passed since he'd been with a man, and it was simply second nature.

For both of us, apparently. We frantically pumped each other's cocks, our kisses reckless as we moaned in unison. My balls were throbbing, and I imploded after another twist of his wrist near the underside of my glans.

He groaned into my mouth, unraveling a moment later, our tongues tangling as his warm seed spurted over my fist. Our lips remained fused together long after he went soft in my hand, but it was hard to drag myself away.

We cleaned up in the third-floor half bath, his skin flushed the entire time.

I helped fix his hair, swiped at my swollen lips, then followed him toward the stairs, hoping that guilt wouldn't find its way inside Delaney tonight.

But he kept his cool in front of Grant and even winked at me as he walked me to the door.

17

DELANEY

HALLOWEEN FELL during the week this year, and I told Marcus he didn't have to show, especially after hearing how busy work had been lately. Grant would've understood even through his disappointment, and I'd be lying if I didn't say I'd have been a little bummed too. Though it might've been for the best, since that intimate moment between us the other night was all I could think about. Thankfully, I'd gotten my wits about me afterward, and Grant didn't seem to notice how distracted I was once Marcus left.

But Marcus was nothing if not dependable. He'd shown right after work, even insisting on picking up dinner on the way so we didn't have to fuss with dishes. We chowed down on our burgers, taking into account the looming six o'clock hour. Kids from the neighborhood would be ringing the doorbell any minute, followed by droves more, and it wouldn't let up for a couple of hours at least.

Marcus had gone above and beyond when it came to Grant's costume as well. He'd made a call to one of his customers and was able to get his hands on a historically accurate knock-off crown and scepter, and paired with Grant's red satin coat with the gold brocade, the ensemble made Grant look amazing.

When Grant came downstairs in his costume, I made a big deal about it, clapping and whistling, which produced a toothy grin—a different kind of smile than the one my corny jokes elicited. Marcus, for his part, had shown up in a King George Hamiltonesque graphic tee that read: *I Will Send a Fully Armed Battalion to Remind You of My Love*. Grant got such a kick out of it, he took a photo of the design and immediately texted it to his friends.

"Oh, and I bought you one too," Marcus told me, conjuring a bag. "We're all in this together, right?"

"Uh-oh," I said with a laugh as I took the package from his outstretched hand. He'd obviously been doing some secret online shopping.

"What is it?" Grant asked excitedly as I tugged another T-shirt out.

I read the print out loud: "What did King George think of the American Colonies? He Thought They Were *Revolting*."

"No way," Grant said. "The perfect pun for Dad."

"I thought so too," Marcus replied, high-fiving Grant.

"It's awesome," I said, holding it up. "Just give me a minute to throw it on."

When I came out of the bathroom, wearing the shirt, I could see a brightness in my kid's expression that'd been missing the past couple of years. My eyes suddenly stung, and I looked away, willing myself to get it together. Fuck, I was being too emotional. It was only a stupid shirt.

A very thoughtful, awesome, stupid shirt.

The weather held up, no rain or wind in sight, which meant more neighbors were out in their yards, with their lawn chairs and portable fire pits, making it feel all the more festive. Ruby was behind the screen door like always, watching the world go by, but tonight she had way more activity to keep her interested.

Marcus switched places with me on the stoop to help Grant pass out more candy while I sank down with a cold one in my favorite wicker chair. Most of the kids had no idea what Grant's costume was—and sometimes vice versa because pop culture was so not Grant's thing—but a few of the parents did, which wasn't surprising. The musical was all anyone talked about the first couple of years after it debuted.

I couldn't keep the grin off my face as I watched Grant and Marcus chat and interact with the neighbors, a few waving to me and glancing curiously at the three of us. It didn't really matter, though, because it was none of their business, and besides, the atmosphere in this house hadn't felt this celebratory since...well, since Rebecca was alive.

Marcus brought his own kind of spark to this family, and tonight it felt so overwhelmingly bright, like an incandescent light filtering through all the cracks in my heart, creating a profoundly warm and penetrating glow.

Grant seemed pretty taken with Marcus, which wasn't something that happened easily or often. It took him years to find loyal friendships, and that was something we'd wished for him for a very long time. Not that Marcus was his friend, more like a good influence, and I would hate for it to be ruined or spoiled.

My thoughts immediately transitioned to what happened in the attic the other night. We were kissing and touching—jerking each other, for Christ's sake—with Grant downstairs. Taking a risk like that was so unlike me. What if, by chance, Grant had found us? Would he be appalled or angry? Would he accuse me of betrayal? He'd sounded so vulnerable that time we'd talked about me dating. He'd encouraged me to invite friends over more often, and even though I'd made it clear to Marcus that I didn't want to turn my kid's world on its axis again, it still felt too close for comfort.

As if I needed another reminder about the sensitivity of the topic, a car pulled into our driveway, and I stood on shaky legs, having forgotten the possibility that my mother-in-law might stop by tonight. Especially once she'd heard how excited Grant was about his costume. Fuck.

I waved as she got out of the car, and Marcus glanced back at me, his eyebrows drawn together. No big deal, he was only a friend, and maybe it was good that they finally met.

She was alone, likely because my father-in-law had grown mostly homebound since Rebecca's death. I mentally kicked myself for not visiting more often. At least he hadn't criticized my every move like my own father did.

"Grandma!" Grant called, bounding down the steps to greet her.

I stepped beside Marcus to help pass candy out to several newcomers as I watched her fawn over Grant's getup. "That's my mother-in-law. They live in Shaker and used to always stop by on Halloween night."

"That's cool," Marcus replied, smiling as they headed up the stairs toward us.

"Oh, hello there. I'm Donna," she said, then looked at me. "I didn't realize you had company."

"This is my friend, Marcus. He actually helped Grant with his costume."

"And your shirt," Grant pointed out, and I could see the confusion in Donna's eyes as she took in my graphic tee, as if trying to line it all up in her brain. I supposed I hadn't shared much the past month or so, outside of some general information about Grant and school, but I thought for sure Grant would've blabbed the rest to her.

"Marc is the guy who owns that cool shop I told you about," Grant said once he filled a kid's pumpkin basket with candy. So he *had* shared some things.

"It's called Worthy's Salvage Shop," I said. "And Marcus is also helping us update the kitchen."

"Ah, now it's all falling into place," Donna said with a smile in Marcus's direction. "How do you two know each other again?"

Marcus glanced briefly my way before replying, "From the grief group, ma'am."

Her eyes widened with surprise before softening in sympathy. "I'm sorry for your loss."

"Thank you," he replied. "And for yours as well."

A loud group of what looked like middle-schoolers approached the stairs—the boys dressed in NFL sports gear and the girls in soccer outfits, which looked to be authentic—their chatter drowning out Donna's response.

Fuck, this was awkward, but I didn't know why it should be, other than it was a buzzkill. Just because Marcus and I had fooled around didn't mean anyone had to know. But it almost felt disingenuous in front of Grant's grandmother. And truth be told, I felt a little queasy, as if I'd betrayed someone instead of simply grabbing on to a bit of joy in the form of warm lips and strong hands.

"You're King George III from that musical," a parent holding on to a toddler's hand said in an animated voice. Grant looked back at Marcus, the two of them sharing a knowing grin. Even that felt uncomfortable. Christ.

"And from, like, history," Grant replied with a laugh as he placed a snack-sized chocolate bar in the kid's bag.

"Yes, of course," the parent replied. "*Hamilton* wasn't exactly accurate."

"True," Grant said, and I wondered if he'd go off about all the ways the musical had taken liberties. He loved to debate pretty much anything, and I tensed, suddenly wanting this portion of the evening to come to an end. Her child had wandered away from her, however, and she needed to catch up with her across the lawn.

Marcus took a seat on the porch, allowing Donna to sit with

Grant on the stoop, and we watched silently while sipping the remainder of our beers. He could definitely tell the mood had soured, and I couldn't find it in me to fix it. Not even with a corny joke.

"Looks like the crowd is dying down for the night," Donna pointed out when there was a lull in the traffic. From the looks of it, she was right. The crowded sidewalks had cleared, and a couple of neighbors across the street had already shut off their porch lights, likely because they were out of candy. We were running low as well, but I knew to buy extra so Grant would have plenty of his own stash to snack on later. He needed a reward for his efforts.

"I think you're right," I replied, just as Jeremy walked up with his younger siblings, both in angel costumes. Grant jumped up, a huge grin on his face upon seeing his friend, and I absently wondered why Jeremy had chosen our neighborhood since his was probably plenty busy.

I waved to Grant's friend, and they talked for a couple of minutes, Grant motioning excitedly about something as Jeremy reached out to touch his crown.

Marcus pulled out his cell, possibly to check the time, then stood with his empty beer bottle. "I should head out. Got an early morning."

My stomach tightened. "Are you sure? You don't have to—"

"Thanks so much for inviting me," he said loud enough for Grant and Donna to hear. "I just need to grab my bag."

"I know where you left it," I said, following him inside. Ruby trailed behind us to her pillow, officially tuckered out from people-watching.

He retrieved his things from the kitchen, barely looking at me. "Marc—"

"You're acting strange," he whispered. "I'm sorry if I'm contributing to that."

"You're not. It's just that…" I motioned between the two of us.

"It's okay to take care of your own needs, Lane, and eventually, they'll have to come to terms with that." He shook his head. "But I actually get it. It's hard to talk to my own family about this stuff. Just remember, they don't know anything, and they never have to."

"You're right." I frowned. "This is so much harder to navigate than I ever imagined. I'm sorry."

"Don't be." His fingers skimmed my shoulder. "I'll always follow your lead. Your friendship is important to me, and I never want anything to ruin it."

Thank fuck. I breathed out. "Me neither."

I followed him back to the porch, where he said his goodbyes to Grant and Donna, who were still sitting on the stoop, waiting for any stragglers. Grant had already broken into the leftover candy, as was evidenced by all the empty wrappers in the bottom of the bowl.

"Marc seems nice," Donna said after Marcus got in his car and pulled into traffic.

"He's actually great." Grant had tucked a piece of chocolate in his cheek, so his voice sounded garbled. I almost—almost—lectured him about his teeth and too much sugar, but I stopped myself. No way I wanted to ruin his mood after such a nice evening. Besides, he was still a kid and deserved to stuff his face on Halloween.

"He's a good man." I averted my gaze, afraid to see that look in Donna's eyes—that bald sadness, or maybe fear, that we were moving on with our lives. I didn't want to disappoint any of them, even if it was about something as simple as a new friendship. Fuck, what would their reaction be to something akin to a relationship?

I thrust it from my thoughts as Grant stood with the empty bowl and headed inside.

Donna stayed seated and leaned closer to me. "How did... Marcus's wife pass?"

I thought about the first time he recounted the incident with me, over drinks at a bar. That haunted look in his eyes was one way I could relate, and only too well. It was the first time I knew with great certainty we'd forged a connection. "In a car crash, about two and a half years ago."

She frowned. "That's terrible."

"Definitely." In group, people shared all sorts of stories about how their significant others had passed, from peacefully in their sleep to murder, which was heartbreaking, really. I'd once suggested to my in-laws that they attend the parent version of the group, but they'd never followed through for their own personal reasons. "One of the things we have in common is...is the desire to feel some normalcy, to feel human again."

She stared at me a long moment before she asked, "And having him around does that?"

"Yeah, I suppose it does." I felt my cheeks grow hot.

"Then I'm glad you found a new friend."

The silence grew between us as she stared out at the night sky, maybe working through her own shit. It was hard not to say something, anything, to make her understand—or maybe to assuage my own guilt.

I said, "We're all working on our own timelines, you know that." She grew rigid as she listened. "Grief isn't something you get over. Your life just absorbs it, incorporates it deep inside you, I guess. I will never not love her. I'm just trying to find my way without her." I blinked away tears as she swiped at her eyes.

"Grief is just love with no place to go. That's what my therapist told me," Grant said from the other side of the screen door. Fuck, how long had he been standing there?

"That's beautiful," Donna said with a watery smile, then patted my hand. "Give some of it to your dad. He needs it."

My mouth opened and closed, but I couldn't find the right words. And neither could Grant, it seemed, because he only stared, wide-eyed.

"You two are more alike than you think. Stubborn, but good through and through." She stood and adjusted her jacket. "And we all need to find happiness wherever we can. Rebecca would want that."

18

MARCUS

NOVEMBER

"Do you think people have room in their hearts for more than one great love?" Frank asked in group, creating a stir around the room. Even Delaney grew still to listen. Before that, he kept checking his phone—he'd told Judy he'd likely leave early to pick Grant and his friend up from the mall. Frank continued, "It's something I've been thinking about lately. Well, since Marc told us he'd joined a dating site."

I smiled, trying to gauge Delaney's expression. Would he care one way or another if I pulled the app up again and flirted with anyone? Made plans? I supposed it shouldn't really matter because we didn't owe each other anything. If us being intimate muddied the water for him, then I didn't want any part in confusing him.

The truth was, I'd avoided any deep conversations with Delaney since Halloween. Last weekend, we'd kept it mostly professional, the three of us choosing a new countertop and sink before getting back to work. It was hard, though, not to remember how full of joy he'd looked that night while passing out candy with Grant and me. As if he'd finally let go and allowed himself some happiness. But when his mother-in-law arrived, I could feel the insidious guilt worming its way back inside him.

And I got it. Fuck, I got it. He was a widower with a teenager, his wife's parents were involved in his life, and they were all still suffering from the loss. But grief would swallow you whole if you didn't allow yourself some selfish moments. That's how I'd describe what happened in the attic—us greedily giving in to our needs.

"Is that something you're interested in doing?" Judy asked Frank. "Joining a dating site?"

He shrugged. "I asked my daughter to help sign me up, but I'm not exactly sure what I'm looking for."

"For action in the bedroom again?" John asked in his irreverent way, and Frank rolled his eyes.

"Not sure my pipes work very well anymore," Frank said, and some group members snickered.

"Well, then you need a doctor's appointment," John scoffed. "There's medicine for that."

"Okay, we're getting off-topic here," Judy said in an amused tone. "Let's get back to Frank's original question about our hearts having room for love. Anyone have an answer?"

I'd admit it was a topic I was interested in. I wouldn't have been a year ago, and from the looks on some of the newer members' faces, neither were they. Not yet. Maybe not ever. But the more I put myself out there, the more I wondered if I'd ever feel that way about someone again. Living for their smile and their laughter.

Delaney's cheeks were flushed as he glanced at his cell, and I couldn't read his expression. It wasn't a topic that'd ever come up between us, even in our rawer moments. Sure, we'd both admitted not knowing how to go on without our spouses, but we never discussed finding real love again.

"I think it's possible," Harmony said. "Plenty of us have felt love for other people before our partners, and maybe even after." She glanced at Walter, who'd remarried and divorced someone all within a year of his spouse's death. "The feelings might've been different than what you felt for your life partner, but they were real all the same. I mean, none of us will ever stop loving the people we lost, but that doesn't mean we can't care for someone else again."

"That's if you put yourself out there again. I know I won't," a woman named Rose said. She'd been with her husband for forty years if my memory served me well.

I thought of my mother and Delaney's father, who'd never found anyone else to share their lives with, and even still, my mother led a full life.

"I think that's okay too," Harmony said. "Relationships are not the end-all, be-all. People can find comfort in plenty of other things, like friendship or hobbies."

When Delaney smiled, it felt like it was only meant for me, and warmth flooded my stomach. He was so fucking attractive and didn't even know it.

"All good thoughts," Judy said when the chatter died down. "Many think intimacy has to involve sex, but that's not true. It's more about feeling safe enough to bare yourself to someone." She gave John a stern look. "To bare your soul, is what I mean. To flay yourself open and have someone offer you safe refuge. That's real intimacy, and if you can find that again, hold on to it with both hands, no matter what form it comes in."

Holy fuck. I held in a gasp as my chest screwed tight.

"I love that," Harmony said, and several people in the group concurred.

"That's something to aspire to," Frank said. "Thank you."

"So, let's move on. Does anyone want to share any small victories?" Judy asked, but I was still stuck on her profound words. Delaney was staring at a fixed spot across the room, so maybe he was too. I felt guilty for tuning out the other group members, but I couldn't help feeling like her words hit home in more ways than one.

"Now that Frank mentioned the dating site, I want to know if Marc has any new prospects," John said, bringing me out of my thoughts. I nearly rolled my eyes because he was all about the salacious details.

"*Maybe,*" I replied in a coy tone, and Delaney stiffened. Undoubtedly, I was still moved by Judy's description, so that might've explained my next confession. "There's this guy I consider a good friend, and...that intimacy thing Judy was talking about? I think we have that—even without the physical part."

Delaney sat rigid in his chair, much like he did the night I announced my date with a guy. So maybe he was processing again, or maybe he was pissed that I'd brought up our friendship. Hell, for all I knew, he didn't even realize I was talking about him.

Shit. Now I was regretting bringing it up in the first place, but I hadn't been able to discuss my feelings with anyone, not like this. What better place than this group?

"Quiet down, everyone," Judy said in a scolding tone when there was a sidebar of whispers. "Friendships can definitely change after a tragedy, Marc. For better or worse. One or both of you might suddenly see things differently or begin realizing what truly matters in life—namely having that sort of connection with someone."

"You're saying you already have an emotional connection to this friend, right?" Harmony asked, and I nodded. "So what's the problem?"

"I don't want to ruin our friendship by bringing in other aspects, like romantic feelings or, you know, *desires*. That would be devastating in its own way," I replied, my face heating as many pairs of eyes were on me. Of course, Delaney and I had already jumped to the desires part, but that wasn't something I was willing to share. "Somehow, he's been able to find the softer parts of me. Like he's digging his fingers into the most bruised and barren areas of my soul and showing me there are places where I'm starting to heal."

Fuck, had I really admitted that? I could feel Delaney's gaze on me, but my skin was still flushed, and I thought it might get worse if I looked at him right then.

"I like that description," Harmony mused. "So why not seek comfort in him if it feels right in this moment? Maybe that's the only thing any of us can hope for. A bit of happiness after being devastated for so long."

Judy nodded. "I'm sure you'll know right away if your assumptions are wrong, and hopefully your friendship is strong enough to withstand the miscalculation."

"I hope so too."

"Or maybe your friend feels the same way and he's scared too. Or the timing just hasn't been right," Delaney's voice rang out across the room. "Maybe you're also the one bright spot in his life, and the most important thing you can do is keep an open line of communication so that you're on the same page and no one gets blindsided or hurt."

"That's good advice, Lane," Judy said, looking between us with a strange expression. "Keep us posted, Marc."

Judy moved us along to another topic, but I couldn't take my eyes off Delaney. Even as he tried to listen to other participants, his gaze still traveled back to mine. No doubt it was risky to bring the topic up in group, but fuck if I didn't also feel twisted up inside about what he'd said.

Maybe he feels the same way and he's scared too. Or the timing hasn't been right...

Delaney's cell buzzed, and he pulled his phone out of his pocket, read the screen, then stood up. *"Grant,"* he mouthed to me and then was out the door.

I sagged against the seat, feeling emotionally spent from

this session, which was not uncommon, but still, I wished I could've at least talked to him afterward.

Once group ended, I walked out to the parking lot with Harmony.

"Good luck with your friend." She winked. "Whoever he is."

I drove home in a fog, glad I'd kept some lights on in the living room.

After downing a glass of water, I washed it in the sink, almost dropping it when the doorbell rang. Was it my mom? I lifted my cell, but there was no message.

I strode to the front door, stunned to see Delaney standing there.

"Surprise?" He shifted uncomfortably on his feet. "I should've called or asked you first, but after I dropped off Grant at Jeremy's, I just...my car drove itself?"

I laughed, joy blooming in my chest. "Now you sound like me the night I showed up on your doorstep."

Pink dotted his cheeks. "And now I know how hard that was. Even without bourbon in hand."

"Which is why you should come inside immediately." I held open the door, wishing I'd straightened up the living room a bit more. But his house always looked lived in too, their kitchen currently in boxes, so he would understand.

"I don't have a lot of time..." he said, glancing around. "I need to make it home before Grant does, but I just wanted to see you, to...to..."

"To what?" I asked, then winced. "Hopefully I didn't make things awkward by bringing that stuff up tonight."

"Nah, you're allowed to rely on the group for help. And besides, you didn't out me." He swallowed. "I'll admit, I like what you said about me. I also like the idea of being your safe harbor."

"You already are," I said around the boulder in my throat. "And I hope I'm yours."

"Definitely." He took a step closer. "So here I am, standing bare before you, and...I'm desperate to kiss you again."

"So do it." I closed the distance between us, my pulse throbbing.

Delaney gripped the front of my shirt as our mouths collided in a frenzied tangling of tongues. It was so fucking hot, I couldn't resist digging my fingers into the small of his back and hauling him even closer. And there it was, the feel of his warm body and hard cock as his shaft slotted perfectly against mine. His groan was deep and throaty, a sound that had become one of my favorites.

"Damn, that mouth of yours," he said against my jaw. "But I need more...I want..." He struggled for the right words, but his gaze was filled with pure desire, and it stole my breath.

"Show me what you want," I murmured against his ear.

He backed me toward the couch, and as soon as I sat down, he sank to his knees in front of me. "Is this okay?" He palmed my cock through the front of my jeans, pulling a gasp from me. His fingers shook as his knuckles grazed my nuts, and I didn't know if it was from nerves or need.

"Hell yes," I said as my fingers fumbled with my button and zipper. I lifted up, and he folded my waistband down my hips along with my underwear. My dick sprang free, stiff and already leaking precome. He gazed at it appreciatively as his thumb swiped my slit, making me shiver.

"Wait." I stilled him with a hand to the shoulder. "Wanna see you too."

He wasted no time getting his button and zipper undone and hauling his pants and boxers down to his knees.

"Such a nice cock," I said, taking in his thick shaft, but before I could appreciate it further, his fist had latched solidly onto my length. I hissed when his breath wafted over my shaft as he angled his head closer.

"Love the way you smell," Delaney said as he buried his nose in the wiry hair at my groin.

I moaned, my fingers burrowing in his hair as he inhaled me, his scruff tickling the top of my thigh. "You're killing me, Lane."

"Just wanna taste you." His husky tone went straight to my balls.

"No way I'm fucking stopping you," I growled, my fingers tightening in his hair.

The first flick of his tongue was jarring, and I nearly sprang off the couch as a zing of electricity traveled up my spine. His fingers gripped my thighs, effectively holding me in place as his tongue circled the underside of my glans where I was most sensitive. It felt so fucking good, I couldn't help rocking against his mouth, already desperate for release.

My nails dug into Delaney's scalp as his tongue played clever tricks up and down my shaft. His mouth felt like the perfect amount of suction against my swollen head, and I felt no shame as needy pleas escaped my lips.

"You sure you haven't done this in years?" My voice was rough and breathy, my fingers finding his jaw, enjoying the feel of scruff there.

"Thanks for the boost of confidence." I felt him smile against my thigh. Fuck, he was so unassumingly sexy.

I spread my thighs wider to give him more room, though I was barely hanging on now that his warm mouth, wet tongue, and firm grip created the perfect cocktail for me to slip off the edge into pure oblivion.

"I'm not sure how much more I can take. It's been too damn long."

"I want you to unload in my mouth." He licked my glans, keeping his eyes firmly latched to mine, more self-possessed than I'd ever seen him. My nuts felt heavy and full, that familiar prickle at the base of my spine mounting right before I erupted like a volcano that'd been asleep for years.

"*Lane,*" I called out as I spurted into his mouth.

His eyes widened in surprise, but he swallowed my load, his lids closing, his throat working to get every drop.

I was spent as I sank against the couch, my chest heaving. "Not sure I can ever move again. That was incredible."

"It was." He pushed to his feet with his pants still hanging open, his cock jutting upward toward his stomach. The head was practically purple, a cobweb of precome leaking against his abdomen.

"Where the heck do you think you're going?" I said, clutching his thigh as I caught my breath. "Need to taste you too."

"Oh God," he moaned as I wrapped my fist around his hardness. His breath was erratic, his hand grasping my shoulder while I stroked him root to tip.

I leaned forward to kiss his hip, then that so-called paunch that really wasn't one at all, just a softer part of his abdomen. "You're so sexy here," I said, and he shuddered, obviously reveling in the contact instead of offering a self-deprecating remark, which I'd fully expected.

And now I could smell his enticing musky scent. It'd been so long since I'd been with a man, I'd forgotten it was such a powerful aphrodisiac. My eyes rolled back, savoring it as his wiry hair tickled my chin.

Delaney bit back a curse when I angled my mouth to lick his glans. My hand curved around his hip to his firm ass, my fingers digging in as I moaned. I was desperate to consume him, to hear more of his noises, so I yanked him closer and engulfed his shaft.

"Fuck, Marc," he groaned as his thighs quivered. "I can't... it's too good..."

He was so far gone that all it took was my tongue and throat working in unison before ribbons of come hit the roof of my mouth. His fingers twisted in my hair as I swallowed, keeping his cock between my lips until he was totally spent and his shaft had softened.

When I looked up at him, his eyes were screwed shut, his lips parted, and I loved that I could give him this—one moment of pure bliss when he was constantly on the edge of worry about holding his family responsibilities together.

He was still shaky, his pupils dilated as he leaned down to kiss me, and I could taste the mix of us on our tongues, which was pretty heady.

When he tugged his pants up and mumbled something about the bathroom, I pointed him down the hall. He obviously needed a moment to compose himself, and so did I. Once I got myself together, I headed to the kitchen to pour us some of the sweet tea my mom had made.

"Thanks," he said as I handed him the glass. He gulped it down, then wiped his mouth with his forearm before turning wary eyes on me. "Was...was that okay?"

"That was more than okay." I pumped my eyebrows, which made him blush. "I haven't come that hard in forever."

"Tell me about it." I reveled in his shy smile—as if he hadn't just done filthy things to my cock a minute before. When his gaze darted to the clock on the wall, he frowned, and I knew the moment had come to an end. "I'm sorry, I have to go."

"It's okay." I kissed him one last time, treasuring the sweet and salty taste of his lips. "Maybe someday we'll have all night."

"Wouldn't that be nice?" he mused as I walked him to the door, then stood watching him, my chest achy with emotion.

19

DELANEY

By the time I got home from shopping for dinner, Marcus's truck was already parked on the street. My stomach dipped like I was in grade school and had a crush. And I supposed that was sort of what this resembled, except more layered and way more complicated. What I'd done the other night by showing up at Marcus's house and going down on him felt good—for him too, obviously—and that was all that mattered. To live in that moment. Wasn't that what Harmony had said? I'd reveled in it all week, that was for sure.

It was a rainy day, so I expected to find Marcus in the garage instead of the kitchen when I came through the door with my grocery bag. But there he was, along with Grant, whose laughter rang out, both of them crouching on the floor near a can of white paint. Each was holding a paintbrush as they stared at the row of newly sanded cabinets near the sink. My chest squeezed tight at the sight of them together. The two guys I felt closest to. They certainly both consumed my every thought.

"What's going on here?" I bent over to pet Ruby, who'd risen from her perch to greet me.

"Grant decided to help me paint," Marcus said with a hint of a smile. "We're just about done."

"I can see that," I replied as I made room for the bag on the table near a box of pots and pans.

"The white color makes everything pop," Grant said. "I see now why you chose that silver-gray for the walls."

I stiffened. "Wait a minute, didn't you agree when we looked through the swatches?"

"Yeah, but I still wasn't sure." He glanced at Marcus, seeming a bit embarrassed. "It's so different from what Mom would've picked."

"I know it is." My chest throbbed. "If you'd wanted to choose something that reflected more of her style, I would've been okay with—"

"No, Dad." He gritted his teeth. "This is your house, so you should decorate it the way—"

"It's our house, Grant," I replied, wondering where in the hell this was coming from. "You have a say here too."

"Do I?" He carefully placed his brush in the paint tray, a scowl on his face.

"*Grant.* If this is about curfew the other night—"

"Just...*never mind*," he replied, his cheeks pink, likely because this was playing out in front of Marcus.

He was still pissed at me, though, and now it was spilling over into the weekend. The night I'd gone over to Marcus's, Grant was late for curfew and didn't respond after I texted him, which made me worry. We'd argued when he finally showed up, looking a bit out of sorts, which he couldn't easily explain, and I'd grounded him for a couple of days. I resisted picking up the phone to call Jeremy's parents and inquire about the rules until I remembered that curfew was on Grant and he'd be an adult soon enough. Besides, I didn't know this kid's mom and dad like I did Ellie's, though they seemed pretty decent, and I would probably sound like an overprotective jackass, including them in my unfound worries. *Christ.*

"Anyway, Marcus knows what he's doing," he grumbled. "So if he thinks you chose the best color for the walls, then he's probably right."

"I definitely do," Marcus said, warily meeting my eyes, and I cursed myself for putting him in an awkward position. "And your input on the kitchen island was great."

"What's the status on that, by the way?" I asked, hoping it was a good segue out of this uncomfortable conversation.

"I'm in the middle of staining it, and once the counters come in, I'll drop it off."

"Great," I said just as Grant's cell buzzed with a text.

He wiped his hands on one of the messy towels they were using, then went to his phone, which was sitting on the table. Smiling, he looked over his shoulder. "I'm just gonna..." He jogged upstairs to talk to one of his friends.

"You all right?" Marcus asked when the room grew quiet.

"Yeah, of course. He's still mad I grounded him over curfew," I replied in a steady tone as if this sort of friction didn't keep me up at night. "He always thinks I'm too hard on him."

"Don't all teens think that about their parents?" he mused.

"Probably." I blew out a breath. I reminded myself that my father could be brutal with his words, so I tried to tiptoe around Grant as much as I could. At least Grant didn't mince words. "Soon enough, he'll get distracted by his computer game, and all will be momentarily forgotten."

"Speaking of which," Marcus said as he replaced the lid on the paint can, "Grant mentioned some of the games you used to play on your Xbox, which has apparently been neglected lately."

"True," I replied, wondering what had brought that on. I used to blow off steam after work sometimes, but Grant was right. I hadn't picked up a controller since Rebecca passed.

"Is that something you and Grant used to do together?" he asked as he washed his hands at the sink.

"Rarely. Grant loves strategy games, and I'm only good at first-person shooter."

"You're good, huh?" He motioned toward the living room. "C'mon, let me introduce you to my skills in *Mortal Kombat*."

"Ooh, old-school," I said, following him. I had to dig out the controllers and dust them off before we got settled on the rug in front of the screen. Ruby sniffed curiously around us before curling near Marcus, who was giving her plenty of attention. Traitor.

Soon enough, we got lost in slashing each other's characters with swords and daggers as they died in outlandish ways. We laughed our asses off at the cartoonish amount of blood the game produced as we each tried to get the upper hand. But Marcus was definitely better at it. The bastard.

I startled when I heard Grant chuckle from the doorway.

"Want to play the winner, Grant?" Marcus asked. "Which will obviously be me."

"So humble," I replied, then held my breath, expecting the same excuses Grant always lobbed at me. I even tried to play in his *Minecraft* world for a few weeks, hoping it would be something that bonded us, but it was short-lived.

"Sure," Grant replied, and I felt a stab of envy that Marcus had more rapport with my own child than me. But I also felt grateful that he provided us a neutral zone where I was able to interact with Grant through a different lens.

Of course, Marcus beat me and then Grant in turn, but at least there was a lot of laughter in the process.

"I'm sorry you ditched your friends only to get spanked by me," Marcus said after winning for the umpteenth time. He lifted his arm and pretended to show off his guns while Grant and I rolled our eyes and laughed.

"You dork," Grant said. "Actually, Ellie's parents are making her study for her SATs. Her brother goes to Franklin U in California, and she might apply there too."

The mood in the room shifted when Marcus asked, "What about you?"

"I, uh..." Grant looked at me, then away. "There are a couple of local colleges I'll be considering."

"Only local?" Marcus was asking the sensitive question I couldn't easily navigate with my son, and he was getting away with it. So I held my breath and focused on the screen instead of on Grant. Though I could certainly feel the heat of his gaze.

"For now," Grant replied. "Sticking around here feels less..." He trailed off and looked away.

"Scary, overwhelming?" Marcus asked, and my stomach constricted painfully. "Safer?"

"Yeah, I guess so."

"I get it. I'd probably do the same," Marcus said, petting Ruby, who was practically lying in his lap now. "Though I might consider a tour of at least one far-away campus just so I could visit someplace cool."

"You would?" Grant asked. "Is that because you like to travel?"

Marcus smiled. "I haven't done it enough, but heck yeah."

"I heard NYU was cool," Grant said with a shrug, and I suddenly recalled our conversation about the subway and his driving lessons. "That's where my mom went to school."

I wanted to add my two cents but was afraid the conversation would sour with my input. I'd sat through the parent night at school where they'd provided us deadline dates, but anytime I'd brought up college visits in the last couple of weeks, he'd shrugged me off.

"What do you think, Lane?" Marcus asked, prompting me to say something.

I cleared my throat. "I think Rebecca would love the idea of

Grant visiting her alma mater. We discussed it a couple of times."

"You did?" Grant asked, his eyes widened in wonder, and I had the urge to hug him. I refrained, unsure if it would be reciprocated. More so, I would only embarrass him.

"Yep," I said with a small smile. "I mean, the final decision is obviously yours. But she thought it would be fun to take you to the city during one of your breaks."

"That would've been fun." He frowned, then looked at Marcus. "Did you go to college?"

"I attended Tri-C for a couple of years," Marcus replied, referring to the local community college. "I always knew I'd take over my grandfather's shop, so I wanted to take some business courses."

"Awesome," Grant said. "My dad went to a trade school and then became an apprentice for a master electrician."

Warmth flooded my chest. I was never college material, but plenty of people weren't. I was grateful I hadn't wasted years trying to figure that out because I was doing something I enjoyed and was darn good at.

"And that's why you need to forge your own path," I said. "If you want, we can visit New York in the next few months."

His eyes grew comically large. "Really?"

"Just to see the campus and the city, even if you still decide to go local," I said, knowing he'd be feeling a bit freaked about the prospect. "It wouldn't mean anything other than that, okay?"

"Yeah, okay. I like that idea."

I blew out a breath, fucking relieved that we'd made some sort of headway. Besides, a trip would do us good, even a quick one. When I met Marcus's gaze, I hoped he could see the gratitude in mine—for opening the door to this discussion, even if he hadn't realized it.

"Okay, I gotta get back to work," he said, standing up. "I can kick your butts again another time."

"You wish." I laughed when he walked out of the room with an exaggerated swagger.

Grant leaned closer to me. "Hey, maybe Marcus would want to come with us to New York?"

I stiffened. "I'm not sure, kiddo. Maybe it would be wiser to invite your grandparents, or at least extend the invitation?"

He frowned. "Grandpa wouldn't be able to make the trip, and Grandma wouldn't leave him home alone, even for a weekend."

"You're right. I almost forgot how hard it would be for them." I sighed. "It makes me thankful they were able to retire early and travel the world. They already have lots of good memories."

"Which is why I wanted to ask Marcus," he countered. "He admitted he hasn't traveled a lot, and he'd be fun to have around."

I was reading between the lines again, wondering if Grant wanted Marcus there as a cushion between us. But maybe I was completely off base. It would be nice for Marcus to join us, but no way I'd put that sort of pressure on him.

"We can talk about it later," I said, then pushed to my knees to store the controllers in the drawer beneath the television.

But Grant ignored me, rushing to the kitchen and asking Marcus to join us.

Shit. I walked in just as Marcus was telling him that the holidays were a busy time for him at the shop, so he'd have to see when his schedule died down.

"Sorry," I mouthed to him, seeing his wary expression.

Grant frowned. "Okay, but maybe just think about it?"

"I absolutely will. Thank you for the invite," Marcus said, patting his shoulder.

Grant avoided eye contact with me as he made his way back upstairs to his room.

"Don't feel obligated at all," I said, hoping he wasn't too overwhelmed by the suggestion.

"It's not that," he said, meeting my gaze. "A trip would be good for the two of you, and I wouldn't want to intrude on your quality time or the memories you'd be sharing with him."

"I understand your reluctance." I opened the fridge, pulled out a couple of sodas, and handed him one. "And the trip *would* be fun, something all of us could use."

"Definitely." He angled the soda can to his lips.

"I just think Grant enjoys your company." I dipped my head. "We both do. So I can understand why he asked."

"The feeling is mutual." He lifted his paintbrush, then crouched down to the lower cabinets to finish the job they'd started. "Thing is, it was Grant who asked, not you. So I'd never presume—"

"I would love to have you come along. It would be a blast," I replied, then lowered my voice. "Guess I'm always nervous to give Grant or my in-laws the wrong idea. Hanging out is one thing, but a weekend trip? We're already sneaking around, and if they ever caught wind of whatever this is between us..."

"It's being there for each other and enjoying ourselves in the process, right?" he grumbled. "No strings attached. You've made that very clear."

I took a step back at his tone, which had an edge to it. "Wait a minute, wasn't that mutually agreed upon? Are you saying—"

"What I'm saying is that I get it now, more than ever"—he glanced toward the stairs—"the weight of your responsibility. Grant inviting me made me realize it, and I wouldn't want to disappoint him either."

My chest was crowded with all sorts of emotions I couldn't make heads or tails of. "Is this too much for you—our friendship and you getting to know my kid?"

"No, of course not. I'm probably enjoying myself a little too much. I look forward to seeing you—both of you. I'm only saying I understand you better, okay?"

"Yeah, okay." But I could still see the melancholy in his eyes, so I stepped closer and crouched down by him. "For what it's worth, sometimes I wish...fuck, never mind."

What in the hell was I saying? Way to muddy the waters even further.

I stood up and backed away, my pulse going crazy.

"Wish what?" he asked over his shoulder. "I thought you said communication was important, remember?"

He was right. I took a deep breath. "Sometimes I wonder what it might be like if the timing wasn't off."

He arched an eyebrow. "Are you asking if I'd date you?"

Our eyes met and held. "Maybe I am."

"Eh, I'd have to think about it," he said, waving me off with a cocky smirk. "I'm pretty particular about who I choose to spend my time with."

"You dickhead," I said with a laugh.

"I've been called worse." He grinned. "Now let me get back to work. You've already distracted me with the Xbox." He laughed when I scoffed. "Don't you have dinner to make?"

"I do." I turned toward the bag of spices I'd left on the table. "Did you want to stay? I'm going to try and make—"

"I actually have plans with my mom and sister. And no, that's not an excuse because you asked to date me."

I barked out a laugh. "I'm gonna kick your ass."

He winked. "I look forward to it."

Later that night, I still couldn't shake our conversation. I didn't know how to do this. How to juggle the task of keeping Grant's new normal intact with no major disruptions, yet also enjoy my friendship with Marcus without letting messy romantic feelings or desires get in the way. I lifted my cell and scrolled to Marcus's number.

Why can't you hear a pterodactyl go to the bathroom?

I held my breath as I waited for his response.

Why?

My chest throbbed as I typed: **Because the *p* is silent.**

LOL. I've been craving your corniness tonight.

Fucking hell. *I've been craving you too.*

Glad to deliver. We missed you for dinner. Shit. I probably shouldn't have worded it that way.

Missed you and your home-cooked meal too.

That just shows how hard up you are if you miss my awful cooking.

It's not terrible. But I'm definitely hard up.

As if I'm not.

There was a long pause, and my gut churned over our conversation. Sometimes it was easier to share my deepest fears when he couldn't see the bald emotions in my eyes.

I typed: **I'm sorry if you think I'm not being brave enough, regarding Grant and my sexuality. Or dating in general. And maybe you'd be right. Maybe I can't muster the courage right now when things between Grant and me feel like we've found some common ground on the sharp edge of a knife.**

My pulse throbbed as I waited for his reply.

I don't think *brave* is the right word.

What do you mean?

I adjusted the covers, wondering again what it might be like to have him beside me for an entire night. My chest ached with so much longing, I could scarcely breathe.

You're already brave. It takes so much fucking courage to carry on and raise an amazing kid after such a devastating loss. I think the right word is *love*. You love Grant so much that you're willing to protect him at all costs. To make sure life is a little softer for him, even if it's you absorbing the shock. And if it were me, I'd probably do the same.

My eyes burned, and I blinked away the tears as I typed with shaky hands.

Fucking hell, Marc. How do you do that...see inside me so well...

I could ask you the same.

I exhaled roughly because fuck, this conversation hit me square in the chest. I didn't want to disappoint Marcus any more than I did Grant. Not for anything in the world.

Night, Lane.

Night.

20

MARCUS

DELANEY TEXTED that the countertops were being delivered. It was two days before Thanksgiving, which meant a shortened workweek. But I didn't mind because the kitchen island was finished and ready to be loaded in my truck. Luckily, I got some help from Marian and her husband, who'd come by to take her to lunch. Normally I could handle hauling stuff on my own with the help of a furniture dolly, but this sucker was heavy. It would be a perfect addition to their kitchen, though, that was for sure.

As I drove to his place, it struck me that the kitchen was nearly finished, so I'd no longer be spending every Saturday at their house like I had for the past two months. Although, they would probably be thankful to not be living out of boxes and skirting around drop cloths and paint cans any longer.

But maybe the distance would be good for all of us. The truth was, I was afraid of becoming too attached. As it stood now, my affection for Delaney had grown exponentially, which might've explained why the conversation that took place after Grant invited me on their trip had stung. Obviously, I didn't think it was a good idea either, no matter how enticing it sounded. If our friendship ever went south, it would kill me to hurt Delaney, let alone Grant, in any way. I now understood a hell of a lot better the sorts of worries that kept Delaney up at night. And sometimes—dozens of times—I wished I were there to hold him instead of pulling up to an empty house and lying in a bed that felt too big for one person.

But I'd learned that I only had agency over my own thoughts, actions, and feelings. Everything else was beyond my control. For now, I'd be grateful for all the gentler—and rougher—moments with Delaney because he was instrumental in helping me find myself again.

Delaney met me at the door, and it took the three of us to get the island inside. The old table had been moved out of the way, and they'd have to buy some barstools to make it work as a seating area, but just as I'd predicted, it looked great in their kitchen.

"That's so cool," Grant said as we stood back to approve the placement, but the admiration was cut short by the doorbell ringing.

"Perfect timing." Delaney headed toward the front door. "Looks like our counters are here."

Thankfully, I didn't have to assist with the hauling of those heavy slabs of granite, the company having plenty of helping hands of their own. So we stood out of the way and watched, pleased with how it was all coming together.

When Delaney's phone buzzed with a text message, he looked at Grant. "It's your grandmother."

"I forgot to ask about your Thanksgiving plans. Who's cooking dinner?"

"Donna always insists, but I'm not sure it'll happen this year. Howard has the flu, and given her hacking cough on the phone today, it looks like she caught it too," he said as Grant's expression turned sullen. "I was gonna run to the store after this to get them stocked up on soup and medicine."

"I'm sorry to hear that," I replied with a frown.

"Eh, no biggie, right?" he said, squeezing Grant's shoulder. "I'm gonna look for a small turkey while I'm at the store. At least we'll have a working kitchen."

"You can't do that," I replied absently, an idea taking shape.

"Huh?" Delaney's eyebrows knitted together. "Do what?"

"Sorry. What I mean is, you can't spend Thanksgiving alone. I'll be heading to my mom's with my sister and aunt, and she'd love to have you."

"No, we shouldn't. It's such short notice. We can't just—"

"Yes, you can." I pulled out my phone. "I'm texting my mom right now."

When he shifted uncomfortably beside me, I worried I'd overstepped. But this was different from a weekend trip. This was inviting a couple of friends to dinner because their plans got canceled. Thankfully, my mom responded right away.

"She says you're more than welcome." I tilted the text message toward him. "No pressure. It's up to you. But they've already heard all about you, and...you won't want to miss her stuffing."

He bit his lip warily. "What do you think, Grant?"

Grant looked between the two of us, his smile spreading wide. "Let's do it."

"Awesome." There, it was settled. My family would meet them and maybe understand why I felt such a connection. Or maybe they'd set me straight. Either way.

Once the counters were in place and we'd signed off on the work, Delaney motioned toward the door. "I need to get to the store, Grant."

"I'll be in my room," he replied. "See you on Thanksgiving, Marc."

We fist-bumped, and then Delaney and I walked out together.

"It was really nice of you to invite us for Thanksgiving, but you didn't have to. We would be perfectly fine here by—"

"Your leaves are piling up again," I said, pointing to the lawn covered in an array of golds and reds, and given the barren trees near his curb, they were the last of the season.

"I know." He sighed. "I plan to rake this weekend. And... nice distraction."

"Would it also be a nice distraction if I said I want to kiss you so bad right now?" That got the desired effect of making him blush.

"You better watch yourself, mister. I might surprise you and jump your bones right here in my driveway."

"Jump my bones?" I pumped my eyebrows. "Is that what the kids are calling it nowadays?"

He laughed. "Grant would be mortified."

"By you sounding old as fuck? Or the idea of you trying to date me?"

"Shh." He glanced over his shoulder as if Grant or the neighbors would hear through the windows. "And were we even talking about dating, or...other things?"

I shook my head, amused that he couldn't even say the words out loud.

"Don't tempt me," I said with a wink as I opened my car door.

"Don't tempt *me*," he responded in that bolder tone I enjoyed.

We shared one last smile before he went to his car. Once I pulled out of the driveway, I headed back to work to take care of a couple of things.

I got home late, finished up some leftovers, then worked out. After I showered and got ready for bed, I felt restless, so I pulled out my cell.

How are your in-laws?

Pretty sick. I didn't go inside, but I could hear them coughing through the door.

Bummer. Hope they'll be on the mend soon. Maybe you can bring them leftovers from my mom's house.

There was a long pause, which made me rethink my reply.

My bad. That might be awkward.

No, it was a nice offer. Why should I let it be awkward? You're my friend, and you invited me to dinner at your mom's house.

True. Wanna talk?

Yeah.

I pressed video call by accident and almost hung up, except Delaney answered on the first ring.

"Well, this is new." His chest was bare, and his sheets were tucked in around his waist.

"Sorry, I didn't mean to—"

"No, it's okay. We should actually do this more often. It's nice to see your face."

"It's nice to see yours too. As well as the rest of you." Delaney flushed at the comment. "Looks like you're also in bed."

"Yeah, I was gonna find a *Dateline* episode to watch."

"Good idea. Maybe I'll do the same." When his eyes met mine, I asked, "Is Ruby in Grant's room tonight, or is she keeping your feet warm?"

"She's with Grant," he replied, glancing across the room, then lowering his voice. "No one here to keep me warm."

"I'd keep you warm if I could," I said, my voice growing a bit husky.

"Fuck, that sounds good," he replied, then looked away so I couldn't see his eyes. "Lots of other things do, too, especially when you look like that."

"Yeah?" I liked it when he told me exactly what he was thinking. "Like what?"

"Like maybe sex. I'm a bit out of practice—with men, I mean."

"Have you ever gone further than a blowjob?"

"Actual penetration?" Delaney asked, and I nodded. "Once. It was rushed, he came way too fast, and it hurt like hell, so..."

"Just like anyone's first time." I absently scratched an itch on my chest, thinking about my first time fooling around with a guy and how messy and awful it was, but also sweet and hot. My first time with a woman was a little better.

"True. But I'm certainly curious," he said in a raspy voice that went straight to my groin. "And it definitely turns me on."

"Imagining being fucked?" I adjusted myself beneath the covers, already feeling overheated from the conversation.

"Yeah." His cheeks were pink. "I like the idea of blanking out my mind and letting someone else call the shots for a change. I know that's not what every bottom does or wants, but for me, I just...need it."

"I get it," I replied, thinking about how crushing his responsibilities must've felt sometimes. "And fucking hell, I'd top you. All you have to do is ask."

"Goddamn it." He squirmed beneath his covers. "Thanks a lot for that visual."

"Sorry, not sorry?" I teased. "Guess I'll have to add jerking off to my routine tonight."

"Same." He groaned.

"Maybe we should do it together?" My pulse throbbed as the question hung suspended between us.

"I'll have to be quiet," Delaney said, and I breathed out in relief as he glanced somewhere off-camera. "Let me put in my earbuds and get something to prop my phone."

"I will too."

I could hear him breathing as I pushed my briefs down, then stacked a couple of pillows across from me to angle my phone against. When he created a similar setup, my mouth ran dry because now I had a better view of him completely bare. Of his meaty thighs and thick cock surrounded by that dark patch of hair at his groin. He also had a good dusting on his chest and legs. So damned sexy.

"Fucking hell, Lane. If only I could touch you right now."

"The feeling is mutual." His voice was husky, and my shaft was growing stiffer by the second. His fingers twisted his sheets nervously, and I wished I could kiss him and make him feel more comfortable.

"Show me how you get yourself off," I said, and his eyes flared with heat, suddenly looking more confident, as if he'd just needed help getting started.

He gripped his cock and stroked roughly. "I've been practicing...with my fingers."

"What do you m—ah, hell, stuffing them in your ass?" I groaned.

"Yeah, it feels good, even without lube, and...makes me shoot faster."

My balls ached just picturing it. "Lift your knees, show me your hole."

"Ah, fuck." He adjusted himself on the pillow, his legs shaking as he exposed himself to me. "I can't believe I'm doing this...holy shit."

I gripped my cock at the root, trying to stop myself from shooting too early. His furry hole was now on display as he sucked on one of his fingers, then circled around his rim.

"Christ, Lane. That's so hot. Keep going."

He looked away, the bloom of color now spreading across his neck and chest, his nipples stiff as he dipped one finger inside, then two. He groaned and rocked a little, a string of precome sticking to his stomach. And I wasn't much better, so I used my thumb to swipe at the slit and help me along.

I watched as Delaney lost himself to the sensation as he stroked his cock, fingered himself, and shut his eyes. His self-awareness had faded to the background, and I loved seeing that. Besides, I was being treated to an amazing show. "You're gorgeous, Lane. Just look at you."

"No, you are." His eyes opened, his gaze latching on to mine. "I haven't given it much thought before—the beauty of a man. But every time I'm around you, I can't help being drawn to you, to how beautiful you are. And not just on the outside, but the inside too. Anyone who gets to have you would be lucky."

I was struck dumb in that moment, my chest aching with affection and longing.

"What if..." I swallowed roughly, my whole body trembling. "What if I hope it's you who gets to have me?"

"Fuck, Marc." His eyes softened as he bit his lip. "I pretend it's you. Every time I do this, I pretend it's you."

"Goddamn it." I started stroking myself faster.

His moan was sensual, carnal, as he fingered himself. "Every time I stuff my fingers inside me, I hope it's gonna be you who gives me this."

"I hope so too." I shuddered, my balls aching and my spine tingling. "Now make yourself come, Lane. Because I'm about to shoot."

His face was so serious, his gaze so hungry as he stroked himself into oblivion. He groaned as his seed spurted all over his chest, and I felt like I was in the center of a lightning storm, my shaft the main conductor, shooting off with a force I hadn't felt in quite some time.

As we slowly came back to ourselves, I reached for my underwear to clean the come off my stomach, and he did the same with a T-shirt. He got under his covers and reached for his phone to give me a close-up of his face—his dreamy eyes and rosy cheeks. "You okay?"

"I'm perfect," I said in a jumbled voice as I got under the warmth of my own sheets. "You should get some sleep."

"Will you stay on with me a little bit longer?" he asked

around a yawn as his arm stretched to shut off his bedside lamp.

My chest throbbed at the sweetness of the request. "Of course."

I shut off my own light, then closed my eyes. A minute went by, then another... He was silent, so I thought maybe he'd already fallen asleep.

But then I heard his thick voice. "Will you come to New York with us?"

My pulse pitched. "You don't have to inv—"

"The truth is, I want you there. And so does Grant. Why do I need any excuses for that? So...at least think about it?"

"I will." I sighed, wishing more than ever that I was there in person. "Now go to sleep."

"You won't hang up?" he asked, his voice growing drowsier. But I heard the underlying neediness too, to not be alone, and I certainly didn't want to be either.

"Not a chance. Sweet dreams."

When I startled awake sometime in the middle of the night, my cell was still in my hand, but the call had ended.

21

DELANEY

Fuck, had that really happened between Marcus and me? Talk about dating in the twenty-first century. Well, not really dating, just...what? Sexting? Hooking up via video? I had never done any such thing in my life, but it was easily one of the hottest in my memory. And the fact that it was with Marcus added an extra layer of...everything.

It was Thanksgiving morning, and I'd just gotten off the phone with my mother-in-law, who promised me they were both on the mend and would be fine with the chicken noodle soup and crackers I'd dropped off for them last night.

I jumped in the shower, my dick immediately growing stiff as I thought about the other night. I swore to God, it'd better calm down before we arrived at his mom's house. To help it along, I jerked off fast and came hard, thinking about Marcus's voice urging me on and how he'd looked ruined afterward, which made me feel satisfied in a way I hadn't in quite some time. I again wished it'd all taken place with him being in my bed without any fears of repercussions.

Afterward, I didn't want to let him go, and I felt a bit childish asking if he'd stay on. But it'd also turned into one of the most romantic things anyone had ever done for me. Some-how, we'd gotten disconnected in the middle of the night, and when I'd woken from a dream starring Marcus, which hadn't ever happened before, I'd felt that same sort of lightness in my heart I always did around him.

I met Grant in the kitchen, and we made sure the apple pie we'd made from Rebecca's recipe had set. Marcus's family hadn't asked us to bring anything, but it didn't feel right to show up without food in hand.

My hand faltered as I tore off a piece of plastic wrap to cover the dessert. Why the fuck was I so anxious about today?

Grant might've been nervous, too, because he wasn't dressed in any sort of historical outfit. He only wore his newsboy cap, a graphic tee that read: *I Hate Repeating Myself. Signed, History*, and a button-down shirt over it with the sleeves rolled up. For the first time in a long while, I found myself smiling at his selection. The truth was, Grant was a cool kid, period, and his collection of T-shirts and historical outfits was endearing. I wished I'd been a lot less fussy about it his whole damned life.

But that moment of clarity was all too brief. As we piled into the car and got on the road, I couldn't help thinking about Marcus's relatives and hoping they'd see Grant that way too. I also hoped they hadn't invited us out of obligation. I turned up the radio to drown out my thoughts, but I couldn't find it in me to hum or sing like I had that one day with Marcus. And from Grant's stiff posture, he obviously couldn't either.

"Maybe when your grandparents are feeling better, you should stay the night. They'll be bummed they missed out on spending time with you," I said as I turned into Marcus's neigh-borhood. His mom lived right around the corner from him, and now I could picture how easy it would be for him to walk over in a couple of minutes flat.

"Good idea," Grant replied, his shoulders relaxing. "We could make some cookies together. Grandma would like that."

"She would." I smiled as I found a spot to park on the street. "Just not oatmeal raisin."

He smirked. "I think Grandpa might like them, though."

"At least we know where she got it from." I glanced at the bungalow, which resembled the majority of houses in the neighborhood. The driveway was lined with cars, so we might've been the last to arrive.

I pushed open the door as my stomach performed dive-bombs, either about meeting Marcus's relatives or seeing him in person after the other night.

But most of my nerves fled when Marcus opened the door, wearing black jeans, a blue button-down shirt, and a huge smile. Damn, he looked good. "Glad you could make it."

"Me too," I said as he took the pie from Grant, and we discarded our coats on the hooks near the door. Four people were seated in the living room near the large television, watching today's NFL game.

Before Marcus could make his introductions, we were warmly greeted by a lady with shoulder-length black hair and deep-brown skin, wearing an apron and a grin that resembled Marcus's.

"Mom, this is Delaney and Grant."

"Please call me Arlene."

"Nice to meet you, Arlene. Thanks for inviting us."

"Of course. The more, the merrier. Make yourselves comfortable."

Marcus led us to the living room, and one of the women waved from a reclining chair. She appeared to be around Arlene's age, was wearing trendy tortoiseshell glasses, and I could only assume she was her sister.

"I'm Aunt Sherry, and the man who can't take his eyes off the screen for one minute to greet you is my husband, Luis."

Luis scoffed before acknowledging us from his perch near the game. He had a mustache and a toothy grin.

"No worries," I replied. "Football is probably synonymous with Thanksgiving."

"Not for all of us," Arlene said with an eye roll.

"Glad to have you," Aunt Sherry said. "Marc never mentioned how handsome you both are."

"*Sherry*," Arlene hissed. "Always starting trouble."

"Where's the lie?" Aunt Sherry winked, and I didn't dare look at Grant or Marcus, especially since my face felt as warm as the bottom of the pie tin.

Someone cleared their throat from the couch.

"That's my sister, Keisha, and her boyfriend, Jeff." Marcus stepped toward them, we followed behind, and I was glad for the reprieve from the aunt's scrutiny.

"Nice to finally meet you," Keisha said with a smirk, and I wondered if there was some story behind it. She had Marcus's coloring, hazel eyes, and her hair had a bit more of a wave to it. It again made me curious about Marcus's father, but all I knew was that he passed away when they were young.

"Hey, nice shirt," Jeff said, pointing to Grant's graphic tee.

Grant dipped his head, but I could tell he enjoyed the compliment. "Thanks."

"Which reminds me," Marcus said, handing the pie to his mom, then unbuttoning his shirt to reveal the graphic tee under it.

"*I'm just here to spill the tea,*" he said, reading his shirt out loud, and all I could do was stare, noting the photo of a ship beneath the words. It was meant to represent the Boston Tea Party but with a modern twist.

"Ooh, good one," Grant said, and they high-fived.

Keisha was also watching them with a strange expression, and that made me snap out of it. Marcus had gone out of his way—again—to make my kid feel welcome. I almost expected him to produce another tee for me to wear like he did on Halloween, and I was glad to be wrong, honestly. I nearly teased him about it, but I didn't think Grant would take it too well that I had no desire to match them. At least not in this setting, when I already felt like we were intruding.

"What can I say?" Marcus shrugged as I finally got my mouth to lift into a smile. "Grant has a kickass T-shirt collection, and I wanted to join him."

Keisha and Aunt Sherry exchanged amused glances, and I shifted uncomfortably as my gut churned. Could they see it now? How close we'd all grown? Marcus had mentioned how close Keisha had been to Carmen. Would she feel the same as my in-laws? Like Marcus was moving on?

Once Marcus got us drinks and Arlene brought out appetizers to tide her guests over, we hung out in the living room for a bit, watching football and chatting about general stuff, like my job and Luis's love of any and all sports.

Grant wanted nothing to do with sports, so he ended up sitting near Keisha and Jeff, discussing his trip to Worthy's in his chatterbox way, telling them how much he liked the shop. Keisha told him more about their grandfather, who, like Marcus, was always tinkering with one project or another, and Grant listened with rapt attention, which was heartwarming.

I stood at one point and went to look at the family photos hanging on the wall near the couch, noting younger versions of Marcus and Keisha, as well as several from Carmen and Marcus's wedding. The largest picture was one I'd already seen on the end table at Marcus's house. I thought I'd have probably liked Carmen, and I had a feeling she and Rebecca would've gotten along famously. Both were strong, smart women. I could see now how they'd married their counterparts—me, way less self-possessed than Rebecca, and from what Marcus had told me of his marriage, he'd been pretty laid-back, sometimes to his detriment. I wondered what that meant when it came to our friendship and how we just seemed to fit.

Marcus came to stand beside me, offering me a glass of red wine. "Sorry, no bourbon," he quipped.

"Probably for the best." I took the offering and sipped slowly, enjoying the mellow taste.

"There must be a story there," Keisha said with an arched eyebrow.

I looked over at Grant, who was talking to Jeff about his classes, and thought he'd likely remember the night I'd had too much to drink.

"Never mind," I said, and Marcus laughed, winking at his sister. She shook her head as she went into the kitchen to assist Arlene with the meal. Earlier I offered to help, but was practically run out of the room because I was considered a guest.

"Is this your father?" I pointed to a photo of a white man sitting on a dock with a younger version of his mom. Their fishing rods were leaning against a pole beside a tackle box.

"Yeah." His shoulder pressed against mine, making my stomach flood with warmth. "That's the 55th Street pier."

"Seriously?" I looked closer, noticing the familiar Lake Erie horizon as well as the boulders lining the shore that broke the waves during storms. Sometimes they got so high that water would splash on the freeway as you were driving by on Interstate 90.

"City fishing," Aunt Sherry said. "Those two loved sitting on that pier together, watching the sunrise."

"That sounds nice." I glanced over my shoulder. "Did you ever join them?"

"Heck no." She made a face. "It's boring sitting there for hours. I gotta keep moving."

"She's got that right," Luis said, and we all laughed. Guess he'd been listening all along, even though he rarely contributed to the conversations. I had an uncle like that—my dad's brother. Quiet and kind and drastically different from my father, who was very opinionated. No wonder they'd had a falling-out.

"Time to eat," Keisha called from the dining room, and we made our way to sit around the table. Arlene was at one end, and Marcus at the other, near the turkey, which he began carving, so it must've been a family tradition. There were all sorts of side dishes in the middle of the table, from sweet potatoes to collard greens, and soon enough, they were being passed around, and we were all digging in.

"Marc said your stuffing is delicious," Grant said around a bite, and I almost reminded him to keep his mouth closed while chewing, but I didn't want to embarrass him. Besides, it was a nice compliment.

"It is good. Everything is," I added, and she smiled. "Do you have the recipe, Marc?"

The room went silent a second before his family burst out laughing. He looked away sheepishly. "Pretty sure I'd ruin it. But I bet you'd do it justice."

"Yeah, my dad is a pretty good cook," Grant said, then shoved another forkful into his mouth.

"Not sure about that," I replied, my face flushing hot, but I appreciated the approval. "But I'd love the recipe."

"I'll send it along with Marc," Arlene said, seeming pleased. "I hear he's been helping you remodel your kitchen."

I wiped my mouth on the napkin from my lap. "More like I'm helping him. All I know is electrical work. I certainly don't have his skills."

"You do all right," Marcus said in that low, soothing tone I liked too much.

When he looked at me across the table, his eyes crinkled at the corners. I grinned and probably held his gaze for way too long. Fuck.

"Anyway..." I cleared my throat. "He refinished the cabinets, and I painted the walls. Grant helped too. Let me show you a photo."

I tugged my cell from my pocket, then flipped to the most recent photos I'd taken the night the counters and kitchen island were dropped off. I handed my phone to Grant, who passed it to Keisha, and around the table it went.

"Well, damn. You're hired," Luis said, swiping through the photos. "Come help us with our kitchen, Marc. It needs an overhaul."

"Hell no," Marcus said, and everyone laughed. "I was only doing a favor for a friend."

"I thought you liked working on side projects." I smirked. "Were we too much for you?"

He motioned to us. "Between the *Hamilton* music and the home-cooked meals, I don't think I can take much more."

The three of us shared a smile, but I could feel everyone's eyes on us. Damn it.

"Can you pass the black-eyed peas?" I asked, trying to change the subject once my phone was back in my possession.

I loaded some on my plate, then passed the dish to Grant, who was well into his second helping of turkey and stuffing. "You could use some vegetables on that plate. I think you'll like these."

"They're actually legumes," he countered but took the bowl from me.

"And legumes are considered starchy vegetables." I certainly hadn't meant to argue with him, not in front of an audience, but his smugness sometimes rubbed me the wrong way.

"Reminds me of Keisha when she was a teen," Arlene said, giving me a knowing look.

"Little Marc was a bigger pain in the butt than me," Keisha scoffed, and Marcus stuck his tongue out as if they were still ten. When Arlene clucked at them, I laughed.

"Little Marc?" Grant asked. "Was your grandfather's name Marcus too?"

"Yep." Marcus smiled. "And don't you dare, or I'll come up with a silly nickname for you too."

Grant grinned in a devious way, as if to say challenge accepted. It occurred to me then that we'd never had a nickname for Grant outside of using his full name when we meant business. But Grant was just Grant, and I liked it that way.

"You're a junior?" Jeff asked, and Grant nodded. "You'll be off to college before you know it. Any ideas where you might apply?"

For some reason, I held my breath as he replied, "I think I want to stick close to home."

"Nothing wrong with that," Arlene said, loading her plate with more turkey.

"You're young, so you should explore your options," Aunt Sherry said, and Arlene gave her a look I read as a warning. Seemed these siblings were as different as night and day too.

"Maybe," Grant said, his eyes on his plate. "Actually, we're gonna take a trip to New York City. My mom went to NYU."

"Nice," Jeff said. "I love the city. When are you doing that?"

Grant looked at me, and I said, "Not exactly sure. Need to look at dates and ticket prices."

"That sounds fun," Aunt Sherry said. "It's better to travel early before life gets in the way."

She threw Luis a cursory glance, and I had to wonder if some of their plans had gotten spoiled over the years. Much like mine had with Rebecca. And for plenty of others too. It was once a topic of conversation in the grief group.

"Marc might come with us," Grant said, putting him on the spot, and I stiffened.

"Only if he has the time," I said in as gentle a tone as possible in front of Marcus's family. I had no idea if he'd even thought more about our conversation from the other night.

And besides, that didn't mean he wanted his family to know about the offer.

"Oh, he can make the time," Aunt Sherry said, avoiding her sister's eyes. "All the man does is work."

"Leave Marc alone," Luis said, nudging his wife. "He can make up his own mind."

"I'll discuss dates with your dad, and we'll see," Marcus said, and that seemed to satisfy Grant for the moment.

"Sorry," I mouthed over Grant's head.

Marcus shook his head, and I noticed Keisha watching our interaction. She stayed silent throughout the conversation, and again I wondered what she might be thinking.

Soon enough, dinner was over, and we helped clear the dishes from the table before retiring to the living room again. Grant and Jeff were involved in a conversation about college— Jeff had attended Kent State and was telling Grant about the campus. Keisha and Aunt Sherry had taken over dish duty, and it was nice to hear Marcus and his mother interact, even though I could tell she was itching to get back to the kitchen, much like my mom used to do.

"Want to help me serve dessert?" Marcus asked, and I was grateful to have something to do with my hands. I still had some nervous energy buzzing through me, and I wasn't sure why.

I followed him into the kitchen, where we cut slices of the sweet-potato pie Aunt Sherry had made, along with our caramel apple.

"Who's ready for dessert?" Marcus asked as we passed the plates around, then sat down to enjoy some of our own.

"I'm officially stuffed," Grant said, standing up with his empty plate.

"Me too." Marcus patted his belly. "I loved your apple pie."

"Thanks. It's my mom's recipe." Grant looked at me with a vulnerable expression. "But we decided to add walnuts."

"We're making it our own," I said in a hoarse voice, suddenly emotional.

I stood too and began collecting plates, swallowing down the boulder in my throat.

We stayed about a half-hour more before we decided to hit the road.

"The food was delicious," I told Arlene as she and Marcus walked us to the door. I waved goodbye to the other family members standing behind them. "Thank you for having us."

She patted my shoulder. "Anytime."

22

MARCUS

O<small>NCE</small> I <small>CLOSED</small> the door behind Delaney and Grant, I could feel their eyes on me. Well, not everyone's. Luis and Jeff had wandered back to the living room to watch the game.

But Mom, Keisha, and Aunt Sherry followed me into the kitchen, where the inquisition would undoubtedly begin. I picked up a towel, wiped down the counter near the sink, trying to look busy but knowing they were watching me until I couldn't take it anymore.

"*What?*" I said, rounding on them.

"You are so wild about that man," Aunt Sherry said as she stored the leftover whipped cream in the refrigerator.

"And his son," Keisha hissed, already in protective mode. "The T-shirt, the trip to New York, the inside jokes."

I threw my hands up. "First, you tell me I'm not getting out enough, and now you're complaining because I've grown close to a friend from grief group? A friend who understands what I've been through?"

"It's more than that, and you know it," Keisha replied, and Aunt Sherry concurred under her breath. "Even his son has you all wrapped up. Does Lane know...that you...?"

"That I...what?" I huffed.

"You know what she's trying to ask," Aunt Sherry said in a softer voice as if she had to tiptoe around the subject. "That you...whatever you call it...also like men."

"I call it bisexual." I nearly rolled my eyes. "And of course he does. I consider him a close friend."

"How close?" Keisha arched an eyebrow.

"None of your goddamned business." I folded my arms. "What's with this line of questioning? What am I on trial for, exactly?"

Keisha finally backed down, her stance dropping, and she sighed. It might've had to do with my mother's stern look.

"Just be careful," she said with a wave of her hand. "Don't want you getting hurt."

"What makes you think I will?" I reached for a soda from the fridge.

"You're just...you'll get it twice as bad now," Keisha said, digging through Mom's Tupperware drawer. "We both struggled to find our place in this community because we aren't Black enough—or white enough, for that matter—and being a bisexual person of color only adds to it."

Mom and Aunt Sherry stayed silent, but I could see the sympathy in their eyes.

"It's not like I haven't already dealt with my fair share, especially as a biracial teen figuring out my sexuality." I glanced at my mother, whose eyes had softened. "Not that many people knew, outside of the guys I was messing around with, but still. I knew back then, and I'm fully aware now of how some people might see it."

"Back then, you hadn't inherited a Black-owned business." Keisha raised a slotted spoon at me, then scooped leftovers into a plastic container.

"So fuck 'em." I took a sip of my soda. "I'm not going to hide who I am. I'm also not going to announce anything either. I don't know the background of any of my customers unless they choose to share it. Business is a commodity, plain and simple. If they don't like it, they can take it elsewhere."

"That's the spirit," Aunt Sherry said as she began divvying up the pies to take home. "I just want you to have fun. And if that involves a handsome man who has a teenage son, then so be it."

"It's not like that," I said, exasperated. Besides, Delaney wasn't here to defend himself, and this conversation had already gone off the rails. "He's a parent, first and foremost. And even if there were something between us, he wouldn't want to uproot Grant's life."

"That's noble but unfair to you," Aunt Sherry said, reaching for the plastic wrap.

"Wouldn't you do the same?" I asked as Mom handed Keisha a large spoon for the mashed potatoes. "Grant lost his mom, and he's still grieving. So I'm hanging out with them and being a good friend. End of story."

"Whatever you say." Keisha stacked her containers and called for Jeff in the other room to round up their coats. "But I know you. When you fall, you fall hard and you're all in."

"Don't be ridiculous." I barked out a laugh that sounded fake even to my own ears. "Nobody's falling."

But that was exactly what was happening, no matter how much I tried to deny it. My crush on him had turned into something way deeper than I'd ever anticipated. At this point, I should've probably pulled back, made myself scarce, but the idea of hanging out with them less had my chest aching something fierce. Besides, our Saturdays in the kitchen were coming to an end, and that would help. And hurt in equal measure.

"I pretend it's you. Every time I do this, I pretend it's you."

After everyone left, I stayed behind to remove the extensions from the dining table and put the chairs back in order. I fluffed the couch pillows and picked up the empty glasses, smiling when I found Mom in the kitchen, enjoying a second helping of sweet-potato pie, her favorite.

She urged me to sit down across from her and handed me a fork so I could pick at the remnants of the apple pie wedge left in the tin. I liked the added walnuts.

Damn, the way Grant had sounded when he'd announced that. Like he'd betrayed Rebecca for changing her recipe. I wanted to hug him. But Delaney's response was perfect. He thought his parenting barely measured up, but I wished he could see himself the way I did. Compassionate and generous, and fucking beautiful.

Jesus Christ, maybe Keisha was right.

"You can't always pick the right timing. Some things are beyond our control. You know that," Mom said after she'd swallowed another bite, and holy fuck, it was as if she'd been privy to my conversations with Delaney. "But if someone makes you happy, Carmen would approve."

"I can't..." I swallowed roughly. "It still feels surreal that we're even having this conversation."

She set down her fork. "Honey, she's no longer here, no matter how protective your sister is. She's in a better place, with your dad...we have to believe that."

My heart ballooned with the idea of all our loved ones somehow meeting in the afterlife and offering comfort to one another.

"And if she's looking down at us right now," Mom continued, "she is kicking you in the ass."

"Huh?" I nearly choked on the flaky crust. "What do you mean?"

"This coming spring, you'll have been without her for three years," Mom said, and I felt that same churning in my gut, but more muted now. It didn't make me flinch as if it had just happened yesterday. Now it felt like I'd tucked the worst of the heartbreak away in a vault, and unless I opened that door, I could swallow down the truth of it without gagging. "And tonight, I finally saw you smiling."

"What? C'mon now. I smile."

"Not like that." She patted my hand. "You keep to yourself. You work late hours in that shop, and I've been worried about how much time you spend there."

"I love my work. It means a lot to me. That's worth something at least."

"It's isolating," she countered.

"I have Marian." I sniffed. "And my customers."

She sighed, likely knowing she wasn't going to win this argument. "Just promise me you'll keep your heart open."

"Of course I will." I cleaned the remnants off my fork. "I told you I went on a date with a guy."

"Uh-huh. And he didn't measure up to this man because you haven't been on another one." She arched a brow. "Does Lane feel the same about you?"

"I...dunno." I shook my head. "Besides, it's not my business to tell."

"All right, I don't want to pry. Just remember your mama is always here if you need an ear or a shoulder."

"I know you are. You've been amazing." I stacked our plates. "When Dad died, we were so young. Did you ever...?"

"I suffered in silence, mostly. So in that way, I understand Delaney." She frowned, and my heart went out to her. "There was no grief group, not one that I knew of, anyway. That sort of thing wasn't discussed as openly as it is now. I'm glad that's changing. That's a good thing. And I'm glad it's helped you."

I stood to go to the sink with our dishes. "Why haven't you remarried?"

"I would if someone special enough came along."

I glanced back at her as I ran the faucet. "How would you even meet them?"

"I have my ways." Her cheeks turned rosy. "You don't know everything about me."

I laughed as I dried my hands, then kissed her head. "I love you, Ma."

When I got home, I felt that restless energy I always did lately. I poured myself a drink and put on some music, but the house still felt too quiet. I looked at our wedding photo and smiled, remembering that night, how much we danced, how we sang at the top of our lungs... I'd like to dance with someone again. Someone who meant something to me.

I lifted my cell and scrolled to Delaney's number.

My family loved you, by the way.

They were great. The food was good too.

I told you about that stuffing.

Don't forget to give me the recipe. Grant will be in heaven.

Will do.

Can I call? Delaney asked.

Please.

"Do you think they suspect?" Delaney asked as soon as I answered the phone.

"How could they not?" I teased. "Do you see the way you look at me? Like you want to date me."

"You ass." He smirked. "I'm being serious."

"So am I," I replied in a pouty voice, and he laughed. "They hinted, but I didn't take the bait."

"Damn, okay." He was quiet for a long moment, and I could tell he was stewing on something. "Some days, I wonder if Grant knows. The way he looks at me sometimes, like he's about to confess something."

"Well, it could be anything. Teenagers keep lots of secrets."

"True," he mused. "I had plenty."

Speaking of teenage years... "Keisha is concerned about me presenting as a gay Black man in my community."

It was obviously more nuanced than that. I was biracial and bisexual, but it was all about people's assumptions. And you know what they said about those. Imagine if they knew I loved rimming and sucking cock. Toxic masculinity was rampant and intertwined with politics and religion. It was one hot mess. We may have come pretty far, but we had a ways to go.

"Holy shit," he replied in a serious tone. "I hadn't thought of that...and I guess that shows my privilege. I'm sorry."

"It's okay. Just glad I can talk about this stuff with you." I took a breath, grateful for the listening ear. "The thing is...sure, it was tough as a kid having a Black mom and a white dad, figuring out where I fit. It was the one big thing that brought Keisha and me closer together. We stuck up for each other all the time."

"Because kids could be cruel?"

"Uh-huh. Adults too," I admitted. "But I actually get it— where the bitterness comes from. Because we have privilege, too, just because our skin is lighter. Racism is ingrained in our society, and I get that now, as an adult, but back then, that shit hurt. Still does."

"Yeah, of course. Nobody can change their physical attributes—for the most part. And I hate when people use that as a weapon to hurt someone."

"Exactly. And now that I'm a mature, responsible adult, I'm not gonna tolerate that bullshit. Even if they take their business elsewhere."

He was quiet a beat, then said, "I like that about you. How you're always unapologetically yourself. You make me want to be brave."

"I already told you—you *are* brave. Everything else will follow when you're ready."

"Yeah, guess you're right."

I wouldn't remind him that some things happened even

when we weren't ready because life was shitty. But it could be beautiful too.

I got settled on the couch, feeling more at peace than I had just a few minutes ago. "Want to find a true-crime episode and watch it together?"

"Sounds perfect."

23

DELANEY

THE SATURDAY MORNING AFTER THANKSGIVING, we were at the assisted-living center, where my father had just finished his breakfast. He was as ornery and dismissive as ever, complaining about the runny eggs and scowling at Grant's WWI-style army jacket and garrison cap, barely engaging him in conversation, no matter how much Grant tried.

"We're gonna get going." I motioned for Grant to head to the door. "We've got lots of chores on our plate, including raking the leaves piling up in the yard."

"See you later, Papa." Grant frowned slightly, waved to him, then stepped into the hallway.

But I turned back to meet my father's eyes. "You could've at least made more of an effort with Grant. I'm used to your sour moods, but he doesn't deserve it. Neither do I, for that matter, but I'm an adult and can deal with it. He's still a kid."

"He looks ridiculous in those outfits. They're a distraction, and you're too soft on him." He sniffed. "You've always been too soft, no matter how much I tried to toughen you up."

"I'll take that as a compliment," I replied, and he scowled. "This has nothing to do with me, and you know it. You're taking out your awful mood on us. I tried talking to you about whatever might be bothering you, but you've never been much for sharing. I have no idea how Mom put up with you." I balled my fists, but he didn't refute me, though I saw the flicker of pain in his eyes, that soft spot he'd always reserved for my mother. She had always defended him, telling me he was just old-fashioned and set in his ways while she overcompensated for him. "Dressing that way makes Grant happy, and he's not hurting anyone. Why squash his joy? He's a good kid."

"You're free to stop visiting if that's how you feel." He waved dismissively. "It's a chore for you anyway."

"When you act like this, it sure feels like it." I clenched my jaw. Way to turn it around and play the victim again. "Grant just wants to know his grandfather, and though you won't admit it, I think you like him visiting. But acting like this will only push him away, like you've done to me my whole life."

When he turned toward the window, refusing to meet my eyes, I strode out of the room, wondering why I even bothered. But no matter how frustrating my father was, I couldn't leave him alone at the most vulnerable time in his life. And Grant might've had the same idea because once I'd given him the option to stay home next visit, he was resolved to come along anyway.

"Mom told me that she visited Papa to support you, most of all, and I didn't really understand what she meant. But now I do," he said in this matter-of-fact tone, not realizing how the sentiment made my heart skip a beat. "So I'll keep coming."

When I reached out to squeeze his knee, he didn't shrug me off. "I'm sorry he's not who you need him to be."

"I'm sorry for you too," he replied, briefly glancing my way.

It was one of Grant's most mature and unselfish moments, and fuck if it didn't make my eyes sting.

As I turned into our neighborhood and noted the fallen leaves, I knew they had piled up long enough. It was a yearly chore I didn't look forward to, but it needed to be done. Now that the kitchen was mostly back in order, outside of some last-minute touch-ups, I couldn't put it off any longer.

I handed Grant a rake, and we started in the backyard, where our large maple had shed its leaves. We had a system going after living here so long, and since Rebecca passed, Grant had stepped in to help, something I greatly appreciated. Marcus had offered as well during our most recent text conversation, and I had a strange inkling he would actually enjoy it. But no way was I going to take him up on his offer. He had his own chores to deal with, and from what I'd gathered, at his mom's place too. She had been so lovely to us at Thanksgiving, and her cooking was damned good. I'd heard Grant raving about it on a call with his friends.

I could tell how close Marcus was with his family, and the concerns he'd mentioned later that night still weighed heavily on my mind. I wasn't brave, not when it came to my sexuality. Maybe I hadn't known what to call it back then, and once I married Rebecca, I was easily able to sweep it under the rug—and obviously pass as straight. But now it just sounded like a cop-out, and I was disappointed in myself that I hadn't done more—to normalize it, or support the community, or...something.

Grant's generation was definitely more accepting and proactive, and whenever he'd casually refer to a gay, nonbinary, or trans kid at school, my stomach would flood with warmth. Had society been more open when I was a kid, I might've felt safe enough to figure myself out a lot sooner. Still, had I come home spouting those sorts of terms, my father would've made me feel small and ridiculous—and sorry for ever opening my mouth.

I gripped the rake, thinking about my visit with my father again. I hated that I still tensed up whenever I was around him. But at least I was stronger now and had learned how to confront him, even if little ever changed.

"I'll grab the tarp from the garage. We'll need to put Ruby inside," I said as Ruby was having herself a good old time running through the pile like a puppy. Grant was no better, egging her on and dumping the leaves over her head as she came barreling toward him. She'd no doubt be tuckered out after this, and once we got her back in the house, she would retire to her pillow for the rest of the day.

We raked the piles of leaves onto the tarp, then opened the gate and lugged them toward the curb, where they'd be collected by the city. If we were lucky, a storm wouldn't blow through with gusts big enough to scatter them back into our yard. Sometimes it was a never-ending battle with the Northeast Ohio weather. "One more load from the front lawn, and then I'll take you driving."

"Can we do it tomorrow instead?" he whined. "Jeremy never gets Saturdays off, and he was gonna come over."

I gave him a stern look for forgetting to tell me. "Now that you've got your temporary license, I need to start teaching you the basics before the winter season moves in and you've got snow to contend with. We'll practice tomorrow too, as much as we can on the weekends."

I spotted the tic in his jaw and wondered if this had more to do with avoiding the driving thing altogether. But I certainly didn't want to deal with a crabby teenager for the remainder of the day. "It won't take us long. Invite Jeremy over for pizza, and then you can hang out for the rest of the night."

"Okay." His expression brightened as he pulled out his phone, no doubt to fire off a text. "In my room?"

"As long as you leave the door open," I replied out of habit, and he rolled his eyes, but I saw that tic in his jaw again. I'd admit I wavered a moment, wondering if the rule Rebecca and I had established long ago should be lifted or maybe adjusted. I knew I was probably doing this all wrong, so relying on some of the structure we'd set up when we became parents always helped me relax a bit if I was feeling overwhelmed. I'd definitely think on it more. But my parents had a similar rule for me when I was a teen, which made it awfully hard to fool around or sneak alcohol or whatever else I got up to with my friends. Grant, however, was way different than I was, or maybe he was just getting a late start, given everything we'd been through the past couple of years.

It took us practically all afternoon, but we got the last of the leaves to the curb just in time for a downpour.

"Looks like we can't go driving," Grant said almost gleefully as we jogged back inside so we didn't get too wet.

"Nice try. We're only gonna practice in a parking lot, and it's good to learn the basics in this kind of weather since you'll be driving through it your entire life." I looked out the window toward the clouds. "Besides, it'll probably die down soon."

"Whatever," he grumbled.

"And then we'll pick Jeremy up on the way home."

He bit his lip, thinking on the idea. Jeremy had his license, but he came from a blended family with lots of kids, so he and his stepsiblings were on a schedule with the two vehicles in their family. He only got access to one a couple of times a week.

"I can drive him home too," I added.

He pulled out his phone and began texting.

"Plans all set?" I asked as his smile returned.

"Yep, let me jump in the shower." He pulled his clammy shirt away from his neck. "Unless you wanna go first?"

"Go for it. I have some bills to pay online."

After we fed Ruby—who was as tuckered out as I'd predicted, barely finishing her bowl of food before lying back down—we got on the road. Grant practiced pulling in and out of an empty parking space while getting used to the brake and gas pedals. I would need a stiff drink when it came time to get on the road with him, but this I could handle.

Once he'd had enough, we traded places, and I drove to

Jeremy's house. I waved to his mom, who was standing at the front door, corralling one of his younger stepsisters as Jeremy slid into the back seat.

"Thanks for the ride," he said, and I smiled in the rearview mirror.

Grant and Jeremy talked gamer language the whole way home, so I was able to tune them out, though it was sweet how much they seemed to connect on that level. Once inside, they retreated to the living room with their laptops instead of his room, sitting side by side on the couch so they could peer at each other's screen and strategize, apparently.

I put in a load of laundry, and once the pizza delivery came, we ate around our new kitchen island. I'd ordered dark-stained wooden stools, and when they were delivered yesterday, Grant agreed they matched pretty well.

"It looks awesome in here," Jeremy said, glancing around the room.

"Right? Marc did a great job," Grant said, then looked at me. "You should've invited him over."

"He had a few projects to finish at the shop." He didn't normally work full-time on the weekends, but the holiday season brought in more customers wanting to give sentimental gifts. "He'll stop by whenever he's free to put the finishing touches on the cabinets and take all his supplies home."

When Grant frowned, I understood the sentiment. Marcus wouldn't have any reason to come over unless we invited him. So we'd have to do more of that. I was dying for his company, to be honest, though our nightly talks helped us stay connected.

"Which reminds me," I said after swallowing the last bite of pizza crust, "how about we visit the city sometime after the New Year? Ticket prices are crazy-high right now because of the holidays."

Grant wiped his mouth with his forearm. "Is that when Marc can make it?"

"He'd have more time, that's for sure."

Grant fist-pumped. "Then let's do it."

"I'm jealous," Jeremy said, pushing his empty plate away from him. They had wolfed down four slices each. "That's gonna be so fun."

"I'm sure I'll text you constantly," Grant said with a shy grin.

"And send photos?" Jeremy asked, and Grant nodded.

I stood with our plates, my cheeks feeling warm, but I wasn't sure why. Maybe because it was strange to be privy to their more intimate conversations, no matter how sweet and how much I'd always wanted Grant to have a companion.

They went back to the couch, and I cleaned up the kitchen, then headed upstairs to change into sweats so I could get on the treadmill. My arms were sore from raking leaves, so why not have my leg muscles join in the fun? Besides, it felt good, like I was working off the last bits of tension from the day.

Once I powered down the machine, I padded to the kitchen for some water.

"Wanna head up to your room?" I heard Jeremy ask, and I stopped in my tracks to listen despite feeling guilty for eavesdropping.

"We'd still have to keep the door open, and my dad would probably walk by just to check." Grant made a frustrated noise. "His rules, remember?"

"Even with guys?" Jeremy's tone was teasing.

"Guess he's covering all the bases. An equal opportunity parent," Grant scoffed.

"That's not a bad thing, but...it doesn't help our situation."

"I'll come to your house next time," Grant said with a groan.

"Good idea. My sisters are good at keeping my parents distracted."

"We'll have to keep track of time, though. I got in trouble for curfew because of you," he said in this teasing tone that made my hair stand on end.

Jeremy laughed. "Yeah, sorry about that."

"My mom would've been cool about it." Grant's voice was strained. "She wouldn't have treated me like a little kid."

My thoughts swirled as I tried to make sense of their conversation. This was why I shouldn't have snooped in the first place. I forced my legs to move toward the stairs as my gut churned. I'd just head up to my room until it was time to drive Jeremy home.

"What if your mom knew what we were up to?" Jeremy asked, and my feet faltered. They were obviously not discussing video games. Something else on the computer?

Rebecca and I always knew that Grant would be exposed to stuff we never were as kids. We used to keep parental controls on his web surfing when he was younger, but Grant was at the age where his curiosity would be piqued about all sorts of things. Other kids were undoubtedly way ahead of him, so it shouldn't have surprised me that Grant was finally doing normal teenage stuff.

"Mom might've lectured me about being responsible, but she was always cool about everything."

"Your dad seems cool too," Jeremy said, and I felt silly being relieved that someone was in my corner.

"He just...worries about everything," Grant said, and my fingers gripped the railing. "He'd be totally stressed out and probably impose even more rules."

They got lost in their gaming talk again, but I stood frozen, thinking about when I was a teen and tried sneaking in alcohol and cigarettes. Should I be concerned and ask Grant straight out? Talk to him about being responsible? Whatever that meant.

I grabbed my laptop and clicked around different parenting sites, trying to figure out the best way to handle this. Rebecca had been the one to give him the sex talk, and she would've known what to do in this situation as well—likely figuring out what situation we were dealing with in the first place. It could've been anything from alcohol to porn. So maybe a lecture about responsibility would cover all the bases.

The conflicting information and advice frustrated me, so I eventually gave up and went downstairs. Still reeling from what I'd overheard, I needed to appear as normal as possible. "It's getting late. I'll drive you home."

Grant sighed, shutting the lid on his computer while Jeremy began gathering his things. "I'll come along for the ride."

Grant decided he wanted to sit in the back seat with Jeremy, so I felt like a chauffeur to a couple of teens. They were chatterboxes, mostly about gaming, but this time I tuned in to their conversation, listening for any clues.

"Thank you for the ride," Jeremy said as I pulled into his driveway.

"No problem."

Jeremy walked inside while Grant opened the back door to slide into the front. "Wait. Jeremy forgot his earbuds. Be right back." He jogged over and was let inside by Jeremy's mother, who waved to me.

When he finally came back out—which felt like a full five minutes—he avoided eye contact with me, and as I pulled out of the driveway, his knee was jiggling a mile a minute as if he was trying to rid himself of nervous energy.

"Everything okay?" I asked when I got back on the road. "You seem..."

"Jesus, Dad. Everything is fine. Why does there always have to be something wrong?"

Apparently, I was already blowing this big-time, so I kept quiet the remainder of the way home. I could force the issue, but where would that lead us?

I'd barely gotten the car in Park when he bolted out the door, and by the time I got inside the house, he was already up in his room with the door closed. I retreated to the couch to click through the channels and get my mind off this strange night.

But I couldn't sit still. Who had nervous energy now?

I texted Marcus: **Talk?**

Definitely.

"You sure it's not too late?" I asked when he picked up.

"No, it's okay." I could hear music in the background, so likely he was chilling out too. "Everything all right?"

"Ugh, I'm sure it's nothing and I'm just being ridiculous."

"I'm all ears, no matter how silly you think it is."

I propped my feet on the coffee table, forcing myself to relax. "It's just that Grant had Jeremy over, and I overheard part of their conversation."

It sounded like he turned down the music. "Tell me about it."

So I did, even though recounting it made me feel like I was being overly dramatic. "And when I tried to ask him on the way home, he got mad and shut me out."

Marcus was quiet for a long moment, making me regret telling him. He was sure to have better things to do than listen to my parenting woes.

"I'm curious about something," he finally said. "Where has Ellie been?"

"I...don't really know. Maybe busy with other things? I think they still message each other, but she hasn't been over in a while."

"So Grant's mostly been hanging out with Jeremy?"

"Yep. And a lot more in the past few weeks." They seemed to constantly be in contact too.

"Sort of like us?" he said in a hesitant voice.

"Huh?" I sat up, trying to make sense of his question. "What are you trying to—holy shit."

"I might be completely off base," he said in a rush, "but when I was a teenager and wanted to be alone with—"

"No need to spell it out." I cringed, finding it as difficult to imagine my own child as it probably was for him to picture me and his mom—or anyone else for that matter.

Though some of it was starting to click. Their shy smiles, sitting close on the couch—*and the back seat*—Grant missing curfew and their conversation about privacy in Grant's room.

"He'd be totally stressed out and probably impose even more rules."

Was that why he took so long dropping off Jeremy's earbuds?

And then I remembered his words from an earlier argument: *"I'm not like you."*

Did he think I'd disapprove, like my own closed-minded father?

"Ah, fuck." My head was reeling.

"You okay?" Marcus asked, bringing me out of my thoughts.

"Yeah, sure. If this is what's been happening with him..."

"Remember, it was only a hunch."

"So what do I do?" I asked earnestly. No way I wanted to blow this too.

"I definitely wouldn't push it. Wait for him to come to you. In the meantime, remain open to the possibility."

"Damn, you're good at this. Thank you."

"It's easier looking in from the outside. I don't envy you. But I'm here to support you whenever you need me."

Fuck if I didn't wish he were here with me, holding me, so we could figure it out together. But he wasn't my partner, or co-parent, no matter how enticing it sounded right then. The best thing to do would be to make Grant feel as safe and comfortable as possible. Especially if he was figuring himself out for the first time. He deserved that.

Once we ended the call, I paced around the living room, trying to wrap my brain around the idea that my child might be more like me than I'd realized.

I headed upstairs to bed, but when I saw his light was still on, I couldn't resist knocking.

"Come in," he said in a grumpy voice. When I pushed open the door, I noticed how he hid his phone.

"The reason I've been so strict with you is because I'm sort of winging it here, and I don't always make the right decisions," I said, leaning against the doorjamb. "I've been overprotective because I've always been terrified of losing you too."

"What? You're not going to—"

"It kills me to think you wouldn't feel comfortable sharing certain things with me. I know you had your mom for that, and you probably wish... I'm sorry she's no longer here." Goddamn it, I was getting too emotional. I cleared my throat. "I just want you to know that I'll always support you and root for you. You're amazingly cool just the way you are."

His face flushed red as he gaped at me. "Dad, I...uh..."

"You're gonna be an adult soon enough, and you'll be facing all kinds of stuff for the first time. So maybe I need to stop treating you like you're still in middle school." I motioned with my hand. "Like with the no-upstairs rule when I'm not home. And maybe you can even have a sleepover, stuff you haven't gotten to experience yet."

"Really?" He arched an eyebrow. "Where is this coming from? Did you—"

"I'm just trying to be a more understanding parent than my dad ever was to me." Having said my fill, I stepped back to close the door. "Good night."

"Wait," he called out, and I froze to listen.

"I just...um...thank you." His eyes softened when they met mine. "Night."

24

MARCUS
DECEMBER

IT WAS THE FOLLOWING SATURDAY, and I was laying down a drop cloth in the kitchen. All that was left were touch-ups on the paint and replacing hardware. They'd selected brushed silver door handles that would complement the other updates well. It'd been a long week, and I'd looked forward to hanging out with Delaney, even if it was under the auspices of more work.

Obviously, today was different, and my stomach had buzzed with anticipation the whole way over. As soon as Delaney had opened the door, in his worn jeans, hair damp from his shower, his smile vibrant, the butterflies in my stomach whirled up a storm. I wanted to pull him into a tight hug just to take in his scent and warmth. But I restrained myself, and it seemed he was too because he'd lifted a trembling hand to touch me before pretending to knock some lint off my shoulder.

Grant had greeted me warmly and told me how excited he was about the trip to New York, which Delaney and I thought might work better closer to spring. Then he'd gone up to his room to prepare for his plans with his grandparents, which involved a visit to the park, followed by a sleepover. Apparently, it'd been a yearly tradition for Donna to snap some photos of

Grant for their holiday card, and they were finally resuming the practice after a hiatus the past couple of years.

We got straight to work, so when Donna's voice rang out from the front door, it startled me. Delaney strode over to greet her, calling up to Grant as he went. "Your grandmother's here."

"Hi there," Donna said as she came through the kitchen. "Wow, this looks awesome."

"I think so too," I said, trying to rid myself of the leftover awkwardness from her Halloween visit, which was likely all on my part. Okay, on Delaney's part too. "The cabinet and wall colors they chose are great, and Grant suggested I stain this island a dark shade."

"It's perfect," she replied, likely a little too enthusiastically because she began coughing, then turned away when the spell went on too long.

"Delaney said you and Howard are both feeling better, but I know how hard it is to shake those symptoms," I said as Delaney moved to the sink to pour her some water.

"It's just a leftover cough," she said, accepting the glass and taking a long sip. "Ah, much better."

"Glad to hear it." I retrieved the screwdriver from my toolbox as Delaney went to the stairs again to check on Grant.

"Thanks for inviting them, by the way," she said when Delaney was out of earshot. "For Thanksgiving."

I dipped my head. "My family was happy to have them."

There was something raw and painful in her expression that I'd recognized in Keisha's, too, whenever I brought up Delaney. I wished I could say something to assuage the ache, but I didn't have the right words. Maybe none of us did for this sort of situation. When life moved on without them, there was nothing any of us could do to stop time.

Grant came down dressed in a black suit, bow tie, and stovepipe hat that resembled Lincoln's ensemble. "Wow, you look amazing."

"Right? This year's photos will be great," Delaney said, which made Grant's expression brighten. "Especially since the weather has held."

"I'll need one framed, Abe." I fist-bumped Grant. "You'll totally rock it."

"Thanks." The blush on his cheeks was endearing.

"You got everything you need?" Delaney asked as he handed him his bag.

"He'll be fine," Donna said. "Don't worry too much."

He offered a tight smile. "Let me know how the shoot went."

"I'll text you," Grant said as he followed his grandmother to the door. "Don't have too much fun without me."

I tried not to stiffen and lifted the paintbrush. "You'll have more fun than me."

"Don't worry, I'll make Marc take a break so I can kick his butt in *Mortal Kombat* for the both of us."

"You wish!" I replied with a laugh that Grant shared. His grandmother looked a bit uncomfortable as she turned away to walk down the steps.

Delaney stayed planted at the door as they pulled out, then waved one last time.

As soon as they were gone, I was pinning Delaney against the wall, stealing his breath with a kiss I'd waited for forever. At least it felt that way. He moaned against my lips, his hands in my hair as we made out for who knew how long. When Ruby whined at the back door, we broke apart, our lips swollen.

"I'll let her out," I said, heading toward the kitchen as he stood there in a daze. "Then I'll get back to work."

"No fair," he said with a chuckle, finally snapping out of it and following me.

Once Ruby was back inside, Delaney fed her, then helped me screw in the hardware, which was tedious work.

"Anything new on the Grant and Jeremy front?" I asked, reaching for another knob.

"Just the usual." He knelt down to start on the bottom cupboards. "Texting or gaming after school. But now I can't help seeing it in a whole new light."

"So you think my observation about them was spot on?"

"Yeah, and I feel like I need to do something, like hug him and tell him it'll be okay so I can be a soft place for him to land." He sighed. "I don't know if he's afraid his grandparents would have a hard time with it. Or even me. And I feel guilty about that."

"He probably knows you'd be cool while also worried for him as a parent," I said, having gotten to know their interactions well by now, as well as Delaney's train of thought. "What parent wouldn't worry about homophobia?"

He winced. "Obviously."

"But coming out is hard for anybody regardless, as we both know. Give him time."

"Maybe if I told him about me..." he said hesitantly. "It might help him feel more comfortable."

"Yeah?" I grew still, making sure I'd heard him right. "Are you considering coming out to him?"

"I am," he replied in a resolute voice. "Just...telling him about when I was younger...for starters."

I squeezed his shoulder. "I'll support you all the way."

"Thanks."

He wasn't saying he was going to tell Grant about us, no doubt still worried about rocking the boat, but it was a start to bridge the gap between father and son.

Once we finished up and loaded my supplies in my truck, we ordered Hunan, with the brown sauce, of course. After it was delivered, we ate it on his new stools in the kitchen.

"Thanks for this opportunity to work on your kitchen. You know how much I envy your house."

"Thank *you*. Maybe someday, once Grant is an adult and

settled in college…" He trailed off, his unspoken words hanging in the air between us.

"I'll own a house just like it?" I teased to move past the awkwardness, not really sure where he was going with his thoughts, which was probably for the best. "Or maybe you'll have another project for me?"

He pushed his plate away as he made a frustrated sound. "I'm sorry I can't promise…at least not yet."

"Shh, don't. It's not necessary. One step at a time." I stacked our plates. "Now let's watch something so I can snuggle with you on the couch."

His cheeks remained flushed as we cleaned up.

Afterward, we retreated to the living room. He fiddled with the remote before getting settled, this time with his arms around me as we faced the television to watch a British murder mystery.

"I have something to ask you," Delaney said against my temple. "And I guess I'm sort of nervous."

I glanced back at him, my stomach dropping. "What is it?"

"I don't get this opportunity often—to have an empty house," he said, his voice tentative. "Will you stay over?"

Fucking hell, this guy. "Are you sure that's a good idea?"

"No, but I know I want it—I want *you*." He kissed my head. "I wanna enjoy your company for longer. All night if I can."

I shivered and turned in his arms to look at him. "I'd like that."

When I sealed my mouth to his, our tongues brushing and winding, the butterflies in my stomach were somersaulting in a flurry of activity. I pressed his shoulders flat on the couch, then sank down on top, my stiff length grinding against his.

His hands grasped my ass, his fingers digging in as he thrust upward, making me groan. It felt so damned perfect to be next to him again, and knowing he wanted me to stay the night…it only made me greedier for him.

Delaney's fingers curled beneath the hem of my shirt, and I leaned back enough to help him lift it over my head, doing the same to him so we were chest to chest, then lips to lips as I fused our mouths back together. I kissed across his jaw, then down to his throat and collarbones, smelling his clean, soapy skin. I brushed my tongue against one nipple, then the other, loving how they instantly swelled as he shivered and moaned.

"Feels so good," he said, angling his mouth to feather his lips against my neck.

"Your smell is driving me crazy." I nibbled at his hip bones, sucked a rosy mark beside his belly button as I fumbled to unbutton his jeans. "I can't get enough of you."

"Marc." His fingers tightened in my hair as he squirmed against me. "Take me to bed."

I sat back on my heels to look at him, at his softened eyes and glossy skin from where my mouth had practically devoured him. Standing, I stretched out my hand to pull him up with me, and hand in hand, we padded upstairs to the bedroom, where I hemmed him against the wall outside the door and kissed him breathless.

Delaney yanked at my button and zipper and helped me push out of my jeans and underwear while he dropped his own to the bedroom floor.

Completely bare, I couldn't help pulling him to me, burying my face in his neck, the hairs on his thighs tickling my own. Delaney sighed against my ear, kissed it, then pulled me toward the bed and urged me to lie down.

He climbed on top, and I stared into his eyes, my hands cupping his face. "What do you want, Lane?"

"I want you to fuck me," he said with so much resolve, I shivered.

He kissed my lips and jaw and ear before licking down my neck to my chest. He sucked a nipple into his mouth, and I cried out, my fingers grasping at his scalp.

"You make me so fucking hard." He lifted his glittering eyes to mine. "I need another taste of you." He feathered kisses all over my stomach and hips and thighs, finally burying his nose in my groin and sniffing deeply. "Your smell drives me wild too."

"Fucking hell," I groaned, completely turned on by his admission.

My stiff cock was making a sticky mess against my stomach, and when he gripped the root, I hissed. I practically came unglued when he lapped at the tip, then engulfed me in the heat of his mouth. I arched my back and gasped as my cock nudged the back of his throat. He gagged a little but got an *A* for effort, using the perfect amount of suction as he brought me right to the fucking edge.

"Wait." My fingers against his skull stilled him. "Don't wanna come yet."

When he drew back, I angled myself enough to flip him to the mattress and show him the same attention. I took his thick length in my mouth, and his hips thrust upward, urging me on. But we'd only gotten started, so I relaxed my jaw, letting go of his shaft, and panted into his skin, trying to rein in my pulse. He made a frustrated noise, his hands cupping my cheeks and urging me back to his cock, which was slick from my saliva. I chuckled, loving when he was self-possessed like this. Letting go and just feeling every sensation.

"Condoms and lube?" I asked, hoping he was prepared because I sure as hell wasn't.

Red dotted his cheeks. "Bedside table."

I rooted around in the drawer, wondering if he'd banked on me agreeing to tonight. There was little chance I'd say no—not for a shot to have him all to myself like this.

I tossed the supplies on the bed and met his eyes. "On your stomach, Lane."

His eyes flared, his cheeks even redder as he twisted toward the sheets and buried his head in his pillow. I shuddered. Seeing him laid out like this for me was surreal.

Was this really happening?

"You're gorgeous." He groaned as I kneaded his ass, relishing the downy fuzz on his cheeks that was reminiscent of the hair on his chest.

When my thumbs parted his crease, he trembled, swearing under his breath.

"There's that pretty hole you teased me with the other night," I groaned.

"Goddamn, Marc," he moaned, his hands balling into fists as if he was trying to control his urges. "I've never...never had anyone..."

"I'm gonna make you feel good, baby," I said with a little growl, my balls already tight and aching. I spread him wide, took in that puckered hole covered by fuzz. I couldn't wait to soften it with my tongue. "Trust me?"

He trembled all over as he nodded. Leaning forward, I teased the rim with my tongue, and his hips thrust against the mattress, seeking friction. "Ah, fuck."

I took my time making him feel good, licking around the rim, then pressing in with light jabs of my tongue. I loved drawing those pleading sounds from him and feeling his muscles contract as I fitted my tongue farther inside.

Allowing him a bit of a reprieve, I reached for the bottle of lube and messily doused my fingers. I leaned forward to kiss down the knobs of his spine, then nibbled the meaty part of one cheek. "I'm gonna stick a finger inside you. I think it'll be easier if you get on your knees for me."

He did as instructed, lifting to all fours and jutting his ass out, which made me lose my breath. "Fuck, just look at you. I want to eat you whole."

"You're practically already there," he teased, and when he

looked back at me, his eyes were soft and playful, making my chest ache something fierce.

"Mmm." I squeezed a cheek. "Someone likes my tongue."

"Maybe a bit too much," he confessed.

"Then let me eat you out a little more." Without waiting for a response, I went at him, licking, kissing, and spearing him with my tongue until he was a begging, sobbing mess.

When I drilled my finger inside his hole, he gasped, his head dropping forward. Gooseflesh lined his spine as I added a second digit and sawed in and out of his ass. His knees nearly gave out when I found his prostate, so I firmly held on to his hip. "I've got you."

My own cock was aching, so I released my grip on him to give it a good stroke. I moaned as I watched my knuckles disappearing inside his hole, making sure he was nice and ready for me. Then I slid the condom toward me and tore it open with shaky fingers before lubing my cock and pouring the silky wetness on his rim, which only made him squirm more.

"*Lane.*" I wound my arm around his chest, lifting him to me, my lips against his ear as I lined up my cock to his hole. "Tell me again how you always wished it was me."

"Every time I touched myself, I pretended it was you." He shivered and angled his cheek against mine. "Only you."

It hit me square in the chest how much I adored this man. How much I wanted him all to myself. But I only had tonight.

"Fuck, Lane." My hand cradled his skull as I tilted it just far enough to smash our lips together in a sloppy, needy kiss. "I need inside you."

"*Please,*" he pleaded against my mouth. "Need it too."

His mouth opened on a silent gasp as I pressed forward, just the head of my cock stretching his hole, giving him time to adjust to the girth. I clenched my teeth, trying to hold myself back because it already felt amazing. "Does it hurt, baby?"

He shook his head. "It feels different this time. Better."

I reached around his waist for his cock, gripping it firmly and stroking upward since it'd waned a bit, likely from the sting of our initial contact.

"I wish this was us all the time," I whispered against his ear as I rocked my hips, my cock stabbing shallowly inside him. "You can't fault me for that. This is too fucking good."

He moaned and swayed, completely lost to the sensation, but his hand reached down to where mine was anchoring his hip, and he tangled our fingers together.

Maybe I shouldn't have uttered those words, but I had no regrets. I'd thought about him and this very scenario too many nights to count, visualizing the sort of intimacy we'd talked about in group. Having a second chance at happiness.

I pulled out a bit, then worked my way back inside him with slow, steady thrusts of my cock. He was tight and warm, the connection between us only heightened like this. Before I knew it, the rhythm grew faster, my shaft driving deeper as he moaned.

My hand left his cock to trail up to his throat. I kissed his head as my fingers found his pulse. He trembled, vibrant and alive, our heartbeats nearly synchronized, galloping in our chests.

Delaney began rocking backward, pleading with me to go harder. Every time my dick brushed that spot inside him, he clenched and shuddered, spurring me on.

My breaths ragged, I was barely hanging on yet hoping to prolong this bubble of perfection. I licked at the line of sweat at his nape right before he fell forward onto his elbows and thrust backward, impaling himself on my cock. "I need you, Marc."

I watched as my shaft split him in two, disappearing between his downy cheeks. My fingers tightened on his hip, my orgasm building like a lit fuse, the intensity nearly blinding. His hand was working his cock, and his skin flushed a rosy pink as he bowed his back and shuddered, coming apart at the seams.

His hole squeezed my shaft like a tight sleeve as my vision blurred and the spark ignited into a raging wildfire inside me. I spilled my load into the condom as I groaned and shook, eventually collapsing to the mattress beside him. My limbs were rubber, sweat pooled at my temples, and my pulse thundered in my ears.

Delaney reached for me, sliding his lips and tongue against mine in a breathy, fervent kiss. Our arms and legs were entangled, sticky sheets beneath, as we slowly came back to ourselves.

"Thank you," he said. "For giving me tonight."

I drew him against me, unwilling to let him go, not yet. Maybe not ever.

25

DELANEY

I STIRRED when I heard Ruby jumping down from the bed and knew it was just after dawn. Normally I'd start rousing at this hour, but this morning I felt heat surrounding me on all sides. Waking up with Marcus was too perfect, and I didn't want it to end. Not when I felt his soft breaths against my neck, his warm limbs...everything only made sweeter by his scent.

Last night had been mind-blowing. I could still feel the aftereffects if I shifted a certain way. Not that I minded. In fact, it felt like I couldn't get enough. *Would I ever get enough?*

It was the weekend, Grant was at his grandparents', and I felt at peace for the first time in years. I wasn't sure when I might have my heart-to-heart with Grant about my sexuality or how it might go, but for now, I was going to enjoy myself and push all the doubt and worry aside.

Apparently, I'd squirmed enough to rouse Marcus too because suddenly I was on my back, looking up at sleepy eyes and enticing scruff that felt coarse against my fingers. His stiff cock rested against my thigh, and just thinking about what he'd done to me last night made me flush hot all over again.

"Mornin'." His voice was raspy, affection and concern in his expression. "You sore?"

"Even if I were, I wouldn't care." I lifted up and nipped his jaw. "I'd want you to stuff your cock back inside me."

The longing in his gaze was so achingly powerful. Those fractures inside my heart felt mollified once again, soothed by the warm, penetrating light he exuded almost effortlessly.

Incandescent.

"Don't tease," he said with a growl. "I love being inside you. Being connected to you like this."

"I'm not teasing. I want you again. *Please*," I begged, and when he leaned forward to fit his mouth against mine, I was in heaven. Our cocks were slotted together, and as he rutted gently against me, I groaned, my fingernails digging into the small of his back.

He sat up. "Don't move." I heard him tearing open a condom, and then he was back, looking down at me with softened eyes.

I lifted my knees to my chest in invitation, and without missing a beat, he lined up his cock and pushed inside, stealing my breath in the process. There was an initial sting and then pure fucking bliss.

We groaned in unison, and from my vantage point, I could see the flaming desire in his irises and the quiet desperation in his expression as he thrust solidly into me. "It feels too good this way."

"*So* good." His hands gripped the backs of my knees as he drove in hard and fast, hot lava scorching through my veins. My cock was leaking between us, so I encircled it with my fist and began jerking myself. The combination of his shaft and my hand made for a potent cocktail, and before I knew what hit me, I was calling out his name and erupting all over my abdomen.

Marcus wasn't far behind. His hips faltered, his motions

erratic, and his face contorted in pleasure. He groaned deeply as he came, falling forward, and rained breathy kisses all over my face.

Settling in each other's arms, I sighed, enjoying our quiet embrace as we caught our runaway breaths. "Suppose we better clean up."

As he disposed of the condom, I reached for the washcloth from last night to wipe us down. Sore but satiated, I dabbed at the dried come on my abdomen.

"I should probably leave soon," Marcus said as he pulled me to him for a kiss. "When will Grant be home?"

"Not until noon. You should stay." My knuckles brushed against his scruff. "At least for coffee? You can shower too."

He sank against the sheets with a sleepy smile. "Sounds good."

"Awesome. Be right back." I sat up. "Need to feed Ruby and let her out."

"Only if you promise to warm me up again," he said in a groggy voice, and I kissed his head, smiling to myself.

I slipped into sweats and a T-shirt and headed toward the hallway. "C'mon, girl."

Ruby ate while I started the coffee machine, and then I let her out to do her business in the backyard. She liked to take her time and sniff in her favorite spots along the fence in the morning, so I headed back upstairs, telling myself I'd check on her in five minutes.

Marcus had rolled onto his stomach, which was quite a nice view. I slid under the covers, brushed my fingertips down the knobs of his spine. "This okay?"

"Hell yes."

I squeezed his smooth cheeks, my hand trailing over the fuzz on his thighs, giving myself permission to explore a little. "I'll admit, it's nice having you in my bed."

"Told ya you wanna date me," Marcus said into his pillow. "I'm irresistible."

"And so modest," I said with a laugh against his nape.

That was when I heard the screeching of tires outside the window.

"What the hell was that?" Marcus asked as his head sprang up.

"No idea." My heart throbbed as a terrible feeling washed over me. I pushed off the bed and strode to the window.

A woman was in the street, crouching over something, her car door wide open. When I angled my head, I saw a dog lying on its side. *Ruby.* I couldn't believe my eyes. "Holy fuck."

"What's wrong?" Marcus asked in an alarmed voice.

"Ruby got out and was hit by a car!" I bolted from the room, ran downstairs, and out the front door, my gut churning wildly.

"What happened?" I asked as I made it to the woman holding her phone and hovering over my dog. I could hear Ruby whimpering, so I immediately squatted to check on her. I saw no signs of blood or injury, but she was obviously in pain. "Oh God, Ruby, honey."

"This is your dog?" The woman's voice was panicked. "I'm so sorry. She just came out of nowhere. I slammed on my brakes, but my reflexes weren't fast enough."

"It's gonna be okay," Marcus said from behind me.

But was it? How could he be so sure when Ruby was lying in the street, unable to move?

"I can drive her to the vet," the woman said.

"It's closed on the weekends." I stroked Ruby's muzzle, trying to soothe her. "But there's a twenty-four-hour emergency center in University Heights."

"We can load her in the back seat of my car," Marcus said, and fuck, right then, I was so grateful for his calm demeanor. "We'll need to be careful about moving her."

"How can I help?" the woman asked. "I'll pay the vet bill. I feel terrible."

I stood up, my gaze traveling up the driveway to the back-yard. "Damn it. Looks like the latch wasn't properly closed on the gate. The wind probably blew it open."

Marcus squeezed my shoulder, but I barely felt it, I was so numb. "How about we get your number, and we'll let you know what the vet says about her condition?"

"Are you sure?" she rummaged through her purse for a business card and handed it to Marcus. "I could—"

"It's okay," I said, finally meeting her eyes, and I saw the panic there. "We'll be in touch. I promise."

I tried soothing Ruby as I waited for Marcus to back his truck into the street, hoping like hell she was going to survive. Her breaths were reedy, her pupils dilated. It was as if she didn't even recognize me. *Fuck.*

We lifted her very carefully and placed her on a blanket in the back seat. I stayed beside her as Marcus drove us to the emergency vet.

"It could've happened to any of us," he said in the rearview mirror. "It was a freak accident."

"No. Had I been more careful and not so fucking"—I waved my hand—"distracted by the idea of getting back upstairs to you, I would've kept a better eye on her and noticed the gate wasn't latched."

"Goddamn it, Lane. I already know where you're going with this. There is nothing wrong with you taking time for yourself and your own happiness." His knuckles were white from grip-ping the steering wheel. "Not everything is black and white. Sometimes life—"

"Is fucking cruel." I buried my fingers in Ruby's fur, willing her to hang on. "But we already know that."

He fell silent the rest of the way as I carefully watched

Ruby's chest moving up and down with effort. *Damn it, Ruby. Be strong, girl.*

Once we pulled up, it was a whirlwind of activity. Two staff members brought out a stretcher to get Ruby inside. They led us to an empty exam room, where we told the vet what had transpired.

She examined Ruby from head to toe, drawing a cry from her when she touched her right back leg. "It looks like she might have a fracture."

"I'm so sorry, Ruby," I said in a pained voice. Fucking hell.

"How old is she?" the vet asked as her assistant typed the information into the computer.

I frowned. "She'll be twelve in a couple of months."

She nodded, patting her muzzle comfortingly. "We'll need to x-ray her leg and then do an ultrasound and some blood work to alert us to any internal bleeding," she said, and I held in a gasp. "The good news is that everything we do is in-house, and we'll have results back as soon as possible."

I breathed out. "Thank you."

"Depending on the results, we'll have decisions to make based on Ruby's age and risk level. Especially if it involves surgery. But first things first." She motioned to the door. "For now, we'll ask for your patience."

I kissed Ruby on the head, then followed Marcus to the waiting room, which was more crowded now than when we'd first arrived. One man was anxiously pacing, obviously concerned about what was happening with his furry family member behind closed doors.

We sank down in two empty seats near a gigantic tank with colorful fish.

I pulled out my cell and called my mother-in-law to tell her the news, my stomach unsettled, and I supposed it was good we hadn't had anything to eat or drink because it might've come right up.

"She said Grant was finishing breakfast, and then they'll be on their way over," I told Marcus. "Thank you for being here."

"Of course," he said absently as he watched the fish swimming around the tank. It felt awkward between us all over again, likely my fault because of what I'd admitted on the car ride over.

I pulled out my cell to check messages and found one from work regarding my schedule on Monday, which had been pushed back due to the contractor's timetable on a new build in Willoughby.

I didn't know what I was going to do if this situation with Ruby took a turn for the worse.

Fuck. I stood up, needing some fresh air. I pushed through the door and stepped into the hallway, closer to the clinic's entrance. I paced in circles, feeling nervous about Ruby. And Grant.

"Lane?" Marcus asked tentatively. "You okay?"

"I just...don't know how to do this if she doesn't survive. Grant will be heartbroken, and I don't know if I'm strong enough to pick up the pieces for him." My fingers forked through my hair, then gripped the strands in frustration. "I don't want to cause him any more pain. He's been through so much."

"I know." He stepped closer.

"I thought we had time with Ruby." I screwed my eyes shut. "She was getting up there but still in good health. And now this. *Fuck.*"

"Hey, come here." When he pulled me into an embrace, I welcomed it. It felt safe in his arms. "I know this won't really register, but believe it or not, you've gotten through a hundred percent of your most awful days, and you're still standing. You'll make it through this too, no matter what happens."

"Goddamn it," I said into his shoulder. "That's true, but

you're right about it not registering yet. All I can do right now is worry about everything."

"It was worth a shot," he said, tightening his hold.

The idea of Ruby suffering was like a hot brand searing my chest. And then there was the matter of Grant.

The door to the clinic opened and shut behind me, but it wasn't until I heard my mother-in-law's voice that I stiffened. "Lane, what—is everything okay?"

Her voice was pitched, and I couldn't imagine what it looked like to her—me being in a guy's arms, in Marcus's arms, in the middle of an entryway. Shit.

When Marcus stepped back, I turned to meet her eyes, which were wide and confused. Grant looked much the same, except more panicked and forlorn. "Dad?"

"We're still waiting on test results to see if there's any internal bleeding," I explained, not wanting to mince words. Not for something this serious. "It also looks like Ruby has a fractured leg, but we'll find out soon enough."

"Poor girl," Donna said, looking between Marcus and me. "I thought maybe something had—"

"I was just...feeling emotional." I winced. Christ, what must they think?

"It looks like you're in good hands, so I'm gonna head home and leave you to it," Marcus said, and my stomach dropped. "Call me if you need anything. Anything at all."

When he patted Grant's shoulder, I realized Marcus was still wearing the same clothes from last night, and they looked a bit worse for wear. Goddamn it.

I opened my mouth to tell him to stay, but he was already stepping through the door and muttering his goodbyes. I considered going out to his car, but that would seem even more strange. Fuck, I hated this.

Turning from the entryway, I followed them into the waiting room, where we sat down with Grant between us.

"It was nice of Marc to show up. He's a good friend," Grant said, and I swallowed, looking away from his grandmother's searching gaze. "Tell me what happened."

"I let her out in the backyard and started the coffee." *Then I went upstairs to be with the guy I'd invited to sleep over.* My mother-in-law must've realized that. How could she not?

Why did the timing always feel off?

"That was when I heard the screeching of tires, and when I looked out the window, I saw Ruby had been hit by a car. The wind must've blown open the gate. I guess the latch wasn't closed." My shoulders slumped. "I should've been more aware."

Grant covered his mouth with his hand as he gasped. I wondered if this was the moment where he'd blame me and tell me he hated me—but I'd already beat him to it. If Ruby's injuries were severe, he'd probably hold it against me for a long time, and I wouldn't even fault him.

When fat tears began rolling down Grant's cheeks, his grandmother put her arm around him. I patted his knee, feeling even more awful and helpless.

"What if we lose her?" he said, laying his head against her shoulder.

"We can't think that way," she replied. "We need to have hope."

"Dad?" he asked, glancing my way.

"Positive thoughts, Grant," I said, even though I was having trouble with the concept myself.

It was awkward, waiting with my mother-in-law, not knowing what she was thinking about the situation with Marcus. I could feel her watching me, and I knew she must have so many questions...

I stood up, went to study the fish, then some of the photography on their walls.

Soon enough, we were called to a back room to meet with the vet. Grant seemed just as jittery as me. Like father, like son.

"I've got some good news," she said, but I held my breath regardless. "It doesn't look like there's any internal bleeding."

"Oh, thank God." I sagged against the wall.

"But the x-ray did show a hairline fracture on her back leg."

"So she'll need to be in a cast?" I asked, trying to think through the logistics.

"Actually, we don't use casts so much anymore," she explained. "Nowadays, we use metal plates and screws to stabilize the bone. It's more effective in helping them heal properly."

"Ouch." Grant cringed. "Will it hurt?"

"Not more than it already does. Though we did administer a painkiller, so she's feeling much better." She smiled. "Animals are more resilient than we think. They even start using their limb pretty quickly after a break, especially when we use this method."

I breathed out. "That's good news."

"Can I see her?" Grant asked, looking relieved.

"Not until we've set the bone. We'll call you back again in a little while. When she's ready to go home."

We retreated to the waiting room, and Grant pulled out his phone, no doubt to text his friends. Though I was bummed about Ruby's leg and how painful it must've been for her, it could've been so much worse.

"The woman who hit Ruby," I said to my mother-in-law, "she was so upset."

She frowned. "I'll bet. I've had close calls with squirrels and birds. I can't imagine a dog."

I nodded. "I told her I'd let her know how Ruby fared."

I lifted my cell to dial Marcus, knowing he had her information and that I had an audience. Walking over to the fish tank, I watched them swim around as the call went through.

"Hey there," I said when he answered.

"Is she okay?"

"A broken leg, but no internal injuries."

"Thank fuck," he said, and I felt relief wash over me again.

I glanced over my shoulder to my mother-in-law, who was pretending she wasn't listening. "So, uh, while we're waiting for her to be fixed up and released, I wondered if I could have the phone number for the lady who hit Ruby."

"Sure thing. I'll text it to you."

I paused, trying to think of something else to say, but now wasn't the time. "Thanks, Marc."

The woman seemed very relieved, and once we'd hung up, I told Grant and my mother-in-law about the call. "She insisted on getting our address so she could refund some of the cost."

It was afternoon by the time we finally got to see Ruby. She came out wearing a cone so she wouldn't fiddle with her leg, and we were given instructions about how to care for her over the next few days. Grant sat in the back seat with her the whole way home, and my mother-in-law briefly came inside with us to make sure we were all set.

"Thanks for waiting with us. I know Grant appreciated it, and so did I."

"Of course." She opened her mouth to say something but then changed her mind.

When she left, my stomach loosened its fist a bit more. I set Ruby up on her pillow and went to my room to change. The evidence of what happened the night before and this morning was visible from the hallway, so I shut the door behind me. I straightened up then changed the sheets, something I didn't have time to do earlier.

Fucking hell.

After everything was back in order, I sat on my bed and texted Marcus.

We're finally home. I'm cleaning up our evidence, if you know what I mean.

Oh, shit. We did leave in a hurry.

I'd laugh if it wasn't so heartrending.

Good God, did that really happen?

Unfortunately, yes. Glad she's going to be okay.

Me too. Thank you again for being there.

No problem.

I stood up and looked out the window, the driver's skid marks still visible in the street.

I'm going to fix the latch on the gate.

Good idea. Promise me you won't be too hard on yourself.

I'll try my best.

But I still felt unsettled, like there was a barrier between us now, and it was likely my fault. Because I didn't know how to deal with any of this. I headed outside to examine the latch, which was slack and missing screws—an easy fix. I cursed myself again for not noticing sooner.

We spent the evening pampering Ruby and giving her plenty of attention. I made a simple pasta dinner, and we ate it in the living room near Ruby's pillow, which was Grant's idea.

"Dad?" Grant said in a wobbly voice. "I have something to tell you."

I placed down my fork on the coffee table, suddenly nervous. "What is it?"

"I think I caused Ruby's accident." He looked down and shifted uncomfortably. "I noticed the latch was loose on Friday after school when I walked my bike to the garage. I meant to tell you when I got inside, but I..." He frowned. "I got distracted by a text."

My pulse was going crazy as I looked him over. My first reaction was some sort of lecture about responsibility, one I'd already given myself, but seeing his worried eyes, all the fight drained out of me. Why pour salt into the wounds?

"Oh, kiddo." I put my hand on his arm and squeezed. "It's okay. I'm not mad."

"How can you say that? It was my fault."

"I was blaming myself too for not noticing the latch was loose." I placed my thumb under his chin to get him to look at me. "Do you think it's my fault?"

He looked at me, eyes wide. "No."

"Walking around with that kind of guilt will make us miserable. We'll need to learn to forgive ourselves for this one."

"But what if it was much worse? What if she...oh *God*." He placed his face in his hands.

"There are so many *what-ifs* in life, aren't there?" I sighed and rubbed his hair. "But we're only human and doing the best we can. You didn't forget on purpose, and neither did I."

Now if only I could buy into the sentiment. I'd been so hyperfocused on making sure Grant was doing okay that I was putting too much pressure on myself.

And it was exhausting.

"If we beat ourselves up over too many things, we'll miss out on how special life can be. And then we'll kick ourselves about that too." I leaned over to rub Ruby's coat. "Life is filled with little lessons to make us more aware, compassionate too, and maybe this is one of them. Ruby will hopefully be around for a couple more years, and we need to give her all the extra cuddles we can so she knows how much she means to us."

He gave me a watery smile as he petted her fur. "She definitely deserves it."

26

MARCUS

"We brought you some lunch," Keisha said as she and my mother came through the door of Worthy's, holding a bag. "You've been working too hard."

It was Saturday afternoon, and they'd been Christmas shopping all morning. It was nice of them to think of me, somehow knowing I hadn't taken the time to eat yet. Besides, all I'd brought with me was a soggy PB&J.

I accepted the bag. "Awesome. Thanks." It contained a Five Guys burger and fries, which only made me think of Delaney and Grant. Again. "You know it's busy this time of year."

We sat in the chairs at the front of the store while I eagerly ate my lunch, not having realized how famished I was, and they told me about their morning, which involved fighting the crowd at the mall.

"Remember, you promised not to go overboard on gifts," I warned them. We'd be celebrating Christmas at my aunt's house this year, and it would be nice to relax with my family, much like I imagined Delaney and Grant would be doing with his grandparents. Aaron had texted that he would be in town, and I looked forward to reconnecting with him, as well as with Carmen's parents on one of the afternoons.

It'd been a week since I last saw Delaney, and it was hard not to relive what happened between us that night—and the morning after. It was one of my most favorite memories with him, and not only because the sex had been emotional and intense and fucking hot, but because it felt like we were actually on the same page, and I loved that he was reveling in our intimacy too.

But I supposed I always knew things might come crashing down around us.

Delaney no doubt still felt guilty that he'd rushed back to me without checking the gate. And from our text conversations this week, Grant had his own stuff to work through. Then there was Grant's grandmother, who'd walked in during our tender embrace and seemed stunned that we were showing each other that level of affection.

Prior to Ruby's accident, Delaney had been ready to come out to Grant, and who knew what the result might've been. It seemed obvious now that the idea had been placed on the back burner. Or possibly scratched altogether. But that was life.

Ruby was recovering well, thank God, and they needed time to just chill together. I would never stop being their friend, but maybe this was a good time to take a step back and regroup—and being swamped with holiday orders would provide a much-needed distraction.

And yet, I couldn't pretend my stomach hadn't been unsteady all week. As strange as it sounded, I'd expected a corny joke to come by way of text from Delaney. At least that would've made me feel like everything was going to be all right. Instead, our conversations were a bit clipped and awkward, as if we were fumbling around each other all over again.

"Don't work too hard," Keisha said as she and Mom stood to leave.

"I could say the same for shopping," I teased, knowing they were off to another shopping plaza in the Beachwood area.

"Come for dinner tonight?" Mom asked, then threw me a knowing look. "Unless you have plans?"

"No plans." I sighed. "I told you, my work on Delaney's kitchen is done."

She arched a brow. "That doesn't mean you weren't invited otherwise."

I shrugged, my stomach tightening. "I'm too busy anyway."

I walked them to the door, promising I'd be over later for some of her chili and cornbread. The wind kicked up the leaves near the door, and I thought about how the fall weather had held. There would be snow on the ground soon, but it was the three months after the New Year that were usually the most miserable.

Then I got lost in reupholstering two wingback chairs for a returning customer who'd appreciated how I'd refinished her dining table last summer. When I found horsehair in the padding, I let her know how that was a common practice in the nineteenth century, which made her even more excited that she'd found the pair in her grandfather's attic.

The bell above the door chimed, alerting me to a customer, so I wiped my hands on a rag and went to greet whoever arrived to pick up their treasured piece. Today it was a couple of ring boxes and old picture frames, which would make thoughtful holiday gifts.

My feet faltered when I saw Delaney and Grant standing near the front desk.

"Marc! Guess what?" Grant exclaimed, stepping toward me. He was wearing his militia coat with shiny silver buttons and a tricorn hat. "I drove part of the way here."

"You did?" I glanced at Delaney, who looked so handsome with his fleece jacket and his hair tucked beneath a beanie that he made my knees weak.

"Yeah, he did. We ran a couple of errands, and then Grant wanted to know if we could visit your shop." His smile faltered. "Hope that's okay."

"Of course it is." I hated this uncomfortable space between us. But I also couldn't deny that I felt instantly lighter in their presence. The truth was, I'd fallen for them both and wanted them in my life, even if Delaney and I could only be friends. I would do the work to make that happen, even if my heart took a direct hit. "How's Ruby?"

"She's doing great and already getting around on her own," Delaney said as Grant checked out an antique world map I'd framed for a customer. "She's also enjoying the extra cuddles and attention."

I grinned. "I'll bet."

"You've, um...got something on your shoulder."

When Delaney lifted his hand to brush it off my shirt, my heart skipped a beat. "It's just batting from the chairs I'm working on."

Our gazes clashed, held for a long moment, and I wanted to close the distance between us and kiss him senseless. It was a feeling I'd have to push aside if this friendship thing was going to work. I couldn't pretend any longer that it might turn into something more.

"Oh, I also wanted to bring you the coils for that standing radio." He dug into his coat pocket and produced a small bag. "Remember I said I could fix it...I mean, if you still want me to?"

"I do," I replied, and his eyes softened as if in relief. He must've been feeling as unsure of us as I was. "Perfect timing too because the customer will be back in town after the holidays. Follow me."

I led them to the back room, where Grant stopped every few paces to check something new out.

"Here's the radio," I said, tapping the top of the curved

wood, which had dried long ago from the cherry stain the customer requested. "Go for it."

"Wow, it looks great," he said, and I couldn't help smiling. The compliment felt good coming from anyone, but from him, it was extra special.

As he stepped behind the radio, I asked Grant if he wanted to see the horsehair I'd found in the chairs I was reupholstering.

"That is so cool," he said, kneeling down to feel the texture. "Is there anything I can help with?"

"Sure."

I put him to work ripping the rest of the old stuffing from one of the chairs. He seemed to enjoy it, asking all sorts of questions while we worked side by side.

We got lost in the work until the bell above the door rang at the front of the store.

"Be right back." I headed toward the customer to hand them the picture frame I'd restored.

After I rang them up at the cash register, I returned to the back room, where Grant and Delaney were fiddling with the dials on the radio and had gotten it to work. "No way!"

Delaney was beaming. "Told you I could do it."

"I had no doubt." I pressed my shoulder to his, and just that brief contact sent my stomach into a free fall. God, I had it bad. "The customer is going to love it."

They only stayed a while longer before Delaney was reminding Grant that they needed to get back to Ruby.

"Thanks so much for the visit," I said at the door, feeling sort of emotional that they'd shown up at all. "Actually, hold on a minute. Be right back."

I headed toward a table under the far window to retrieve something I'd been thinking about for weeks. Maybe today was as good a day as any. Especially since things felt so upside down, I didn't even know when I'd see them next.

"I have something for you, Grant," I said, holding the box in my hand. "Call it an early Christmas gift."

"Why early?" Grant asked in a strained voice, eyeing me suspiciously.

"Why not?" I handed him the present. "A gift is fun any time of the year."

I could feel Delaney's gaze pressing in on me, but I kept my focus on Grant, not wanting to betray how broken up I was feeling right then.

"What is it?" Delaney asked as Grant lifted the cover.

"No way!" Grant said, lifting the spyglass out of the box, and I heard Delaney's gasp. "Dad, look."

Delaney's eyes were wide, and he looked stunned. "That was really awesome of you."

I shrugged. "I came across another one from the same era, and I knew the perfect person who had to have it."

"Thanks so much," Grant said, studying it closely before carefully placing it back in the box. "I know exactly where I'm gonna put it in my room."

When I walked them to the door, my feet felt heavy, and I wished they could stay for longer, even though I had plenty of work to get back to.

"See you at group?" Delaney asked in a hopeful tone.

"Yep, unless I get busy." I didn't tell him I would try my best because it might end up being one of my only links to him.

"Okay." He frowned. "Well, thanks again. For everything."

It felt like a goodbye or the closing of a chapter, and I had trouble breathing. "Yeah, of course. You too."

He held my gaze for one more second, then followed Grant to the car.

Just as I was heading to the back room, the door flew open, and in walked Grant, a little out of breath.

"Everything okay?"

"Since we're giving early gifts," he said, handing me a large envelope, "my dad said it was okay."

My pulse was battering in my ears as I opened the envelope and pulled out one of the photos from his day in the park. He was leaning against a tree with a radiant smile.

"You came through for me, Abe." I felt stinging behind my eyes. "I love it. Thank you."

And then Grant was throwing his arms around me and pulling me in, which really got me choked up. "Thanks again for my spyglass. Will you be hanging out with us anytime soon?"

"Sure I will," I said around the boulder in my throat. "Especially when things die down around here."

"Okay, good." He pulled away, then looked over his shoulder to where their car was parked. "Because Dad's been sort of mopey the last few days."

My chest ached. "Maybe it's because of Ruby's accident."

"I think it's more than that." He bit his lip as if measuring his words. "Your friendship means a lot to him."

When Grant's eyes met mine, it was as if he saw right through me.

"It means a lot to me too. Just like your friends mean to you?" I asked.

"Yeah, like that." He flushed bright pink and looked away. "Well, see you."

I stayed at the door as they pulled away from the curb, feeling overly sentimental. Or maybe like I was grieving all over again, but this time something different.

27

DELANEY

WHEN MY CELL rang Sunday morning, I was surprised to see it was a call from Tristan.

"I heard through the family grapevine about Ruby," Tristan said. "Is she okay?"

"Yeah, for the most part." Grant had wanted Ruby with him most nights, and they were still asleep last time I checked on them. "Thanks for asking."

"We've had dogs come in for grooming who are recovering from similar injuries, and they seem to bounce back pretty quickly."

"That's good to know." I placed a cup under the coffee machine and pushed the button.

"Fair warning...I also heard all about your friend, Marcus," he said cautiously. "That he spends lots of time with you and Grant and helped remodel your kitchen?"

"Yep." I winced. "Gotta love that gossip."

"Right?" He snickered. "Hope Marc is doing well."

I took a moment to compose my thoughts. Tristan was someone I could talk to about this stuff. Why hadn't I thought of that before?

"Did it take a while...for Chris's family to get used to West being in your life?"

"Yeah, of course." He sighed. "Ultimately, they realized I would never stop loving Chris, even though I'd made room in my heart for someone else. Someone I love very much and want to spend my life with. Someone I don't ever want to be without."

Fuck. His words resonated in a way that hit me square in the gut.

"Did that make you feel guilty—that you could love someone other than Chris?"

"Maybe at first, but I never subscribed to the idea of a person only having one soulmate or whatever. I think people connect on different levels, and when it turns into something as profound as love...it's rare and precious and should be treasured," he said, and I rubbed at the ache in my chest his words produced. "Because in the grand scheme of things, life is pretty fucking short."

"I really like that," I said as I doctored my coffee with sugar. "Thanks."

"Is there something I'm missing here?"

"The truth is...I've been with guys back in the day, not that I really understood what being bisexual meant." It felt good to get that off my chest. Actually, it felt great, like taking a load off. "But after I met Rebecca and knew I wanted to spend my life with her, I ignored that other side of myself."

"I've heard similar stories too many times to count," he said, and I marveled at that. "Does this mean there are feelings involved...for a certain someone?"

"I didn't think I was ready to date anyone, honestly, but sometimes stuff sneaks up on you," I said with a laugh. "Besides, Grant has been through so much, and I didn't want to bring him any more stress or heartache. So...I'm still figuring shit out."

"You've been through a lot too, so be gentle with yourself. You'll know when you're ready."

After the call ended, I just stood there staring into space, thinking about everything that had happened with Marcus and how happy he made me—us, really. Grant had been so emotional after our visit to Worthy's, and truth be told, so had I. It felt like his gift was a send-off of sorts, and I could understand why. He'd gotten mixed messages from me all along, and who would want to deal with that bullshit? I might've thought our intimate moments could remain separate from our friendship, but who was I kidding? It was all profoundly entangled.

Once Grant woke up, I made us breakfast, then tidied up the house. My in-laws were coming over for dinner, which was the least I could do after their help with Ruby. She'd stayed with them during the day all week while I was at work and Grant at school.

After grabbing a couple of last-minute items from the grocery store, I started making Rebecca's Alfredo sauce, which I knew Howard enjoyed. Grant helped by setting the table and preparing the garlic bread, and soon enough, they were at the door. Ruby stood from her pillow to greet them, which was how I knew she was feeling much better.

Grant helped his grandfather with his walker, and after showing him the updated kitchen, we got him settled at the dining table, which would be way more comfortable for him than the kitchen island. Howard was a man of few words, and over the years had gotten more set in his ways, so I half expected him to complain about one thing or another, like our new wall color or fixtures, but he seemed pleased instead.

Grant grabbed the salt and pepper shakers he'd forgotten earlier while Donna helped me set the pasta and salad bowls in the center of the table. For some reason, it felt awkward, like there were unspoken things between us. But maybe it was my conversation with Tristan that was still weighing heavily on my mind.

Once we finally dug in, my stomach settled, and the conversation flowed more naturally as we talked about Howard's treatments, my work schedule, and Grant's classes.

"Grant will be taking his SATs soon, and obviously, his scores will be used for his college applications," I said, reaching for the salad bowl.

"It's hard to believe you'll be graduating next year, Grant," Howard said. "Are you excited?"

"It's almost too fast," Grant muttered, his cheeks rosy. "There's so much to do."

"Like what?" Donna asked, passing the garlic bread to Howard.

Grant chewed a bite of his pasta, then said, "Like finally getting my license and making more memories with friends."

"We've still got plenty of time," I reminded him.

"Dad said we'll probably visit NYU," Grant told them, and I was surprised he hadn't mentioned it to his grandparents sooner. Or about inviting Marcus. *Let's not open that can of worms.* Grant continued, "Not because I want to go there—I'll probably consider local colleges like CSU and Kent—but to see where Mom went to school."

"Really?" Donna asked, eyeing me. She seemed delighted with the idea.

"It's something Rebecca and I talked about, and I think Grant would like the city."

"Well, your mother certainly did," Howard told Grant, shaking his head. "I was glad when she decided to move back home."

"Your grandfather always worried about her safety in such a big city," Donna said in an exasperated tone. "But your mom took care of herself just fine."

"She did, didn't she?" I mused.

Grant wore a playful smile, and I wondered what memory of Rebecca he was conjuring up right then.

"Oh, I almost forgot." Grant looked at me. "I might be able to get a job at the movie theater, and you know, pay for my own gas and stuff. Jeremy said there were openings."

That was definitely new information, adding yet another layer of mystery to their friendship, which I was starting to think with increasing certainty was way more. There were probably clues all along that I'd never noticed. Rebecca would've, though. And no doubt, Grant would've already confided in her.

"Have you met this Jeremy fellow?" Howard asked, breaking me out of my pessimistic thoughts.

"Yeah, of course." I twisted the noodles around my fork. "He's a nice kid."

"I'm glad you have a good friend," Donna said with a smile, and it was so reminiscent of what she'd said to me about Marcus on Halloween that my chest ached.

"Yeah, Jeremy is..." Grant trailed off, then swallowed. "He's awesome."

Grant fidgeted in his seat, making me wonder if he was mustering up the courage to say something more meaningful. And why shouldn't he be able to? My gut churned.

We finished eating, and after clearing the dishes, we relaxed in the living room for a bit, but I could tell Howard was uncomfortable, likely because he was used to his reclining chair and his favorite news program that he watched ad nauseam. Donna was a saint where he was concerned. But that was love and commitment. For better or worse.

"I heard Grant's school is doing well in Scholastic Challenge," Donna said. They had made the top twelve in the state, and the teacher who ran the club felt confident they'd make it all the way to the final four. "When are the semifinals? I'll put it on our calendar."

"Not until the end of March," I replied, trying to remember the email sent to parents. "I'll have to look for the exact date. They're allowing only four tickets each because there's limited seating for family."

A pained look passed between Rebecca's parents.

"She'll be with us in spirit," I said in a solemn voice, and I felt Grant shift beside me on the couch.

"She definitely will," Donna replied in a tight voice. "And she'll be so proud of Grant."

Howard murmured his assent, and I squeezed Grant's knee.

It grew silent in the room, but it wasn't uncomfortable. We'd shared many of these smaller pauses over the past couple of years, each of us taking a moment to remember Rebecca in our own way.

"Maybe Marc will wanna come instead," Grant said so suddenly, I nearly choked on my own saliva.

"*Grant.*" He obviously didn't understand how that might feel for his grandparents, as if Marcus would be taking Rebecca's place, but I could see the pain written all over Donna's face.

"Marc is not part of our family," Howard said in a dismissive tone, and I felt a sting of frustration that I couldn't unpack right then. There were more urgent things to discuss.

"No," Grant said, "but he's a good friend, and I like having him around." Grant looked at me. "Dad does too. Right?"

With all eyes on me, I sat there motionless, trying to think of the right thing to say. I thought back to that conversation with Donna on Halloween.

"*We all need to find happiness wherever we can. Rebecca would want that.*"

"When I met Rebecca, it was like I'd been struck by lightning," I said in a soft voice, ignoring Howard's confused expression. "Pretty early on, I knew I wanted to spend my life with her. And nothing mattered more than making that happen."

Grant blinked repeatedly, his emotions so close to the surface since Ruby's accident.

"And we were happy—even more so when Grant came along."

Donna grinned at Grant, likely remembering how excited Rebecca had been to find out she was pregnant with him.

"Even though I almost caused her to die?" Grant asked in a blubbery voice, and my chest seized. Fuck, how long had he been carrying that around?

"Are you kidding me? Neither of us would've traded you for the world. You taught us that love was deeper and more complex than we'd ever imagined. You were her favorite human, her greatest accomplishment." When I reached for Grant's hand, he didn't pull away, only tightened his grip. "So don't think for one minute that she regretted anything, okay?"

He nodded, his eyes shiny and wide. Donna was wiping her cheeks with her forearm, and Howard kept clearing his throat.

I took a deep breath, my heart trembling, but I needed to push through.

"After Rebecca passed, I didn't think I had it in me to go on...I felt so empty...and lost," I admitted, and I heard a sob catch in Grant's throat. "But Grant got me through. And so did you."

"You got us through as well," Donna said, and Howard nodded.

"Sometimes you meet a person, and it feels like you've known them forever. With Rebecca, it was immediate, like I was thunderstruck." I pushed the rest of the words from my lips before I chickened out. "With Marc, it was like a gradual, smoldering flame. His friendship has gotten me through some of my worst moments, and I'll always think he's special." I rubbed at the stitch in my chest. "Do you know what I mean?"

Grant was completely still beside me as Donna said, "I think I do. Your connection is hard to miss."

When our eyes met across the room, I could see the understanding shining in her eyes, along with a thread of melancholy I knew only too well. She'd obviously already been putting the pieces together in her head, and I just gave her the extra push she needed to draw her conclusion that Marcus meant a hell of a lot to me.

"Like I said before, we need to find happiness wherever we can." Her smile was a bit sad. "In the end, it's someone's soul we're connecting with."

"Why are we speaking in riddles?" Howard grumbled, and I would've laughed had my heart not been lodged in my throat.

"I think it's time to get you home." Donna stood unsteadily, then walked over to her husband. "These boys have things they need to take care of, and it's better if we left them to it."

Howard let Donna help him up, even though he kept throwing us quizzical looks. Grant stayed put on the couch, as if in a daze, as I walked them to the door.

Donna pulled me into a hug, then whispered in my ear, "You're a good father, and you were a wonderful husband. Rebecca loved you so much and would want you to be happy. We'll have more time for a heart-to-heart about this later. For now, there's a kid who needs his dad."

"Thank you," I replied in a watery voice. "For everything."

After I closed the door behind them, I turned to see Grant watching me closely.

"*Dad?*" he asked warily as I sat back down beside him, ready to get on with it.

"When I was a kid, my first crush was on a boy," I said, and Grant covered his mouth with his hand. "It was confusing, especially since I went on to crush on girls too."

"Are you saying you're pan or bisexual?" he asked, and I nodded.

"Your generation is much savvier and more open. We didn't really have those kinds of labels back then. I thought maybe I was just going through an experimental phase, so I kept it to myself and never brought it up again, not even with your mother." I balled my fist. "My father would've never been accepting enough to have that kind of conversation, and I suppose that sort of set the tone for me."

Grant winced. "He probably would've said something homophobic or insensitive."

"Yeah, unfortunately." I frowned. "He doesn't make it easy, and I vowed to never be like him. To never create an atmosphere where my kid couldn't seek my advice or tell me important things. I'm sorry if you've felt something different from me."

"No, Dad. I'll admit, sometimes I didn't want you to worry." His gaze connected with mine, and his eyes softened. "And for the record, I never wished for it to be you...instead of Mom."

"How did you...?" *Know my deepest, darkest fear?* I swiped at my eyes, not sure when I'd even started crying. "Well, fuck."

"*Language,*" he said teasingly, and I chuckled. "We might butt heads a lot, but I would've been devastated whether it was you or Mom. I wouldn't trade you for the world either."

I furiously swiped at my eyes, my heart feeling achy and full.

Grant stood and got me a tissue. "You've always been more of a softy than Mom."

"Yeah...yeah, I have."

Ruby had come over to sniff at our feet, obviously sensing our emotions. We rubbed her fur and rained kisses on her head for a couple of minutes, giving her attention and us a reprieve from our heavy conversation.

"The stuff you said about Marc..." Grant's voice was hesitant. "Do you have feelings for him?"

"Even if I did, I was too afraid to upend your life. You're just getting settled again."

Grant stared at me. "You should know by now that things don't always work on your timeline."

I shook my head. "Now who sounds like the adult?"

He laughed.

"Anyway, it's not like I know for sure how he feels."

"Seriously?" He rolled his eyes. "I think it's obvious how he feels."

"Okay, smart-ass." I smirked, then grew serious. "Bottom line...I wouldn't do anything that made you feel uncomfortable."

"I love Marc. He's practically family, no matter what Grandpa says."

"He is, isn't he?" I mused. "We'll see. In the meantime, we've got dishes piling up. Help me tackle them."

Grant followed me to the kitchen, where we rolled up our sleeves and got to work cleaning our mess from dinner. It felt good to be doing something physical to help balance out the emotional turmoil in my head.

When Grant's phone buzzed with a text, he threw the towel over his shoulder and twisted toward the kitchen island to read the message. I watched as a beautiful grin stretched his lips.

"Uh-huh," I said with a wink. "Let me guess...Jeremy?"

He stared at me for a long moment. "You figured it out, didn't you?"

"Maybe?" I said, and relief washed over his face. "Sounds like you should take your own advice."

"Maybe I already have," he quipped.

"Then I approve." I lifted my hand to high-five him. "Will his parents?"

"Yup."

"Good." I breathed out. "Still have to keep your bedroom door open."

He rolled his eyes. "I wouldn't have it any other way."

Afterward, Grant went up to his room, no doubt to get on

the phone with his...what? Boyfriend? Christ, what a night. I sat in front of the television, barely registering what was on the screen.

When a message came through from Marcus, my fingers trembled on the screen. It was a photo of a vintage-style frame he'd found to display Grant's gift.

That looks amazing. And perfect timing because we had a good conversation tonight.

Did it involve someone named Jeremy?

Yeah, among other things, and it felt fucking great.

I'm really glad. I know how much that was weighing on you.

Thank you.

I considered texting more, but there were too many things cycling through my head, and I needed to get it all in order first.

I cut the lights, then headed upstairs to bed, deciding to sleep on it.

Passing Grant's room, I saw that he and Ruby were cuddled up together in his bed.

"Dad?" he said, lifting an earbud away from his head.

"Yeah?" I leaned against his door, suddenly feeling exhausted.

"Why was six afraid of seven?"

A grin pulled at my lips. It was one of my first jokes from his childhood, so I played along. "Why?"

"Because seven eight nine."

We smiled at each other across the space that seemed way less vast than just a few hours before.

28

MARCUS

I PULLED INTO A PARKING SPACE, having nearly missed group this week because the customer I'd been waiting on to pick up his chest of drawers was running late.

Though I regularly caught flak for getting too wrapped up in work, this session felt important, and not only because of the man I so desperately wanted to see and spend time with.

We'd only texted brief messages the past couple of days, but I couldn't fault him for that. I could only imagine how much support he needed to offer Grant after his revelation about Jeremy. To be honest, I was feeling a bit lost about how to proceed with him and our friendship in light of that news, especially if he was going to remain committed to his plan with his son. One coming out story at a time, I supposed.

There was also something else there, in between the lines in his texts, something I was missing, and I was bracing myself for even more disappointment.

But maybe this was how it would go between us—only checking in occasionally and getting together on rare occasions. That was how we'd begun this friendship, after all, and so maybe it was a fitting ending as well.

As soon as I made it to the seat across from Delaney, I hated that my pulse ticked up at the hint of relief in his expression. Having this direct view of him was torture, though, because it only brought back the memories of having him under me, watching that bliss on his face when he finally let go of his tightly wound expectations. Bringing him pleasure was one of my most favorite moments. Holding him all night too.

"Let's get started, group," Judy said, and everyone quieted down. "Today's topic will be the unhealthy things we've done to manage our grief."

She went on to explain how counterintuitive coping mechanisms might only prolong or stifle our grief. I'd learned so much about my own thought processes and behaviors from Judy and would be forever grateful I'd found this group.

"Does anyone want to begin?" She looked around the circle. "Remember, this is a no-judgment zone."

Harmony raised her hand first. "I'll admit I smoked pot way too much afterward, at first to manage my nerves, and then to just get out the door in the morning."

"It was the same for me and alcohol," Frank confessed, his shoulders slumping. "I'd go to the corner pub a lot so I didn't have to be in the empty house without her."

Others murmured their assent and shared they'd done one thing or another to numb themselves and the pain. Pills, non-recreational drugs, all lead them either to this group, treatment, or prolonging their pain. My stomach hurt as I listened to all the stories, and given Delaney's expression, he was feeling the same way.

"What other behaviors besides consuming alcohol or drugs?" Judy asked.

"I was too forward with women I met," Walter admitted. "I thought it would help to have someone to flirt with, but it didn't. It only felt worse. I missed her more. Getting married so soon afterward was a huge mistake too. So I'm learning to enjoy my own company now."

That was one of the most honest admissions I'd heard from him.

"I'm glad to hear it," Judy said, and a couple of group members threw out positive affirmations for Walter.

I raised my hand next. "I work too much. Even when Carmen was alive, I'd stay late at my shop if we'd had an argument, but mostly I'd just lose track of time." I frowned. "Now it's much easier because there's no one waiting for me."

"How does that feel?" she asked.

"Lonely, of course." I refused to look at Delaney because it was too raw an admission. "But it's partly my fault. I could do more outside of work."

"Like what?" she prompted me.

"Right now doesn't exactly count because the holiday season is a hectic time for my business," I explained. "But I could do more stuff that makes me feel good, like working out. I haven't run in the park in weeks, and I should get back to that. I could also take on more side projects that get me out of that setting."

I chanced a glance toward Delaney. His cheeks had turned rosy, and his smile was shy and so filled with meaning, it made my heart stutter.

"You should consider traveling too," Delaney said, biting back a grin. It was true that we'd made plans to visit New York, but...I no longer knew where we stood.

"Or going on dates," John quipped, true to form, and everyone laughed.

"Yeah, I've let that lapse too. Not really interested at the moment." I looked away but not before noting Delaney shifting in his seat. Did it make him jealous that I might date again? I sighed. Didn't he know how hard it would be to find someone as special as him?

"I know what you mean," Frank said. "My daughter helped me sign up, and at first, it was exciting to talk to new people. But it gets tedious too."

"Finding someone you connect with can't be forced," Harmony said. "It takes time."

I wondered what Delaney's response would be on this topic, but he kept silent. And he was fidgety today, which made me curious if something more was going on with Grant, or Ruby, or his in-laws, for that matter. Something he hadn't shared with me by text.

Suddenly I wanted the group to be over so I could ask him directly. Was that why we hadn't had a real conversation since the day they left my shop? Not that it should surprise me. I'd sort of set the tone with Grant's present, as if I wouldn't see them again anytime soon.

Mom had smiled when I'd shown her Grant's photo gift. I'd found a cool vintage frame to use for it and texted it to Delaney. He seemed pleased and the next day messaged that Grant loved it too.

I tuned back into the group, and I'd probably been in my head too much because it sounded like the topic had changed to healthy coping mechanisms, and I'd already missed a couple of the comments.

One woman talked about accepting more invitations from friends because it helped her get out of the house. I'd said no so often the past couple of years that even my childhood friends didn't ask anymore. Good reminder for me as well.

Delaney lifted his hand, which made my pulse gallop for some unknown reason.

"I've thought about putting myself out there more too, but I was afraid my son would suffer from my choices." There was a murmur of assent from others in the group, who were likely thinking about their own kids. Walter looked a bit defeated, and I remembered that he had adult children who'd disapproved of his second marriage.

"It's an admirable plan, but one I imagine is hard to maintain," Judy said in a sympathetic voice.

"It is." He winced. "But I was willing to sacrifice myself for it, which isn't always healthy."

Judy nodded. "How did you overcome this?"

"I'm still a work in progress. But I did meet someone new..." he said, and my pulse thundered in my veins. "Not new...*old*...I mean... Damn, I'm not very good at this."

"It's okay. Take your time." Judy smiled. "What are you trying to say?"

"What I'm trying to say is...there's this guy I want to date."

"Not this again," John said, and there were nervous titters from other members. I could barely fucking breathe as I studied Delaney, but he didn't meet my eyes.

"*Rude,*" Harmony said, throwing John a look.

"Everyone calm down," Judy said in a warning tone before prompting Delaney to continue.

"I thought I had to hold everything together, or our world would spin out of control again." He blew out a breath. "Turns out no matter how much you try, things still happen that you didn't anticipate."

"Are you referring to the guy you want to date?" Harmony arched an eyebrow.

"Yeah. I consider him my best friend...and he's come to mean the world to me. Which is pretty damned scary because I don't think my heart can handle any more breaks. It's pretty banged up already." The ache in my chest only intensified as I listened to him. "But I'm terrified he won't want me in the same way."

"What makes you think he wouldn't want you?" I asked suddenly, my throat tight.

The entire room was so quiet, you could hear the sound of traffic outside.

"All my rules and resistance were probably frustrating as I tried to hold it all together and keep the peace." Delaney finally looked me square in the eye. "As soon as I tell him I'm in love with him, he might think I'm too much for him—that *we're* too much for him. My kid adores him too."

Holy fucking hell. I was openly panting now, just trying to manage my out-of-control breaths.

"What do you say to that?" Harmony asked me, obviously egging us on.

"I say that letting someone in again, despite the fear of losing them, is pretty brave." I sat up straighter. "But I think that's what love is all about. Giving them all of you, baring your soul, and asking them to accept you anyway. I'm pretty sure the guy you're talking about is already in love with you too. Probably was already half in love with you over bourbon and Asian takeout."

Delaney's smile was dazzling as our eyes held across the room.

"I'm confused," John said, his face screwed up.

"Are you dense?" Frank replied, and I held in a laugh. "Lane is saying he wants to date Marc. They're friends, we all know that, and evidently, have developed feelings for each other."

It was as if a light bulb went off over John's head. "You must be the friend Marc was talking about when we discussed second chances."

Judy cleared her throat and smiled. "It makes sense since you already share such a powerful bond. I'm very happy for you both."

"On that note." Delaney sprang from his seat. "Do you mind if we...?" He cut across the circle and held his hand out to me.

"I'm not sure my knees are working properly right now," I

said, clasping our fingers together, and he helped me out of my seat.

The room erupted in cheers as we walked out the door together.

My eyes stung as I looked back one final time and met Judy's smile. Harmony gave me a thumbs-up, and Frank looked pretty emotional.

As soon as the door shut behind us, Delaney backed me against the wall, hemming me in with his arms. Thankfully, the lobby in the community center was empty, so we no longer had an audience.

"So what do you say, Marc?" He kissed my temple. "Will you date me?"

"I'll have to think about it," I teased, but his smile faltered, and he looked so serious. "Fuck, Lane. I was not expecting that...romantic gesture. Be still my beating heart." Red lined his cheeks. Was this really happening? I leaned toward him. "Of course I want to be with you."

I gathered his face in my hands and kissed him with all that I had, pouring into it all my longing and desperation, hoping it would tell him exactly what he meant to me.

When I drew back, a thread of nerves took hold. "What about Grant? Your in-laws?"

"Let's just say they know how I feel about you. Grant is all in, and if my in-laws need a little more time to get used to the idea, then so be it." His eyes softened. "I don't want to be without you anymore."

Our lips met again, our tongues tangling, our hands winding in each other's hair as pure joy filled me. Delaney was digging into the tender places in my soul again, uncovering fertile soil that was finally ready to grow roots.

"So...it feels like we ditched class early." Delaney brushed his lips against mine. "What do you want to do?"

I knotted our fingers together. "You don't need to get back to Grant?"

"I've got a little time." He looked toward the parking lot. "Besides, he has a friend over. *Jeremy.* And they're working on a school project."

"Uh-huh." I kissed the side of his mouth. "Look at you being all chill."

He shrugged. "He knows the rules. The bedroom door needs to stay open."

When our eyes met, I barked out a laugh, and it was contagious.

Delaney arched a brow. "I deserve some sort of reward for my restraint."

"We can always head back to my house and make out a lot more?" I suggested.

"That's what I'm talking about." Delaney yanked on my hand. "Let's go before I change back to anxious-parent mode."

We practically ran to the parking lot and to our separate cars so he could follow me home.

Fuck, I love you, I quickly texted before getting on the road.

His response was immediate: **I love you too. So much.**

I couldn't stop smiling all the way there.

EPILOGUE

Delaney
April

"HERE IT IS, the historic Stonewall Inn," I said, pointing out the famous gay bar known for the Stonewall riots after a police raid in 1969.

Earlier in the day, we'd checked into our hotel in Chelsea—which was Grant's suggestion, not only because the Manhattan neighborhood was known for its art galleries and restaurants but also for its large LGBTQIA population. Then the four of us —Jeremy had joined us in NY—decided to hit the pavement. The first thing we did was walk around the NYU campus, which was poignant for Grant. He'd bought a T-shirt and a few other memorabilia in remembrance of Rebecca. I couldn't help getting choked up as well, recalling my visits there at the beginning of our relationship.

Marc was fantastic in his support, staying in the background and allowing me and Grant to experience it together as Grant asked a hundred questions about his mom. Marc and Jeremy had eventually parted ways with us to wait on a bench in Washington Square Park near the famous arch. It'd been my idea to invite Grant's boyfriend on our spring break trip, which was the perfect opportunity for Marc and me to take time off work. Grant and Jeremy were sweet together and practically tied at the hip, even at school, where they were accepted by peers, for the most part. Apparently, Ellie was very protective if they ever caught any flak.

A year from now, we'd already be planning for college, and both boys had decided to stay local, Jeremy pretty set on Cleveland State. But after a campus tour, Grant had decided to apply to the more academically rigorous Case Western Reserve University. His scores were undoubtedly good enough to be accepted. The school was located on the east side, not far from our neighborhood, but to my utter surprise, he'd decided to try and live on campus anyway. Especially since his teacher had encouraged him to apply for a coveted history-program scholarship, which would help defray the cost. Of course, he could still change his mind, but it was obvious he was feeling more confident in his own skin, and I was so proud. Rebecca would be too.

We walked across the street to stand in front of the Stonewall Inn and take in its history as well as the plethora of rainbow flags everywhere we looked.

"It's how the Pride parade began," Jeremy pointed out.

"And the gay rights movement," Grant added.

I found myself marveling again at the openness and activism of this generation of kids. There was so much I'd missed...and maybe even ignored. So seeing the world from my gay child's perspective was something I cherished and benefited from in my own navigation of a relationship with another man.

Marc and I had been taking it slow, which meant going on dates, spending lots of time at each other's houses, having weekend sleepovers, and running together in the Metroparks.

Marc had decided he was ready to leave group after January's session, but I'd chosen to stay on through spring, mostly to support others, even though I was feeling healthy enough as well.

Marc and Grant had become thick as thieves. Marc had essentially taken over teaching Grant to drive, no doubt because of his calmer demeanor, and even tagged along with us to Grant's driving exam, which he'd passed with flying colors. The plan was to buy him a used car for his birthday that he could eventually use for college. For now, he'd been saving money from his part-time job at Worthy's Salvage Shop on the weekends. It'd been Marc's suggestion since Grant seemed to love it so much, and he'd jumped at the chance rather than applying at the movie theater.

Thankfully, both our families had been pretty accepting of our relationship. There'd only been a few awkward moments in the beginning—and mostly from Howard, who seemed much more accepting of his grandson identifying as gay than of my being bisexual and wanting a relationship with Marc. My heart-to-heart with Donna had definitely helped, and she'd become one of our biggest cheerleaders, together with Arlene, which was pretty heartwarming. Donna had even encouraged Grant to invite Marc to Scholastic Challenge, where they'd finished in third place.

My father was a different story altogether. He'd suffered a heart attack two months ago, had open-heart surgery to repair the valves, and the whole incident seemed to have shaken him. Maybe it made him consider his own mortality or something. At the time, we didn't know his fate, so I'd gotten in touch with his estranged brother, and after he'd shown up to offer his support and some sort of reconciliation, Dad seemed even more bewildered.

He was less ornery now and more humble—well, for him. Or maybe *grateful for the little things* was a better way to describe it. One time I'd even walked in the room to find Grant holding his hand and reading to him from an old Western novel the center kept in their library. I couldn't forget that image for days after. Nor the one of Dad laughing with his brother over some childhood memory. Like a full belly laugh that'd made my skin prickle.

But there were signs even before the heart attack that Dad was softening, that our confrontation might've made something register, however small. He was more engaging with Grant the very next visit and even asked me more questions. He'd briefly met Marc once during an intense discussion after his surgery, but at the time, Dad's focus had been elsewhere. Still, I talked about Marc often, and I could see the wheels spinning. Soon more questions would come, and I didn't plan on holding back. But for now, baby steps.

"Let me take a photo of the two of you," I told Grant and Jeremy, whipping out my phone.

They posed near the Stonewall Inn entrance, and when Grant boldly reached for Jeremy's hand, my stomach tightened even as my heart soared. The anxious parent in me looked around to make sure we were safe. I wasn't foolish enough to pretend homophobia didn't still exist, even in the largest, most diverse city in the country. Interestingly, my worry about Grant's outfits—today it was his Hamiltonesque King George— had retreated to the background. Besides, nobody had batted an eye here. I supposed in a metropolis this large, they'd seen it all.

"Where's a better place for them to be their true selves?" Marc said from beside me as I snapped away, reading my reaction well, as usual.

When we traded places so Grant could take a photo of Marc and me, I was bowled over when Marc knotted our fingers together. But I didn't pull away, instead relishing the moment. I would never take this liberating feeling for granted again, knowing what others had gone through before us.

After we visited Christopher Park across the street, which featured monuments from the LGBTQIA rights movement, we found a low-key Italian place to grab dinner in the West Village.

"My feet are killing me," Jeremy complained after we'd placed our orders.

"I hear you." Marc smiled. "We can go back to the hotel and rest up. We have another big day tomorrow."

Our plans for the next couple of days included all the touristy stuff from the Statue of Liberty to Times Square to Central Park, as long as the weather held. Spring in the city was as temperamental as it was in Cleveland. So we had backup plans, including museums, which seemed to please Grant and Jeremy.

"So far, this city is awesome. I can see why Mom loved it," Grant said, buttering a roll. "But I can tell why it would be overwhelming too."

"Definitely." I took a sip of water. "She thought our city was a tad more manageable."

After we finished stuffing our faces with wonderful pasta, we walked back down Christopher Street toward our hotel, passing a few other gay establishments, including a drag queen bar called Ruby Redd's. The marquee read that Frieda Love would be headlining, and I thought it sounded fun. And given Marc's grin, so did he. Maybe we'd find one in our own city and make a night of it.

As we passed by the Stonewall Inn again, Grant studied a flier near the door before turning to me. "Will you go inside and buy us some T-shirts? They would be so cool to have, but we're obviously not old enough."

Grant and his collection of shirts.

"That sounds like a great idea," Marc said, glancing inside the window.

"Right?" Grant replied. "We can meet you back at the hotel if you wanna stay for a while."

I scrutinized him, wondering what in the world he was up to. Was this really about buying shirts? But I didn't read anything coy in his expression, nor Jeremy's. Maybe he really wanted a shirt but also knew Jeremy and his aching feet needed to get back to the hotel.

Except there was no way I wanted them wandering around the city alone. "I think it's better if we stick together and—"

"I'll walk with them to the corner and make sure they know the way back. It's only a couple of blocks south," Marc said, squeezing my shoulder. "I'll meet you inside the bar."

Before I could dispute the idea, they started toward 7th Avenue, Jeremy looking relieved, and I watched them for a minute before turning toward the Stonewall Inn. Taking a deep breath, I swung open the door and stepped inside, noting the plaque on the wall commemorating the riots.

It wasn't lost on me that I was officially inside my first gay bar.

The interior was a bit dimmer but well-maintained, with wooden tables, stools, and an area to play pool in the center of the bar. It wasn't very crowded for a weekday, but I counted about a dozen patrons, none of whom paid me much attention.

I stepped closer to the bar to look at the shirts hanging along the back wall.

"Can I help you?" the bartender asked. He was an older guy with a friendly smile, and it made me wonder how many tourists they catered to on a daily basis.

"I wanted to buy a couple of T-shirts for my kid and his boyfriend."

Wow, that felt surreal to say out loud but also pretty fucking good.

"Sure." He grinned. "Just give me a couple of minutes to get them from the back room. Feel free to have a seat in the meantime."

I slid onto a stool at the end of the bar and just soaked it all in—not only the bar but the entire day. Pretty damned cool.

A swath of light alerted me to the door opening behind me, and when I turned, I saw Marc approaching. I took a moment to appreciate how devastatingly handsome he was as he closed the distance between us.

"Is this seat taken?" he asked in a flirty voice as he sidled up beside me.

"Depends," I replied, playing along. "Can I buy you a drink?"

He winked. "Only if it's good bourbon."

"Coming right up," I said, patting the seat beside me. Suddenly staying for a drink sounded like a hell of a good idea.

"Are you looking for a hookup tonight?" he asked as he sank down beside me. "I'm game if you are."

I groaned under my breath. "It was your idea to splurge on a stupid suite."

Marc had reserved a large enough space for all of us, with two bedrooms and baths as well as four queen-size beds, likely so we didn't give the kids the wrong idea about expectations. We may not have brought it up directly, but by now, Grant knew that Marc and I shared a bed when he stayed over, and I certainly understood that Grant and Jeremy were not so innocent either.

"We can be quiet," Marc said against my ear, and I shivered.

When I turned to meet his eyes, his fingers connected with my nape, and he leaned forward to kiss me. I stiffened briefly before remembering where we were. And fuck if that didn't feel great. To kiss my boyfriend in the middle of a bar.

"You two are sweet," the bartender said as he returned with

a box of shirts. "Can I get you a drink while you choose which you'd like to purchase?"

"Please," Marc said, then proceeded to order us a couple of bourbons, neat.

By the time I chose the shirts and sizes, our drinks had been served.

Marc held up his glass. "To us and our future."

I smiled as I clinked my glass against his. "A future that involves you moving in with us? Maybe even this summer?"

It was something we'd discussed in very general terms, without putting a date on it—and, of course, I'd run it by Grant first, something Marc had insisted on. Along with the idea of updating more of the house.

"Are you serious?" he asked, his eyebrows practically to his hairline.

"I am. I want you with me." I squeezed his hand. "Always."

"I want to be with you too, Lane." He kissed my cheek. "Always."

We never said the word *forever* to each other, our past wounds still too fresh. We knew there were no guarantees in life and that you could lose someone you loved in the blink of an eye. But in my soul, I knew we meant *until death did us part*.

Maybe we'd even make it official someday.

"And Grant?" His tone was hesitant.

"He's so excited, he can barely contain himself. I'm surprised he hasn't already asked you himself."

Grant had admitted the idea also helped alleviate his fears that I wouldn't be so alone. I told him I'd be fine regardless, but his concern was sweet, really. We didn't argue nearly as much, but we still had our moments.

Marc's grin was so radiant, it lit me up. "Then it's settled."

I clinked his glass again, and we relaxed in our seats and sipped our drinks.

There was some laughter and singing behind us, and when

I looked over my shoulder, a couple of women were locked in an embrace in the middle of the floor.

Marc stood and held out his hand. "Dance with me?"

I hesitated for a split second before taking his hand, my chest achy, and following him to the floor. Never in a million years would I have thought I'd have this opportunity with him. I wound my arms around his neck, he planted his hands on my hips, and we began swaying together to the soft music piping through the speakers. "Damn, this is nice."

"It is." When he pulled me closer to connect our lips, my heart clenched. His kiss felt like *everything*. My stomach was warm, my emotions close to the surface, his scent surrounding me, making me sigh.

After dancing to one more song, we made our way back to the bar to finish our drinks, neither of us able to wipe the smiles off our faces.

"We better head back," I said, noting the time.

After we cashed out, we began our trek to the hotel. We took the elevator to our suite, and when we stepped inside the room, we found two boys asleep on the couch in front of a blaring television, their shoulders pressed together, their fingers intertwined.

Fuck, my heart.

I lifted my finger to my lips as we tiptoed past them to one of the bedrooms and softly closed the door behind us.

We wasted little time stripping down to our underwear and sliding beneath the covers together, ignoring the other bed completely. We were a tangle of arms and legs as our lips and tongues met in a deep, heart-melting kiss.

I could feel his hardness against mine as his fingers dug into my ass, and I bit back a groan, afraid to make any noise. Rolling on top of him, I whispered in his ear, "I want to eat your come, but you have to be very quiet. Can you do that?"

"Fuck, Lane," he swore under his breath. His eyes were

wide, desire coursing through them as he nodded. I wasted no time sliding beneath the covers, shoving his briefs down, and taking his stiff cock in my mouth.

When he groaned and thrust against me, I lifted my hand and planted it against his mouth to shush him. He kissed my palm, then sucked on my fingers as I took him to the brink in record time. I swallowed his entire load, my own cock throbbing, but I ignored it.

He pulled me to him and kissed me lazily.

"Don't think I can move," he said thickly. "But I wanna suck you off too. Maybe you could—"

"Shh." I kissed his temple. "Go to sleep. You can repay me in the morning."

I turned to shut off the bedside lamp, then settled into his arms, my favorite position, as he began floating into dreamland.

"Can't wait for the rest of our lives," he whispered in my ear, and I hummed in agreement. "I love you, Lane."

"Love you too." I shifted to kiss his cheek. "Always...*and forever*."

His arms tightened around me.

"Forever," he whispered into the darkness, but his words illuminated my soul as I drifted into sleep.

OTHER BOOKS BY CHRISTINA LEE

Standalones:
A Breath Apart
Love Me Louder
Kickflip
A Kaleidoscope of Butterflies
Have Mercy
Incandescent

Fated Series
Moon Flower
Moon Spell

Easton U Pirates series:
Bat Boy
Home Plate
Perfect Score

So This is Christmas series:
Beautiful Dreamer
Beautiful Temptation

Under My Skin series:
Regret
Reawaken
Reclaim
Redeem

Roadmap to Your Heart series
The Darkest Flame
The Faintest Spark
The Deepest Blue
The Hardest Fall
The Sweetest Goodbye

Co-written with Nyrae Dawn (AKA Riley Hart)
Free Fall series:
Touch the Sky
Chase the Sun
Paint the Stars

Spinoff from Free Fall series:
Living Out Loud

Standalones with Riley Hart:
Of Sunlight and Stardust
Science & Jockstraps

Forbidden Love series with Riley Hart:
Ever After: A Gay Fairy Tale
Forever Moore: A Gay Fairy Tale

Boys in Makeup series with Riley Hart:
Pretty Perfect
Pretty Sweet
Pretty Wild

Co-written with Felice Stevens
Heartsville series:
Last Call (MMM)
First Light (MM)

M/F books that can all standalone:
All of You
Before You Break
Whisper to Me
Promise Me This
Two of Hearts
Three Sacred Words
Twelve Truths and a Lie

ABOUT THE AUTHOR

Once upon a time, Christina Lee was a wardrobe stylist in New York City. She spent her days schlepping clothes, hailing cabs, and on the hunt for the perfect lip gloss, which became a bit of an addiction—along with books and coffee. You could always find her perched in a corner booth of a favorite diner sipping a dark roast and reading.

She currently lives in the Midwest with her husband and son— her two favorite guys. She's been a clinical social worker and a special education teacher and while very rewarding, they still didn't feel like an exact fit. It wasn't until she began writing a weekly column for the local newspaper that the bells went off in her head. She could finally draw from her real-life experiences and vivid imagination to write fiction—and she's never looked back.

Christina writes romance in different sub-genres, but mostly with LGBTQ characters because representation matters and *everyone* deserves a happily-ever-after.